End of the Tracks:
Homecoming

by Danny Ledonne

"In order to survive these times and stay human, we will have to walk with one hand holding the grief of watching the dying world and another hand holding the light so we can find our way towards the new world which is being born." — *Laura Matsue*

[I – Speedy Car Pool Service]

"Dugen, wake up. We're at Sasha's place."

Nate idled the engine of his beat-up station wagon. The car radio faded in and out of an up-tempo love song, the name of which nobody could remember. It was Dugen's alarm clock.

> *did you know I dreamed about you*
> *did you know I cried*
> *my heart's unredeemed without you*
> *my tears fallen and dried*
> *oh, oh oh*
> *my dearest one*

Dugen rubbed his eyes as his nose whistled from being partially stuffy. Sleeping sideways against the rear passenger-side door panel does that sometimes. It was a sub-optimal bed, but Nate's station wagon had been Dugen's overnight crash pad for months now and finally felt broken in.

"I had nearly completed my metamorphosis into a moth-tiger hybrid. I hope I can resume hypnagogic work on that again tonight" Dugen muttered as he sat up in the car.

Nate was parked in front of Sasha's upscale hippy dorm, Woodgrove Sunbeams. The birds chirped wildly in the spring morning air. Nate's driver-side window was rolled down to appreciate the crisp atmosphere and air out the stench of whatever Dugen had eaten at last night's pork roast.

Sasha stepped out of the dorm entrance with a bounce in her step and waved at her favorite college boys sitting in the dark blue station wagon. Her long brown hair was braided with hints of every color of the rainbow. Her freckles caught the morning sunlight.

"Morning!" she gleamed.

Sasha hopped into Nate's station wagon, sitting beside Nate and rolling down her passenger-side window immediately to take in the fresh air and fumigate Dugen's back seat stench.

"Hey, how was the community bakery sale or whatever?" Nate inquired as he engaged the transmission and pulled onto a quaint side street.

"Oh, it was so lovely. I wished I could take those ginger and spice smells with me... but at least I bought a couple loaves to slice and leave in the common room." Sasha was always eager to bathe her senses in sumptuous treats.

Nate reached for his straight black coffee and took a hearty sip while it was still warm. He wasn't exactly an early riser, and it took a potent kick to get him in gear for their morning commute.

The station wagon coasted through their quiet neighborhood en route to the main campus drive.

"You could probably sell some of those slices at a premium given the sorry state of the campus cafeteria, you know." Nate had never lived on campus, but visited the cafeteria often enough with friends to conclude he would never pay for any questionable cuisine from his own limited bank account.

Dugen stretched and gazed out the window, as if seeing the Salmon Springs College campus for the first time. Dugen often did this as a matter of practice in order to perceive the world anew each day. He also made an effort to rediscover his two best friends each morning, as though meeting them for the first time.

"Oh, the cafeteria isn't *that* bad!" Sasha was sometimes defensive of anything the campus provided, even when it amounted to little worth defending. Her eternal school spirit.

"You just have to check out the salad bar... or sometimes the deli stand is pretty good. Just avoid the preheated meal options because you're better off just microwaving something at home for half the price."

Sasha didn't go out of her way to be a maternal figure, but these two ragamuffins could use some good mothering while away at college.

Nate pulled up to the stop sign with more traffic in a hurry to get to morning classes. Salmon Springs had a "15 minute rule" for professors arriving late, but students would be counted absent if they didn't arrive by the time roll call was made. It was the kind of double-standard that prepared students for the unfairness of adult life.

"How's it going, Dugen?" Sasha looked back at him from her seat. His scruffy facial hair looked red in the morning sun.

"I'm deciding what I should change my major to next semester" Dugen replied while gazing at the fluttering leaves, bright green and fresh off their branches.

"You change your major every semester!" Nate exclaimed with exasperation.

"That practice was established sophomore year, Nate the Great. What remains to be seen is whether the physics department will accept me into their program based on my stellar test scores but absent taking the bullshit prereqs they impose for purely gate-keeping functions." Hopping around majors was a game for Dugen and the deans were onto him by now.

"You want to go into physics, Dugen? That's great! You know, I'm so proud of you and how much you've made of yourself here at college" Sasha swooned with pride.

Sasha had met Dugen on a funkadelic music social media group while they were both in high school. Sasha was living in a suburb of Phoenix at the time and Dugen was completing his degree through an online academy because his dad was stationed at a military base in South Carolina.

Sasha applied to Salmon Springs College because she always wanted to explore the Pacific Northwest. Sasha also applied for Dugen on a dare after Dugen said he didn't want to go to college until after he had walked the entire Chilean coastline.

There was much debate as to whether the distance was 3,999 miles or 4,000 miles and Dugen wanted to decide for himself. With the ongoing political turmoil in the region, that walk never happened because Dugen's father refused to pay for it and Dugen couldn't produce enough blood plasma to cover the travel bill.

That's how people as different as Sasha Fenix and Douglas

Dugen ended up in Salmon Springs. The town was a funky mix of eclectic folks who got along mostly because they didn't fit in anywhere else.

"He doesn't want to go into physics" Nate protested.

Nate had been letting Dugen live out of the back of his car for $200 each month and it seemed a fair deal for both of them, but the shared bathroom and shower access had been a sticking point. Nate had no objection to Dugen getting a hot bath, and Lord knows Dugen needed one, but Dugen insisted on bringing several neon plastic pool toys and a disco ball for no reason Nate deemed justifiable.

"Last year, Dugen rendezvoused as a Women's Studies major before switching to an interdisciplinary degree in Underwater Performance Art and Marxist Political Theory" Nate explained.

"The working hypothesis was that guys in Women's Studies get at least 20% more pussy. I would say from personal experience that a 5% bump in bumping was the ceiling. Max 5%." Dugen added.

"And I'm sure it was just an extended field study for you, Dugen." Nate shook his head as he gripped the wheel.

It was as though Nate and Sasha were in the front seats talking about their rebellious man-child in the rear of the vehicle. It was as though Nate was threatening to pull over and end their family vacation right there and then.

"They really hate it for some reason... when you design your own major, only to abandon it a semester later, but that's just because they failed to acknowledge I completed my major requirements with a thesis project" Dugen explained with indignant candor.

"Oh wow, you completed your thesis project? Did I miss that?" Sasha looked over at Nate, worried she had been absent for Dugen's baccalaureate dissertation.

Nate rolled his eyes.

"It wasn't a thesis project, Dugen. You set up a bunch of blow-up toys in my bathtub, dumped glitter all over a full tub of water, pointed a strobe light at a disco ball you hung from the shower curtain rod, and live-streamed yourself naked, singing a Russian drinking song you plagiarized."

"'Oi Moroz, Moroz' is a traditional song, but I remixed it with more neo-Leninist influences." Dugen worked hard on that, actually.

Nate was visibly annoyed. The traffic had barely budged and it was getting perilously close to 9am.

Sasha laughed. "That sounds amazing! I hope there's a recording of it."

Dugen shrugged and stuck his head between the front car seats. He definitely was not wearing a seat belt. He had to set the record straight.

"So I emphatically deny plagiarizing the song! I remixed it and included attribution with lipstick written on the bathroom tiles. Fair Use. 17 United States Code Section 107. And also, it wasn't especially visible because you only gave me one strobe light."

Nate chuckled as he moved up a car and took another black coffee chug.

"Oh right, this is my fault for not having *multiple strobe lights* on hand when you asked to use the bathroom for three hours and refused to explain why... I forgot."

"Well it sounds amazing, Dugen. I'm really proud of you." Sasha kissed Dugen's forehead like that wasn't a weird thing at all.

"It was a great thesis project. I had almost 400 people watching the stream at one point and then I posted the notice from the dean that I had been suspended from the program as a photo for all my fans to comment on. It validated the subjugation of elite power structures just as Marx predicted would happen in *Das Kapital*. I should have given the keynote address at the annual academic symposium for that. I'm sure I was a runner-up" Dugen gloated.

"I'm sure!" Sasha concurred.

"I'm sure." Nate muttered.

Their station wagon was next in line at the Stop Sign of Eternity. Sasha began humming to herself as she looked out across the street. She loved the vibrant bustle of students hurrying to class, surely as eager to learn as she. A tall, athletic blonde in business attire walked past their car.

"Hey, that's Jillian!" Sasha exclaimed.

Jillian looked over, somewhat surprised but also hesitant to respond.

"Um, hi. Jill, please." Jill stopped and waved, adjusting her backpack across her shoulders. She was formally dressed in preparation for presenting her semester research project.

Sasha was great with names and remembered Jill from their freshman interest group, nearly four years ago now. Jill vaguely remembered Sasha's face.

"I'm Sasha Fenix. We were in the same Future Women Leaders service group together freshman year. Seems like so long ago" Sasha laughed nervously. She was used to people forgetting her name or where they met, so she always offered a social cushion to soften the awkward pause in this situation.

"Oh yeah, of course. Of course!" Jill smiled. She had no time for random street reunions like this, and definitely not today. She was presenting in her Nutrition Sciences course about the metabolic effects of synthetic fats and sugars during a fitness regimen.

"Well, gotta get to class" Jill smiled and started to turn away.

Nate waved farewell politely with one hand still on the steering wheel.

Dugen glanced over and muttered something about a "hot piece of ass for a Thursday at Sam-Co."

Spontaneous gestures of generosity were in Sasha's DNA and this morning was no exception.

"Want a ride to class? We carpool together and park in North Lot." Sasha also never took her benevolent offers with a no; once she was in the giving mood, she was unstoppable.

"Oh, um..." Jill calculated the compounding awkwardness of declining the offer divided by the further awkwardness of getting into a car with two random, scruffy college lads and an overbearing hippy chick from freshman year.

What the fuck, right? It's college.

"Sure" Jill agreed.

Jill smiled as Sasha hopped out of the front passenger seat. She trusted Nate to sit next to an attractive young lady more than Dugen. Leaving the door open for Jill, Sasha opened the rear passenger door. Dugen glared at Sasha.

"Since I rent this vehicle for stationary overnight habitation, I sublease the rear seats during daytime hours for $125 monthly. As the contractual licensor, I hereby grant you access to half this space for the duration of this ride at no charge, but—"

"—I'll make you dinner tonight and it will be the best meal you've had in months" Sasha cheerfully interrupted as she diplomatically slid Dugen's legs off the seat so she could get in.

"Hi, I'm Jill" she offered her best handshake to Nate as she sat in the front passenger seat.

Nate found the forced introduction a bit much for the minimal serving of coffee he had downed. He ran a carpool service now? His next vehicle would definitely be a two-seater pickup.

"Nate. Nice to meet you. And that's Dugen. It's best not to talk to him without an attorney and a hostage negotiator present."

Jill laughed nervously. Surely that was a joke. It was probably a joke.

"Are you a business student?" Dugen launched into the inquiry forthright.

Jill instinctively assumed her professional posture, just like her academic advisor and career counselor trained her to do.

"I'm majoring in Exercise Science with a double minor in Nutrition and Human Physiology. I'm also on the varsity track team. Big meet this weekend!" Jill smiled, then straightened out her grin. Too immodest? Too boastful?

"Jillian, um sorry Jill... she's really smart" Sasha added.

"I've taken some of the foundational exercise science courses and found them too restrictive, unimaginative... but with potential for utility maximization if augmented with cybernetic technology" Dugen declared.

"Oh. They are tough classes but I learn so much and definitely look forward to putting all those textbooks into practice." Jill responded like any accomplished job interviewee would to a largely superfluous statement.

Who was this guy?

Dugen continued, having waited months to say this to anyone who might listen. A slow-moving vehicle is a captive audience.

"My view is that the scientific reduction of human biology to serve broader economic objectives is a dead end, philosophically. But if that reduction is in the service of achieving a lowest common denominator, conceptually and practically, with cybernetic augmentation... well, there's some wild shit there, right?"

Dugen began to laugh wildly, almost uncontrollably. "Some seriously wild transhumanist shit right there!" Dugen gestured with his fist as a loose hand tightening into a robotic grip. He stared at Jill with wide eyes. What a first impression.

"That's really interesting, never thought of it like that..." Jill smiled and laughed nervously, then looked up front.

"You two would have so much to talk about" Sasha beamed. It was finally time to pull ahead from the Stop Sign of Eternity.

Nate accelerated. He found it best to avoid at least half the conversations he could be part of. Including this one. It was a short drive across the campus perimeter to North Lot. Busy morning traffic, as usual.

The car radio continued with another top 40 hit of the age, a hopeful ballad about the future infused with ska-styled brass horns.

> *Jump up on your Saturday*
> *cause you know that's what we do*
> *living wild like a runaway*
> *blasting beats with my rock jam crew*
>
> *don't bother looking back*
> *it's all dust by the time we're through*
> *red in the head, paint the white way black*
> *rip-roaring past the cautionary you*

Nate merged into traffic as Sasha and Dugen discussed what meal would make sufficient payment for her use of "his" back seat.

It was hilarious to imagine how many other ways Dugen might try to monetize the rear of Nate's station wagon. Then Nate contemplated whether it had seen any college indiscretions during Dugen's dubious tenancy. Did Nate want to know? Surely not.

"So what are you studying?" Jill turned to ask Nate, seeking something more like normal adult conversation. Her networking skills had to do something for this sordid situation. Backpack between her legs, Jill reached for her container of gum to covertly manage her social anxiety.

"Forest Management. If all goes according to plan, I'm gonna be working at a National Park this fall. I interned at Yellowstone last semester and loved it."

Nate's eyes glimmered with the fond memories of such majestic natural beauty. The solitude, the quiet peace of winter as the tourism subsided and the rich tapestry of wildlife flourished uninterrupted. He longed for those morning hikes on the trail and the late-night stargazing while bundled in six layers of clothing, breath rising as pillars of steam, dissolving into the infinite black stratosphere. The woods were calling him again.

"That's so nice. I've never been to Yellowstone but would love to check it out." Jill found a topic of genuine interest.

Nate nodded and glanced at the clock radio.

It was nearly 9:00!

Time to pass some slow commuters. Nate loved to drive fast.

Nate changed lanes and accelerated. Blew past three slow cars. A van. A pickup truck. Another slow car. Nate liked to push the speed limit just enough to shave some time off his commutes.

All those minutes added up. And now multiplied by a factor of four. The speedy car pool service.

The turn for Salmon Springs College north parking lot was coming up. Nate prepared to signal.

Click. Click. Click.

Nate returned to the right lane.

Out of nowhere:

Black truck with a flatbed trailer!

"FUCK." Nate tried to swerve as the truck entered his lane.

There was no time.

There was no distance.

The station wagon collided with the truck.

An industrial cacophony of smashing sounds.

Nate gripped the wheel and closed his eyes.

Sasha gasped, put her hands up, and fell onto Dugen.

Jill was blindsided. She screamed in terror.

Their station wagon spun, swerved past oncoming traffic, and settled in the median.

Smoke. Hissing sounds. Car horn blaring. Serene spring tranquility shattered.

"Oh no, oh no, oh God. Oh fuck." Nate was exasperated. He looked back.

Sasha and Dugen were covered in debris and shattered glass. They were breathing fast. They looked back at Nate. They were in shock. A few scrapes and scratches. They looked intact.

Nate looked over to Jill. She was staring blankly ahead of her.

Did this really happen?

What just happened?

What just happened...

It just... happened.

Jill looked down. The hot, piercing pain was immeasurable.

Her legs were contorted, crushed in the shape of the dented front passenger car door.

There was so much blood.

So much blood.

[2 – All Your Boxes]

Jill awoke in a cold sweat. Her breath was fast. Her heart raced.

It was her worst nightmare all over again.

She reached down beneath the sheets. Her legs were intact. Her muscles were strong. Her pulse was flush against her skin. She looked off to one side to see the first pale light of morning creeping in from under her curtains. She slept through the night. That was accomplishment enough.

She turned on the lamp on her bedside table. Unfurling the sheets, Jill traced the surgery scars along her right leg. They had faded so much that it took a close observation to locate them. The surgery team at Salmon Springs General had done a tremendous job.

Jill stretched and slipped into her morning comfortables. Jill brushed her teeth, flossed, and fixed her hair as her AI assistant loaded the daily news bulletin. She voice-activated her tablet as it rest on the charging station. With a monotone delivery, the digital announcer summarized the headlines. Jill only paid passive attention to what was a predictable parade of horribles in headline form.

- There had been another bombing in a foreign capital. The regional governments condemned the attack, but officials conceded further instability was likely, as many insurgent forces were consolidating power and preparing for a coup attempt. Drought conditions led to hunger, hunger led to civil unrest, and civil unrest led to mobilizing militia groups. Food supplies came and went, but guns and ammunition were always plentiful; thus, the ingredients for ongoing warfare were abundant. This was usual for a Tuesday.

- In related news, parts of the Pacific Northwest region have broken off from federal control. A rising group of loosely-affiliated militia movements, calling itself the Reddard Faction, have claimed large areas outside city centers where police control has receded. Named for the fallen militia leader Bronson Reddard, the movement opposed the creation of the National Defense Force and now openly defied their authority in these territories.

- Rolling blackouts were affecting much of North America and Europe as extended summer heat waves pushed aging electrical grids to a breaking point. Towns and cities with independent, distributed solar were less affected, but reporting in those regions was also limited due to a lack of centralized communication networks. "Off the grid" meant that good news and bad news alike rarely carried. This left everyone else to speculate and project their existing prognostications onto the off-grid regions.

- Due to ongoing flooding and hurricanes throughout the Southeast, major league sports like football and baseball have been suspended in order to utilize the stadium space for permanent shelters. This had become a regular practice for decades now, but the severe conditions were now so omnipresent that the facilities were needed year-round. As major urban coastal areas became deluged beyond recognition with sea water, massive population shifts inland were an ongoing occurrence.

- As such, climate disruption created climate refugee populations at an unprecedented scale, the United Nations formed a council on mass migration. This move was long overdue and unlikely to address the scale of the problem. Individual countries vacillated between offering shelters and accommodations or erecting higher walls and fortifying them with armed military forces. But due to the extreme nature of the droughts, floods, wildfires, and hurricanes, no combination of deterrents proved effective at mitigating widespread human travel to more temperate, inland regions.

- The Species Extinction Clock was moved up another twelve minutes. A loss of habitat was the primary culprit, though scientists disagreed as to how much global climate disruption was eclipsing habitat disruption due to human activities. In the end, it was likely a distinction without a difference, given that declining biodiversity served to accelerate other environmental problems in ways not previously predicted. Animals no one much cared for turned out to be the proverbial canaries in the coal mine; who knew the absence of a few tiny frog species could commence the collapse of an entire ecosystem?

- With global temperatures rising and supply gaps in preventative medicines, common diseases were on the rise and, in some regions, at record levels. Regional pandemics were not uncommon, though a dramatic decrease in global air travel and long distance commuting had the effect of a low-grade quarantine. Nonetheless, life expectancy continued to drop as a result of infectious disease outbreaks.

- In economic news, ongoing talks of a wealth tax to fund universal basic income were stalled in the World Economic Forum as several rich countries objected outright. Global poverty was at an all-time high relative to dwindling populations, but the plight of the poor drew insufficient sympathy from key voting blocs in world governments. The wealthiest nations pledged to dedicate more resources to the problem voluntarily, but their free enterprise advocates continued to argue for a privatized philanthropic solution with business leaders – not politicians – determining how best to remedy unprecedented levels of wealth inequality.

"So just get up earlier and hustle for your money" Jill muttered as she stepped out of the shower.

She was in a grouchy mood already. Her hot showers had been cut down from five minutes to four minutes as power supplies were rationed on weekday mornings and afternoons. "Peak usage" seemed to be an ever-expanding definition for utility companies these days.

"Newsfeed off" Jill prompted her tablet.

That was enough bad news for now. Probably for a long time.

Even as things seemed to be getting worse and worse, they more or less felt the same. When the trajectory is decline, decline begins to feel normal. Coping with loss was proof of life.

If you weren't losing something, you were probably dead. Be thankful you had something left to lose. Appreciate what remains. It was the best available mantra, apart from some soothing yet empty religious palliative about End Times redemption.

Good times surely were just around the corner. And if they weren't, decent times were good enough.

Jill opened her curtains and stretched. Even after That Crash, she dedicated herself to maintaining great physical fitness. It wasn't just about being able to run up three flights of stairs for a meeting without being winded or run a half-marathon for charity; it was about control.

In a world of chaos and uncertainty, being able to walk into the gym and pound out a solid workout left her invigorated and de-stressed. It gave Jill control of her immediate experience. And that was more than most people had.

Outside, the entire cityscape of Wynhill Heights stretched almost without end. Jill's upscale condo was nestled in the business district, and that meant her morning commute was a mere four blocks.

Skyscrapers jutted up against the morning skyline, hazy as usual given the ongoing wildfire season. Anyone who could pay for clean interior air did so promptly and without hesitation. Those who couldn't afford or access filtered air struggled more each spring, each summer, each fall. "Wildfire season" might as well be swapped with "clear air filtration season" between November and March. If residents were lucky.

Jill had fallen out of love with her premium view of the city. Wynhill had fared better as a financial center for the East Coast than many other cities. But the problems that started elsewhere crept into Wynhill just as every other community.

Poverty was rampant and tent cities were common. Most commercial and residential real estate was owned by investment firms and transnational corporations. There were no "market pressures" to address the need for more affordable housing; it was more profitable to leave a luxury condo vacant for a few months until it was bought up by speculators than to rent it out as a multi-household residence. The corporate landlord software algorithms made sure of that.

Wynhill marketed itself as an upscale lifestyle experience, and that was still possible – if you could afford it.

Private security, fencing, and perimeter restrictions for unauthorized vehicles or pedestrians created a comfortable barrier between the wealthy and everyone else. If you weren't on your way to being wealthy, or already there, you were probably going to remain broke – whether employed or jobless.

Housing had become a premium experience. Whether the term was a shanty town, a tent city, an urban ghetto, a favela, or a slum, it was where most of the world called home.

Jill used to have a form of economic survivor's guilt. She still did some days, like when she made eye contact with a glassy-eyed, haggard stranger curled up in a blanket on the street while on her walk to work or shopping downtown. What could she do? She worked hard, she paid her taxes, she donated at the annual charity ball at the office. It wasn't her fault. She was just trying to help. Somebody should do something. Maybe they just didn't want to work?

Social scientists in the mid 2030s began to call this era "The Long Collapse."

It didn't commence with some spectacular market crash or global war, though such calamities were built into prediction models, being the subject of widespread academic and popular discourse.

No one could quite agree on the precise cause of The Long Collapse.

Maybe it was the volatility of Peak Oil as petroleum supplies dwindled and the price-per-barrel would spike due to shortages and then crash due to a lack of demand. A global economy run on a centralized commodity was extremely sensitive to price shocks and supply disruptions.

Maybe it was the decline of environmental resources like fresh water, nutrient-dense soil, precious minerals, or protein-rich fish supplies. What once seemed abundant was now heavily contested and often the underlying driver of local conflicts in one hot spot or another. Then another. Then another. Then wider social unrest. Then militarized skirmishes.

Maybe it was global climate change crossing precipitous thresholds too hard, too fast, and resulting in chaotic weather patterns and catastrophic natural disasters. Growing food on an industrial scale requires predictable environmental conditions that no longer existed. Coastal flooding and erosion made many cities uninsurable, unaffordable, and ultimately uninhabitable.

Or maybe it was some combination of all these factors and more. Maybe it was far too many resource-intensive human activities being scaled up all over the world in the same microsecond of geological history. Maybe it was the normalization of rapacious resource consumption with no signs of tapering, insufficient efforts at sustainability, and a booming population of converging globalized civilizations, all replicating the same unsupportable economic, agricultural, and political models.

Nobody really knew what started The Long Collapse.

Everyone argued about it. Who was to blame? Why it wasn't fixed sooner? Who was still in denial about it? Who was over-reacting to suit their ideological agenda? Who was cynically profiting off the pervasive strife? Everyone had a theory. Little of it mattered.

Nothing was turning The Long Collapse around at this point. It wasn't just a few bad years; it was looking like a few bad decades.

Some days, it felt like an emergency. Most of the time, though, The Long Collapse just felt like a new way of life for everyone.

Those senior enough to remember better times would speak of them only in distant, somber ways. It was as though such prosperity and decadence never happened at all. It was as though an orgiastic dream with an abrupt, uncomfortable awakening.

By analysts and philosophers alike, The Long Collapse was sometimes called the hangover of a civilization drunk on infinite growth and unchecked ambition. Decline meant sobriety.

"Whatever." Jill was a survivor. She had survived a car wreck that the doctors said would have put most people six feet under.

Her varsity track career ended that day back in the spring of 2025, but she graduated with honors on a full academic scholarship. She continued on to complete a Masters in Communication and an MBA at the same time. No big deal.

Sure, Jill was resentful of her misfortune but remained undeterred. She used the settlement money from That Crash to move to the East Coast, intern at a big firm, and start her own consulting practice.

Jill succeeded. She was a high achiever. She expanded her consulting firm to several cities before selling her company and taking a mid-level supervisory position at Suncoast Management. She was their youngest hire in the division.

Jill rarely made time for life outside work and always told herself that she would settle down someday, but became so consumed by her work that she eventually questioned wanting anything else. Who has time to start a family? How is that even affordable? And look at the world today. Who would want to bring children into this mess?

When The Long Collapse started, Jill saw major challenges for corporate communications and doubled down. She beat the rounds of layoffs and downsizing at Suncoast. She went from being a sprinter on the track to a distance runner on the corporate treadmill. She was damn good at it, too.

Jill always started her workday early from her home office so she would set foot in the board room already prepped and fully informed.

With a blueberry pomegranate nutritional shake in hand, she opened her virtual office suite across four synced tablets mounted on her fine mahogany desk. The convergence of luxury and function.

The usual daily updates from the corporate headquarters, "right-sizing" various satellite offices, focusing on core quarterly metrics, profit-loss ratios, a reminder from HR about mandatory micro-aggression training, adjustments to the company pension plan...

"Oh, shit."

"Shit, shit, shit."

"No."

Jill's heart raced as she swiped away from the previous messages
and accessed a receipt-verified memo from her division chair.

Even before she opened it, she knew.

She knew because she had circulated these messages to
previous co-workers for years. She drafted this very message to
be sent to someone else. Now, it was for her.

Jillian Tavana   ,

This message serves as a notice of employment termination. Your last day will be today,   Tuesday, September 19, 2045   .

Please suspend all other work in progress. Your tasks today are: 1) write a transition memo summarizing your current client tasks, performance management caseload, outgoing action items, and any key performance indicators your division may have missed, 2) pack all your boxes for an orderly and prompt departure. A complimentary lunch will be provided.

This notice is unfortunate for our team and indeed for all of Suncoast Management. You have been a valued contributor for over   12   years and our company could not have weathered such difficult times without you. Your   supervisory position and the remaining management team reporting to you at the Suncoast Wynhill metro office   were eliminated in the latest round of right-sizing actions. Regrettably, economic conditions have made the board's responsibility to maintain profitability even more difficult and challenging, but necessary cuts were required this fiscal quarter.

You will receive a payout for the remainder of the month, plus any accrued time off through the end of the calendar year   . Suncoast Management will prepare a severance package and termination documents which we trust you will find agreeable.

Best of luck on your future endeavors and thank you again for your dedicated service in achieving the Suncoast vision for a prosperous business climate.

"Corporate Mad Libs."

Jill finally realized how insufferable it felt to receive a badly-formatted form letter as her sole and final notice of termination. She would never send out such a shoddy notice to any of her clients or colleagues.

Maybe she was too good for Suncoast, anyway. They didn't deserve her, anyway. She was overqualified, anyway. She was due for several promotions and was passed over every time.

Suncoast Management wasn't firing Jillian Tavana, because she had already "quiet quit!"

Being let go at work wasn't all that different from being dumped by a longtime lover or getting divorced from your spouse. Your world is shattered in the short term, your outlook is gloomy for the near future, but the next relationship will start the process all over again.

You bargain with yourself for a while, you blame the other person, you settle on a few areas of improvement and conclude within three months that it was better this way.

Jill buttoned up her suit, pulled her hair in a bun, and held her head up as she took the glass elevator to the ground level of her building. She felt herself descend into the depths of Wynhill's grimy, decaying underbelly once again. She vowed this would be her last.

The scurrying and scuttle of the streets were always filled with distrust. Never make eye contact, never stop to engage.

There was stranger danger everywhere now. It felt like it had been like this for so long, there was never any other way for the pedestrian commute. Anyone with big money took an armored car – electric when possible, but gas-powered if necessary – with doors always locked. For everyone else, it was a bike, scooter, skateboard, or sneakers.

Jill had carried mace in her purse for many years, but only in the past few months did she find herself clutching it from the concealment of her designer handbag. Most new handbags worth buying had an inner pocket specifically for a concealed weapon of one kind or another; it was the next best thing to actually fixing the staggering wealth inequality, which made a walk to work more dangerous to begin with.

Jill's last walk from work felt like a walk of shame after a night at the frat house. Was she proud of her work at Suncoast? Any regrets? Would she do it all again from the start?

The usual grieving process commenced. Jill was a high achiever, but she knew her share of setbacks and disappointments, as well.

Nobody makes it to their forties without major losses, even if mixed in with major victories. And Jill had counseled plenty of her own former colleagues in what felt like an ongoing war of attrition by corporate firms against their own employees: make conditions so bad at work that people "quit," so you never have to formally terminate them and trigger unemployment benefits.

The unusual greeting routine gave way to the uncanny feeling of leaving the office forever. Did the empty smiles and perfunctory greetings come from a place of bereavement? Did they know it was her last day?

Jill felt numb. She needed to get through this. It would be humiliating if it didn't feel so inevitable. It was a rite of passage she had avoided for far longer than most people she knew at Suncoast. Hard-working people. People with families. People with mortgages and student loans and credit card debt and medical bills. Who was Jill to complain? She owned her own condo and had no debt, no dependents, not even a houseplant that would rely on her.

Jill banged out a transition memo with ease because all the necessary components were already drafted. It was as though she was a "prepper" of the corporate world; storing a cache of vital information and a "bug-out bag" for when the upper management shit hit the board of director's fan.

The landscape was an air-conditioned assortment of banal designer furniture and sleek computer equipment instead of a frigid taiga, but the mindset was the same. Jill was a survivor. And she very well could be the last person to leave the crumbling office in the disintegrating business district of the Wynhill metro area.

Packing up all your boxes is an act of personal consolidation. The two most impactful events in a person's life are always loss and moving. Losing friends or family, losing a pet, losing a lover or a prized possession. It's all gone now. You can take the memories with you, but you have to leave the physical proof of that connection behind.

Moving means redefinition. Shake up all the pieces of your life and roll them out somewhere else to see where they will land. Packing up all your boxes means intentionally compounding everything you are and carrying it to the next destination.

Maybe that was the saddest part of it. Not the loss of her cushy corporate gig, but how unremarkable it all was. Nothing in those boxes meant anything to Jill. Etched glass awards, achievement plaques, certificates of achievement, notices of recognition.

It was purely corporate conditioning. It was an affirmation that Jill struck all the poses and made all the noises expected of her, like a well-heeled kabuki theater for the one percent. And now that it all fit neatly into two boxes and a mailing tube, it meant less to her than the office plant she could have maintained in the same space the entire time. If living plants weren't prohibited in the décor guideline manual that came with her corner office, that is.

Jill hit 'send' on her transition memo. She cc'd everyone in the office. Maybe it was passive-aggressive, but having nothing left to lose is a profoundly liberating experience. There was no snarky tone in the contents of the document; it was as impeccable as every other aspect of Jill's job performance.

Everyone would wonder how she could write such a thorough and complete memo in less than an hour. The smart people would know she wrote it months ago because Jill knew this would happen; she was as prepared to get laid off as she was to work. That's why she always excelled: she was ready.

That is, she was ready for everything except the next message she got in her inbox. As Jill loaded her two boxes and one mailing tube into the back of a company moving car, her phone pinged again. And instead of being from one of a dozen Suncoast colleagues wishing her well and feigning shock at her departure, it was a name she hadn't thought of in a very long time.

Hi Jill,

Can you believe it's been 20 years? *It's crazy to even think about it. So much has changed, and not just in the cliché ways to which most folks refer.*

As you probably heard or read about, almost all of Salmon Springs College burned down two summers ago in the 44-Cascade Complex wildfire. There isn't money for a rebuild, so the remaining cohort of students are taking classes remotely. It's a sad situation, but we were the lucky ones to have attended SSC during such a thriving time and I'm forever grateful for it.

Anyway, there isn't a broad interest in an annual homecoming event (there aren't sports teams competing right now, anyway). But this is our one and only 20-year class reunion, so why not celebrate?

My husband Rylar and I are hosting an informal Homecoming 2045 event on the weekend of October 7th. We live on a small farm just west of Salmon Springs and would love for you to come!

We are keeping it small. I am inviting Nate and Dugen, just so you know. I realize things worked out as well as they could after that crash, but I totally understand if you are hesitant to attend. If not then, perhaps another time?

Hope you are well! You are so successful and I'm very proud to call you my Future Women Leaders freshman interest group partner!

Yours,
Sasha Fenix

Jill looked out the company car window, past the rows of tent encampments and makeshift cardboard houses, peering into the depths of her own shunted emotional reservoir.

Of all the emails she was prepared for today, this wasn't one of them. A flooding of feelings left Jill awash in excitement, sorrow, regret, resentment, nostalgia, guilt, and anger... but most of all: curiosity.

Should she tell her dad? They hadn't spoken in many, many years. He was still living in their old place in Salmon Springs, the Tavana family home.

Surely these two pivotal messages arrived in her inbox on the same day for a reason, or at least with the opportunity for her to make a reason from them.

Arriving at her posh apartment earlier than usual, holding two boxes and a mailing tube, Jill gazed across the Wynhill skyline as if for the first time.

Perhaps for the last time.

Perhaps she had many more boxes to pack today.

Perhaps it was time to survive something new.

Oh, if only Jill knew what the limit-seeking edges of survival would soon reveal inside her...

[3 – Moral Equilibrium]

The rave at End Party was just ramping up and the drugs were just kicking in. Amid smoke-filled beams of flashing colored lights, writhing bodies grooved to the music in jubilant fervor.

Electric grooves, pounding bass, crooning smooth lyrical melodies blasting from the DJ booth, flying across the room at the speed of sound and back again.

Reverberation sensation sublime.

> *at the bottom of everything*
> *you know what to do*
> *the vibe comes from anything*
> *so gather up your crew*
>
> *tempt me baby*
> *show me a good time tonight*
> *gonna cry when its over*

our ecstasy is gonna bite

oooh oooh yeah you got it
ohhh ohhh yeah you want it
mmm mmm yeah you need it
so mmm hmm yeah you flaunt it

Sweaty and scruffy, Dugen wiped his brow and made his way through the crowd. His body gyrated in a combination of dance moves and stumbling gestures, as if a participant and an evacuee of the same bopping cacophony.

He definitely took double the dose of X-Delight. Synthetic hallucinogens had become safer and more reliable over the years, but only if their chemical purity was guaranteed. And in 2045, nothing was guaranteed.

Well, not quite.

Dugen slunk down in a neon plastic lounger next to a couple of passed out party-goers. He drank whatever was left on the table, since clearly they were done drinking.

"Tastes sweet, still cold going down." Dugen cleared his throat.

He had to yell over the blazing synth beats. His hair was nearly long enough to put up in a bun, so he found himself pulling loose strands from across his face.

"They call this place End Party because it's an abbreviation of a popular phrase. Did you know that?"

Dugen preferred to talk to people who were incapacitated because they were less argumentative and availed him of the opportunity to develop his own thoughts out loud. Dugen still preferred a captive audience.

"End Party comes from the slogan 'the end of the world is the best time to party.' Scholars disagree on the origin of the phrase, which pre-dated The Long Collapse by a decade at least. The most likely source is the lead singer of the techno-punk band Golly-Whopping Gorefest, named Jonny Jundersohn."

Dugen paused to belch.

BUUUUUUUURRRRP!

Nobody heard. Nobody cared.

"During a pre-show interview with Trends e-mag, Jonny was quoted as saying that he doesn't worry about potentially negative cultural influences from his mosh pit shows because the world has already ended... but we can't hear it because the music is still going... might as well keep partying."

Dugen paused to belch again and loosen his necktie.

The thing about X-Delight is that it hits hard and stays active for an hour or two, but then tapers off quickly. Most experienced users could fit an X-Delight trip inside a lunch break – and at a fraction of the cost of a fine martini.

Dugen preferred to stay substance free during the daytime but would take something wild and vibrant during his nightly excursions. He considered these sessions to be a form of psychedelic cultural anthropology. The psycho-activity combined with attempts at socialization to generate more insights into the human condition and the nature of the universe.

That was the theory. Dugen was putting it to practice.

"But I contend that Jonny wasn't talking about literal music; that was just a readily-available metaphor employed by a poetic musician. Merely the medium, my friends."

Dugen waved his finger, then continued.

"Partying until the music stops could be conceived as a broader philosophical framework to think about reverie as a remedy for dystopia. Maybe the world has ended, and maybe we can't hear it over the music, but the void created by apocalypse could be filled by the excesses of celebratory hedonism. Maybe."

Dugen looked over at the passed out party-goers. They were finely dressed for the occasion. A hundred years of unwieldy consumption had created a fashion glut and an embarrassment of riches for those inclined to paint the town red. Black-out drunk with decadence.

"What I'm saying," Dugen tried to summarize "... is that, is the collapse of society merely creates a psychic vacuum. That space is waiting to be filled. And the chaos of unabated pleasure could be the ideal substance to pour into the despairs of The Long Collapse. At least until something better comes along. It's a makeshift solution for an unprecedented problem."

Dugen raised a glass in each hand and clinked them together as a toast to himself. He made his own good company.

"The end of the world is the best time to party!" Dugen drank the last of each glass and set them down dramatically.

The sound startled one of the party-goers from their stupor. She looked over at Dugen with a puzzled, disoriented stare.

"Until next time." Dugen made a clicking sound followed by a double finger-gun gesture.

He stood up and walked like an Egyptian towards the exit. Were there usually inverted purple pyramids falling from the lighting grid and between the ceiling panels? Or was this the next exotic detour of his X-Delight? The fun part was the distinct possibility it could be both.

To friends and enemies alike, Dugen described Blackroot as "a college town on the coast, humid enough to stave off the parched conditions which made more inland regions a tinder box for wildfires." Dugen had been bumming around Blackroot for the better part of a decade after having just woke up there one summer. It suited him well enough for now.

As for tonight's foray on the fringes of sobriety, Dugen had been coming to End Party every week or two. It was the hottest club in Blackroot and had the least power outages. He found that was infrequent enough to keep from being recognized by security.

Nobody could prove it, but there were some alleged "incidents" of partial nudity involving a man in a dinosaur costume. Dugen told police that he didn't know anything about it, but would keep his eyes open "in case such a man were to return." Was it him? Nobody could prove it. Besides, everybody knows that the dinosaurs went extinct. Except for the ones that evolved into rapturous party-raptors. Maybe Dugen was their final form.

Pushing the metal bar on the back door, Dugen stumbled into the alley.

It was still early in the night. He had enough coins in his pocket to procure a few hot dogs from his favorite vendor up the street. The steam rising from the heat and the pungent aroma of sausages and kraut were more than enough to entice a weary club-goer.

Dugen couldn't party quite like he used to. It was starting to rain.

"Dogman! The usual please... and thank you, kind sir" Dugen

stammered as the street vendor pocketed his coins. It was the clinking sound of a midnight dinner bell. Dugen's mouth watered like a Pavlovian mutt.

"What's the usual, my man?" Dogman Alphonse was old and tired. He had no idea what Dugen was talking about.

"The usual is whatever you feel like giving me for what I gave you. That's usually the usual in any voluntary exchange. Plus I'm hungry enough not to be more exacting than—"

"—a'yup, okay... you got it." Dogman Alphonse knew enough to get to dogging.

Out came two steamy sausages, wrapped in buns, with everything on them. All the fixings were tough to get these days, so it was a smorgasbord for the senses when a fully-dressed dog was presented. Dugen reveled in the aroma.

"Yes!" Dugen was thrilled with whatever the universe gave him, especially if it contained enough salt and nitrates to power through the entire night.

"I won't be back for awhile" Dugen spoke with a full mouth and a sense of satiation.

"Oh no? I see you here all the time." Dogman Alphonse had been running this stand for at least 20 years and fed generations of famished college students and drunk club-goers.

It was a minor miracle that his gig was still running strong, but being mobile and keeping his inventory simple was the key to salty success.

"Yeah, but not again for awhile." Dugen rummaged through his pockets, then held up a single sheet of paper he printed from the Blackroot Library that afternoon.

"See this? It's an invitation to a homecoming party from an old hippy friend of mine. It's back in Salmon Springs! 20 years! Crazy, right?"

"Oh, nice." Dogman Alphonse had no other customers and a bit of company was a welcome occurrence at this hour.

"I read that the college had burned down with most of the town. They called it 'Cascade Complex Wildfire Number 44' or something. Seemed like just a matter of time after all the other fires in the area." Dugen wiped his greasy mouth on the sleeve of his shirt.

"Oh well, I had accrued like 300 credit hours there... and now they're up in smoke. Poof. Like that. Degree programs are flammable... but only the knowledge burns on." Dugen let out a long breath so the vapor from his mouth would dissipate in the cool, early autumn air.

"That's too bad, I know what you mean. The fires keep getting worse and nowhere is safe. Half surprised Blackroot hasn't gone down in flames." Dogman Alphonse laughed. "Could take me down with it by now."

"Yeah, but... my friend Sasha's throwing a party, anyway." Dugen finished downing his double dog.

"Well, take care my friend. Come back to Blackroot and tell me how it went – if this place is still here!"

"You got it, but if you don't see me again... it's because the tides of fate have shifted and charted a new course for me." Dugen wiped his face on his sleeve. "Always excellent eats, my friend!"

"Thank you, my man!" Dogman Alphonse nodded and began to close up shop. At this late hour, Dugen was his last customer.

Dugen headed across the underpass and into South End in search of debris. If he was going to raise enough funds for a train ride to Salmon Springs, he would first have to balance the moral equilibrium.

South End was always a mess. To the extent Blackroot still had city sanitation services, they were north of the freeway overpass.

Services like trash cleanup and road maintenance had always been disproportionate in favor of higher property values, but The Long Collapse had forced all municipalities into a triage mode. Keeping the power on and providing clean water was about all most cities and towns could afford to do. Everyone just had to make do with crumbling roads and bridges. All that was once "out of sight, out of mind" had become "clear and present garbage."

For a few years now, Dugen had deputized himself as a kind of dirt cheap, urbanized super hero, a vigilante of the slums. But rather than fighting violent crime like Batman, Dugen vacillated between being a good Samaritan and a petty thief.

In this episode: Dugen knew that, by dawn, he could lift enough bike parts to assemble something worth bartering for a ticket out of town.

First though, Dugen found a crumpled-up black trash bag against the fence line. Fences acted as filters through which a stinky city breeze would pass, but leave behind the wrappers, cans, bottles, and other tattered throw-aways.

If Dugen was in a hurry to fill a bag with trash, he would work the fence line first.

Dugen's favorite part of picking up trash, aside from the occasional discovery of discarded street treasure, was assembling the remnants of a by-gone era. These were the clues of a civilization in decline. They told a story. Who was going to listen?

The most common finds were usually some combination of low-value sustenance packaging and mind-altering substances. An emptied box of crackers and a bevy of beer cans. Potato chip wrappers and tiny plastic liquor bottles. A beef jerky bag and a glass bottle drained of its cheap wine.

Then there was the evidence of overnighting. A mildew-ridden sweater and a flattened cardboard box for a mattress. A discarded sanitation kit containing used-up toiletries. The obligatory feces mound a few feet to one side. Maybe the ashy remains of a fire pit. An abandoned shoe. Where was the other of a matching pair? Widowed shoes were surely a metaphor for something.

Dugen usually scooped up all of it and trashed it. His goal was to restore the area to something resembling its original state – perhaps not a pristine, natural one, but at least how it would have looked before The Long Collapse.

Dugen viewed this as his civilization curator role. He wasn't just picking up litter. He was gathering all the discarded objects representing the excesses of the epoch. Who would be left to assemble all the clues as to what happened here? How did people live during The Long Collapse? Would some future society return to gather these clues and make meaning from them?

Dugen's 300-plus credit hours had to be applicable somehow. It wasn't long before the bag was full. Dugen stretched his aging back and groaned.

The X-Delight had worn off and everything felt a bit dull, numb, and somber. He sat against a pillar of the underpass to rest. The scene was dark, quiet, and tailored for solitude.

Dugen whistled for a few minutes. Whistling in the night was a favorite pastime for him lately.

He tried to play some of his favorite songs with his lips and tongue. Dugen didn't learn how to whistle until high school, but became exceedingly good at controlling his tonal range and pitch.

It was a party trick and a fast way to make friends whilst moving from school to school with a military father and a clinically insane mother.

> *ever go somewhere else?*
> *ever try to come back?*
> *did everything change?*
> *did you change, too?*
>
> *placement on the map*
> *underneath the same stars*
> *spinning a million miles in space*
> *you'll never stand still*
>
> *so get up and get going*
> *knowing you were already en route*
> *cultivate the yell inside you*
> *culminate in outer shout*

A few mice scurried about. One would stop to look at Dugen, then return to sniffing the debris for something to eat.

Dugen loved the night hours because he had the fallen world all to himself. Dugen and the mice. Dugen the Mouse King.

"Scavengers. We've always been scavengers. Skimming, scraping, scrapping scavengers. We managed to fool ourselves for a few millennia, but that was merely the exception to the rule. The turn of times has clarified this illusion." Dugen was explaining this to the rodents, who clearly already knew.

"Civilization is a rock hurtling through the air. Chaos is the gravity that pulls it back down. Anarchy is the ground upon which all civilizations fall." Something he'd been thinking about.

Dugen picked up a chunk of granite and tossed it into the darkness of night. It predictably fell after a brief aerial ascension. Dugen heard the thud in the distance. It echoed back across the freeway underpass. Almost nobody drove on the freeway these days. It wasn't safe and there wasn't fuel and there wasn't any better destination, anyway.

"That's us. That's now." The mice appeared disinterested. "We are living in the echo of our former civilization. But I can still hear it." Dugen pointed at one particularly pugnacious mouse with an apple core. "And you can, too."

Dugen stood up and stretched. It was time to go bike hunting and South End was no good for that. The best bike hunts were in West Valley near Blackroot Prep Academy. On weekends, the campus was largely vacant as the staff were home and the students were away partying.

It was a two hour walk to West Valley and the infrequent transit bus was no longer running past midnight. But Dugen had an inside track on some quick transportation.

Not far from the freeway underpass was Chuck's Moving and Storage. Dugen never met Chuck, but figured he must be a nice enough guy to let Dugen borrow one of his vans.

The keys were always kept above the passenger-side visor. Dugen knew this because one of Chuck's ex-employees knew this and lost a game of high stakes poker to Dugen. This was years ago.

Dugen walked around the worn-down brick building once for good measure. No dogs, no security cameras. There was a high fence, but Dugen knew of a low pit along the north side. Sliding underneath and picking his favorite vehicle, it wasn't long before Dugen was on his way to West Valley. He wasn't stealing; he was borrowing. Back before dawn.

CRASH.

It was a shame about the broken gate, but Chuck shouldn't have put a lock on it so Dugen could have opened it more easily. He would surely take some of the bike hunt proceeds and leave it in the van for Chuck to repair the gate.

It was the right thing to do.

The roads were empty but the streets remained lined with tents. A dumpster fire here and there, scenes of cold alley-dwellers warming themselves around an oil barrel topped with billowing flames, and a herd of deer making its way across an abandoned construction zone and into a thick patch of brush.

The wilds and the impoverished all blended together like an unaired National Geographic special.

Blackroot had been a vibrant city before The Long Collapse. It fell on hard times when a massive flood coming from a Pacific tsunami left the city under 10 feet of water for months. The structural damage was devastating and the initial death toll was high, but the lack of widespread evacuation meant the surviving inhabitants were left to fend for themselves without services.

The stagnant water led to disease and decay. Shortages of vaccines and anti-bacterials made matters worse. The ensuing civil unrest resulted in a breakdown of social order. The survivors formed improvised communes as governmental assistance was delayed and de minimis. Almost every place had some version of this story—already or eventually.

Dugen had found himself in Blackroot in the aftermath of the flooding, which happened around 2035. Nobody could quite remember the year at this point.

Most hallmarks of time are predicated on economic order and social cohesion. When those foundational elements break down, time becomes much more immediate. Fiscal quarters break down into fight or flight. Time is marked by having a full belly and a warm place to sleep.

It was a form of asynchronicity. Dugen planned to explore this topic later.

The crumbled, soggy remains of lower Blackroot suited Dugen just fine. The residue of better times left him many tangible and philosophical nuggets to gather.

More fascinating still was the dedication among its remaining population to return to the previous regimens and rituals: the worship of accruing wealth, the pursuit of status, the imbibing of fine drink and lavish social affairs.

The landscape had changed, but the paradigms of the previous era had not.

Dugen arrived at the edge of Blackroot Prep Academy to find it quiet as usual for the hour. He spotted a favorite bike rack and, sure enough, two prized specimens were sleeping side by side. Minimal cable lock security. Not a problem. Chuck's vans were all equipped with a toolbox well-stocked with cable cutters.

The bike hunter stalked his unassuming prey.

Grinding through the plastic sheath at the base of the lock was usually the easiest point. Dugen had been in the bike hunting business for a couple decades, on and off. He'd had bikes stolen from him, he'd stolen some bikes; it was all part of the great Cycle of Bicycles churning all around him. It was an unbroken thread spanning back millions of years to the beginning of bike history, and surely would span for millions more.

I like the bike I swipe, I swipe the bike I like
the bike likes the swipe, like the swipe of a bike

Dugen hummed to himself as he loaded the two bikes into the back of the van. Campus security would be by in a few hours, the owners of the bikes would be by in a couple days, and perhaps new bikes would arrive soon for the great exchange to continue.

Dugen promised the stolen bike owners that good cycle swipes, like good deeds, could be passed on. "If your bike disappears, the next to appear in its place is surely yours to claim. That's what we call 'the great Cycle of Bicycles.'"

The drive back to Chuck's went smoothly enough.

Gas stations were scarce but still around if one knew where to look.

Freeway exits rarely had a functioning one. Those were raided or abandoned first because roving petrol gangs saw them as under-defended, easily plundered, and quickly evacuated.

But in more affluent, tight-knit neighborhoods like West Valley, gas was still available at a premium. Electric cars were scarce and the giant battery cells were nearly impossible to find, but gas-powered vehicles were still viable for the select few who could afford them and/or resourceful enough to service them from the scrapyard... or for the discerning rental patron like Dugen.

He topped off the van's gas tank with a debit card he had lifted from one of the passed out party-goers at End Party. With the right button sequencing, most keypads could be put into override and the PIN code was always accepted, even if it was wrong.

With no one to maintain the hardware or update the firmware, exploits and bugs made most electronic kiosks vulnerable to apocalyptic hacker types. And if the passed out party-goers didn't remember getting gas? Surely they were grateful to have an upstanding moving and storage company in town and wanted to pay it forward as a down payment on their next visit.

Another rebalancing of the scales for the Moral Equilibrium.

Dugen parked the van back in line with the rest of Chuck's fleet. He wiped it down with a shop rag from the glove box so it was spotless. Better than Dugen had found it.

He was doing Chuck a favor. Whoever Chuck was.

Maybe Chuck was dead.

Maybe this moving and storage establishment was named after the proverbial Chuck, the notional Chuck, the platonic Chuck, the eternal Chuck in the sky, the everyman Chuck who had ever owned a moving and storage company. Maybe Chuck was smiling down at Dugen from above, elated with pride to having his van in immaculate condition and fueled up for its next outing.

Prove Dugen wrong.

Walking one bike in each hand, Dugen shut Chuck's gate so it looked more or less intact. Maybe the next person to use it would notice the damaged lock and latch only after they handled it and would assign the blame to themselves.

After all, the rest of the scene looked clean as a moonbeam.

The walk ahead was short. Dugen whistled and wondered what Salmon Springs was like these days. Those were some of his best years and those were some of his best friends. Being in your 20s meant having constant social exposure in the best possible way – surrounded by those inclined to be intellectually curious and ethically flexible.

Those curiosities diminish with age and flexibility hardens with time. Now early 40s, Dugen did his best to maintain both but it was an uphill battle, like a salmon swimming upstream.

Were the salmon coming back to Salmon Springs? That was the rumor.

At the north end of the underpass, Dugen arrived at a tent encampment known as Top Chop Shop. Locals regarded it as the finest in South End and probably all of Blackroot. Bikes, scooters, skateboards, and other easily-moved items of moderate value arrived here frequently and at all hours of the day and night. It was a 24/7 hub for the underground transportables market.

No one asked questions, no one questioned motives.

Dugen was a frequent contributor, patron, and benefactor of Top Chop Shop. Maybe he would get a plaque someday.

"Look who is rolling up with two fine ladies tonight!" One-Eyed Roderick was happy to see his old friend, Dirtbag Dugen. Roderick was always chewing on a toothpick and nobody had ever seen him eat anything except tins of sardines. Could be the breakfast of bike-lifting champions.

"Yes siree, straight from West Valley and ready to be sold off or diced up for parts. Happy to barter for them either way. Name your best offer." Dugen was a perpetual deal-maker because life was always a bargain.

Roderick cackled with a smoker's cough and looked the bikes up and down. He scratched his chin. "I'm thinking three-fifty is what I can do."

Dugen nodded. "Three eighty-five and they are both yours. I've got travel expenses coming up and still owe for the ride to get these beauties here."

Roderick let out a long, slow moan. It helped him think.

"Yup that works." Roderick extended his hand. Dugen shook on it.

These days, a handshake was the highest form of mutual assent. No paperwork from yesterday, no lawyers today, no revocation tomorrow.

One-Eyed Roderick always seemed to have a wad of bills in the side pockets of his denim overalls. The guy was a walking cash exchange and seemed to know the street price for any item off the top of his fuzzy, wrinkled head. He fanned out a combination of hundreds, twenties, and fives to add up to their exchange price.

"Thanks as always! I may not be back again for awhile. Going back to Salmon Springs."

Dugen pocketed the tender and headed out the deluxe, double-sized tent Roderick had erected for Top Chop Shop.

It was starting to rain again.

"What's in Salmon Springs? Didn't it burn down?" Roderick flicked his toothpick into a coffee can in the corner and instantly replaced it with a new one.

"We'll see." Dugen paused as he stood in the rain. "Probably not all of it."

Dugen pulled up the hood of his jacket as the first light of dawn crept through the storm clouds. Frequent wildfires meant hazy red and gold sunrises. Precipitation usually broke up the smoke enough to have great visibility in the morning.

What was a fair price for a two-hour van rental and a lock plus latch replacement? Dugen thought seventy-five was more than generous. He left it in the deposit box at Chuck's.

Dugen was getting tired. The train station was in the Central District. He could hitch a ride there and catch the afternoon schedule north to Salmon Springs.

Along the underpass was Couch Collective—behind an abandoned furniture store. It had become a regular rest stop for weary travelers without cash but seeking somewhere dry and reasonably safe.

Before The Long Collapse, the destitute and the unhoused would sleep on cardboard right in front of the Mattress Market window display, with mattresses locked up inside the furniture store.

Dugen was always perplexed by this. If some alien explorers arrived to observe human civilization, how could Dugen explain the homeless people sleeping on cardboard in front of a building... while perpetually unused mattresses "priced so low, they have to go" were encased in glass just inside it?

Was this really the best system humans could come up with for allocating resources?

Once The Long Collapse was underway, all pretenses of these putative property rights dissipated like farts in a stiff breeze. The mattresses, pull-out beds, sofas, and love seats were promptly "liberated" for anyone to use. Nobody was going to buy them. They were already made and ready for utilization. The need was urgent. The objections were non-existent.

Due in equal parts to necessity and non-enforcement, the capitalist enterprise of Mattress Market was transformed into Couch Collective.

Dugen found a couch suitably dry and comparatively clean. He sat for a moment and yawned. Several other comrades of Couch Collective were passed out around him.

Dugen looked over at an old woman wrapped in blankets, laying completely still. She didn't appear to be breathing. Dugen stretched and laid down on the couch.

"Yeah, I know what some people think about all this. How can I justify a pattern and practice of petty theft?" Dugen snapped his fingers, if only to hear the echo across the highway underpass.

"The key is balancing the Moral Equilibrium. I make a habit of cleaning up the accumulated debris of our aggregate largesse. I pay forward the dividends of my efforts." Dugen pulled his hood down to cover his eyes. He scratched his scruffy red beard.

"I recognize my methods are unconventional, but clearly... convention is dead. From its corpse, we must all harvest a system of morality fit for purpose... one which meets the demands of our age, not any previous age. When an outdated system breaks down, who will implement a new one?"

The old woman wrapped in blankets looked almost mummified. Maybe she had died a long time ago and her body was dumped here.

Or maybe she could still hear Dugen's pontification even as her brain shut down. That's what neuroscientists had posited in studies of how the brain dies: the sense of hearing is the last to go. Perhaps the old woman could take in Dugen's words as an epilogue to carry into her next life.

Is that how any of this works?

"I'm no expert." Dugen yawned and closed his eyes. "But I do try. I do try."

Before long, Dugen would be on a train to Salmon Springs. To his odd chimera of an alma mater. To his rowdy band of collegiate misfits. Revisiting the past is a discrete luxury of middle age.

The sleepy substances of his suprachiasmatic nucleus were kicking in.

What contours of contemplation would such a journey hold after all these years?

> Dugen
> > fading
> > > fast,
> > > > dreamt
> > > > > of
> > > > > > finding
> > > > > > > out...

[4 – Your Resting Place]

"Looks like this is really it, girl."

Nate stood over Kyla as she panted and whimpered in her grassy plot next to the cabin. Nate had gotten Kyla when she was just a puppy, before Nate and Caitlyn fixed up the cabin together, before Caitlyn's accident, before her overdose. It seemed like so long ago.

Kyla was twelve now, quite old for a Sheprador mix. Her fur had become more matted and her eyes were cloudy, her whiskers gray, her joints arthritic. She had frequent digestive problems and couldn't walk more than a short pace before collapsing in pain.

Nate had given her various supplements and medications, which extended Kyla's mobility for many years. She had been such an active dog and was always eager to go for hikes along the mountain trails or ride in the back of Nate's truck to Salmon

Springs for their monthly supplies. She was also a charmer and made new friends with every trip to town.

Pets had taken on a new meaning during The Long Collapse. Their invaluable service as companions was compounded, given the amount of human loss. With the demise of so many friends, family members, co-workers and colleagues, most people who could afford an animal bond welcomed one.

But aside from consoling humans stricken with grief, pets of suitable ability also retained their service roles in defending livestock from predators, protecting their owners from burglars and roving gangs, and even hunting small game, adding protein to the family diet. A well-trained dog was a priceless contributor to a family or small community fallen on hard times.

Nate knew Kyla wouldn't make it another winter.
Winters in the mountains were hard on anyone's body, regardless of species. The pleasant early autumn weather would soon give way to freezing overnight temperatures, bitter cold winds, and blankets of snow.

As much as Kyla loved the snow, she could not longer manage to traverse in it... yet she was too aggravated to stay behind when Nate went out solo.

Tears welled up in Nate's eyes. Kyla remained still, her breathing forced and raspy. She was in too much pain to get up.

Having a pet means bearing witness to the entire lifetime of a family member in a mere fraction of one's own. A pet could give the gift of novelty and discovery, of bonding and maturation, but also of grieving and loss. Nate was grateful for it all.

Kyla was there at the beginning of Nate's engagement to Caitlyn and the rickety old cabin they bought together after leaving the National Park System. Kyla was there for their efforts to spruce up the cabin and alerted Nate when a beam fell on Caitlyn during the remodel. Kyla was there for Nate when Caitlyn was bed ridden. Kyla was waiting by Caitlyn's side when Nate came home to discover she had overdosed. Whatever Kyla understood about everything that happened, Nate knew their family dog was like a child to them.

Kyla had given Nate everything she had. Nate owed her a peaceful passing in return. He knelt down to pet Kyla one last time. Her fur was warm to Nate's touch. Kyla closed her eyes slowly. It was as though she knew they were saying goodbye. Or at the very least, that the pain would be over soon.

Nate took a syringe from a small, black medical bag. He pet Kyla gently with one hand as he placed the syringe against her fur, then injected the tip deep beneath her skin.

Nate steadily depressed the plunger as the pentobarbital entered her bloodstream. It would all be over soon. Nate held Kyla in his arms.

"There you go, dear girl. There you go." Nate felt the tears rolling off his cheeks.

Getting a dog was originally Caitlyn's idea. Nate had come from an abusive home and fled when he was sixteen. He had never had a pet before. In his darkest fears, Nate would inherit his father's drunken rage and beat anything in sight. A woman, a child, a dog. By avoiding any close relationships like this, Nate thought he could avoid becoming his father.

"But you're just avoiding becoming yourself" Caitlyn had said early on in their dating life. She was right. And she pushed Nate further out of his shell than he had ever been.

After That Crash and the subsequent settlement, Straight-Shooting Nate completed his forestry management degree at

Salmon Springs College and spent a few years with Build-up Together. He learned enough Spanish to get by in Central America and picked up enough carpentry skills to help build more than 300 houses, schools, and medical clinics.

It was satisfying work.

The call of the wild brought Nate back stateside and to several National Park assignments. Like his internship before, Nate most loved the off-season and doing population surveys far from anyone else.

That is, until he met Caitlyn. She had been a park guide specializing in interpretation for youth and family tours. She always had a strand of red hair which fell out of her cap and caught the morning sun and the afternoon breeze. Once Nate saw her at a ranger station while picking up new field maps, he could never look away again.

In some ways, Kyla had come with the cabin and lived there her entire life. When Nate and Caitlyn first looked at the place, the realtor mentioned having a litter of puppies and brought Kyla for a ride-along up the mountain roads and to the "fixer-upper" of a listing. Kyla got out and sniffed around, reached the front entrance, and looked back at Nate and Caitlyn with approval. Kyla was staying, so Nate and Caitlyn might as well write the check, buy the place, and move in with Kyla.

Half of everything is recognizing the opportunities right in front of you. "Seeing things for what they are" Nate's wise mother used to say to him.

Nate had never been much for grand planning or elaborate goal-setting. That never worked out, anyway. Especially since The Long Collapse. Just getting through the day was plenty. Appreciating the time that was left. His beard had grown so long as the years passed.

Nate held Kyla close. Her breath had stopped several minutes ago. He didn't want to let go. Her fur was still warm. Soon, her organs would shut down completely and her body would begin to dehydrate. Her body heat would dissipate and her joints would stiffen.

Nate knew every biological aspect of death. It ultimately came down to physics. To the law of entropy. To the dissipation of energy. To the irreducible complexity of each molecule scattering in all directions. To disperse every microscopic speck of being into the infinite expanse beyond.

Nate had leaned down and pulled Kyla in for one last hug. When he stood up a few minutes later, he looked down only at her body. Where had Kyla gone? Did she have a soul that exited her body during their embrace? Did she lose consciousness, and with that, every ephemeral aspect of her being faded away? The death of every pet provokes these questions.

"It's okay now, girl. Let me take you to your resting place."

Nate left Kyla's body on the grass as he retrieved her favorite blanket from next to the fireplace. Standing in the quiet, empty cabin, Nate felt the twelve years of memories lingering in every corner of the large, single room in which he had lived with his own little family.

He was grateful for all of that time. It was less than he had hoped for, but perhaps more than he deserved. It was somber to have ended, yet sublime to have ever been.
Good times don't last forever, but there is no guarantee of good times, at all.

"Don't look for the gold at the end of the rainbow. Behold all the colors in the middle." That's what Nate's mother had said when he was a boy. He thought she was talking about leprechauns.

She was talking about living life.

The framed photo on the mantle remained Nate's favorite encapsulation of his golden middle years. He and Caitlyn were kneeling together with Kyla as the mountains surrounded them. It was a self-timer shot they took on their first hike to Timberline Bluff. That's where Nate was taking Kyla to rest.

Next to the photo was Caitlyn's urn. He had kept it there since her funeral. It would soon be time to scatter her ashes. But not today.

Nate draped Kyla's worn, red blanket over her body and tucked it in under her, swaddling her in a thick layer of wool. He looked at her face one last time before wrapping the blanket over her skull. She looked so peaceful. It had been a good twelve years together in their cabin at the base of the Timberlines.

"Here we go."

Nate opened the main compartment of his frame backpack and hoisted Kyla's body into it. He set the pack on the workbench beside the cabin and next to the plot of grass. He positioned himself against the pack and slid his arms through the straps.

Click. Click. Lashing the cords. A tight fit.

Nate had only packed water and some energy bars that were always stocked in his front pouch. It would only be a couple hours round trip and Nate couldn't eat right now if he wanted to.

The trail was briskly adorned by the iridescent leaves of early fall. Before their pigments faded, each leaf appeared as a jewel flattened against the soil.

in the sweltering stillness of heat you arrive
slipping in silently between seasonal walls

to whisper cool breezes and night freezes
as the first colored foliage falls

reveal your golden hair, Autumn
and display it a fiery red
until whimsical crimson twirls down upon frozen
ground
and the snow tucks my Autumn into bed

Along with his camera, Nate usually kept a pen and paper with him during his travels, as well as during various field assignments.

It kept him mentally acute and gave longevity to his observations.

He had written many poems about the forest and the mountains and the streams and the changing seasons and the coastal tides and the night's sky and the phases of the moonlight. No one else would ever read them, but that was hardly the point; they were for him to bear witness to his own life, to the passage of time, to the shifting landscapes within a singular shell of longevity.

As the trail narrowed into a canyon climbing up the side of the mountain, Nate imagined the tiny creek off to his right which was once a river so powerful to have burrowed the mountainside down into the canyon walls reaching well above him. Seeing the world in geological time like this was always a humbling experience.

His entire life and everything in it could be measured in mere millimeters of this canyon wall. Nate ran his fingertips up and down the layered rock formations with each step. From present day back to Sumeria in the flick of the wrist. Reach down a bit to get to the woolly mammoths, further still to the era of giant lizards, and all the way to the canyon floor to get to those first trilobites.

Or something like that; Nate only took a couple geology courses.

The shape of the forest was always familiar to Nate even if the particular tree branches might change. A new patch of deadfall near the ridge line this season. Last year's downed trees were already overgrown with mosses and epiphytes. The forest never stood still. It was making grand moves in slow motion if one paid enough attention to notice.

Nate felt his heart racing and his thighs began to burn. He had set a brisk pace for his last hike with Kyla and he was not accustomed to carrying such a heavy pack. But this was always the plan and he was prepared, at least logistically, for putting Kyla to rest.

Near the clearing at the top of the canyon trail, Nate traced the edge of the trees into a small dirt path which only he and Caitlyn had ever explored. It was a favorite spot. And it was going to be the resting place for Kyla. All those years ago, Caitlyn had said so in as many words. Every pet owner knows they are likely to outlive their animal and Nate was realistic about giving Kyla her ideal burial.

The thick brush of the game trail had become so dense that Nate held up one arm to keep the branches off his face. In a few years' time, the way would be closed off entirely if he didn't come back with a machete and a hatchet. But perhaps that was for the best. Their secret forest grove on Timberline Bluff could be sealed away for eons. That seemed ideal.

Nate reached the grove and slid the heavy frame pack off his body. He had broken a sweat and reached for his water bottle. He downed most of it to quench his mighty thirst. Nate dipped his bandana in the bottle to dab and wipe cool water across his sweltering brow.

Nate had left the shovel here in the grove from their last hike. Kyla was getting old but Nate didn't know if she would make it through winter or not. If he didn't dig a hole before the ground froze, it would be impossible again until late spring. With her hole already dug, it was just a matter of lowering Kyla into it and scraping the topsoil off the adjacent pile to fill it.

Snug in her blanket, Nate placed Kyla into her final resting place. He looked around, imagining the view she would enjoy in her endless, serene slumber. Nate remembered their treks through these woods together, before and after Caitlyn had passed, and how Kyla seemed to favor this grove above any other location on the trail. Perhaps Kyla chose this secluded sanctuary of trees as her resting place. Nate understood as much.

The red blanket was buried under layers of thick brown soil, bits of tree branches and leaves, tufts of grass blades and roots. It was a mix of the earth. It was Kyla's eternal bed.

"Take care, girl. See you again sometime." Nate didn't know about any of that, but he wanted Kyla to believe it. It was such an immense suspension of disbelief to imagine a deceased dog could hear Nate and understand spoken English, but it still seemed possible. It felt possible.

Owning a pet opens one up to all sorts of beliefs about intuition and unspoken languages, especially with a dog like Kyla who could read human emotions better than Nate ever did.

That was a bond worth honoring.

And now it was done.

Of his memories, of his emotions, of his sentiment and sacrament, the sum total of what Nate was leaving back in the secret forest grove on Timberline Bluff. He was still sorting that out.

Nate gathered the shovel and packed it away in his bag. The walk down would be lighter and easier. Already planning his final trek back up the trail, Nate's next task required driving along the winding Timberline Bluff road and into Salmon Springs.

Unlike the other Homecomers, Nate had never received Sasha's invitation; she didn't know where to find him. But if they were to cross paths during their 20-year Homecoming weekend, what would Nate even say to her? Or to any of them?

After what had happened with That Crash, well... Nate tried not to think about it.

[5 – Good Morning from Fenix Farm]

Rooster Rodney was always the first up at the Fenix Farm. By the early light of dawn, Rodney had hopped up to the top perch of the coop and began crowing.

"Err-err-err-err-errrrrrrrrrrrr!"

"Err-err-err-err-errrrrrrrrrrrr!"

"Err-err-err-err-errrrrrrrrrrrr!"

This would go on for at least ten minutes.

This is going to be a big month, I can just sense it! There's change in the leaves, there's a stirring in the air. And Homecoming is nearly here! It isn't what anyone might have planned, but what in life is? We will still make the most of it.

Sasha put her journal down on her nightstand.

"Alright Rodney, let's get everyone fed."

Sasha stretched as she sat up and yawned. Rylar was still asleep next to her. She kissed his forehead. He had worked late the night before on re-insulating the workshop addition to the side of the house. Winter's chill was creeping in and the autumn chores were becoming more urgent.

Sasha threw on some sturdy farm clothes. She cracked open the door to the kids room. Acacia was still asleep, but Timo was looking out the window facing the edge of the Salmon Springs woodlands.

"Hey Timo, ready to help with the outside chores?" Sasha whispered.

"In a minute, mom." Timo's gaze was intent and unwavering, especially for a six year old. Sasha took interest in whatever Timo was fixated on, crossed the hardwood floor, and put her arms around Timo's flannel pajamas. His sandy blonde bowl cut was still swirled with the tossings of slumber.

"What'cha lookin at, hun?"

"At the last star. They always go away by morning. I think, I think this is the first time I discovered it."

Timo pressed his finger against the glass pane. He was touching the star now. Timo exhaled against the window. Then he removed his finger, leaving a portal encircled by fog.

"I made a hole for you to see it." Timo stepped aside so Sasha could look. Sasha smiled at Timo. He was such a clever and generous boy. Sasha knelt lower and looked up through the window, lining up the view of the star within Timo's 'breath portal' of condensation before it faded.

"I see it! It's definitely getting sleepy. Would you sing a lullaby for the star to go to bed?" Sasha loved the imaginary world overlapping the seen world and Timo brought out that affinity in her.

Timo nodded. He knew just the right one.

> *good night starlight*
> *slumbering away bright*
> *dream through daytime*
> *gleam against darkness*
> *starlight ready for bed*
> *wake up at sunset red*

Acacia looked over from beneath her layers of blankets. She squinted and wrinkled her nose such that the freckles she inherited from her mom were all scrunched together.

"You two are so silly!" she giggled. Timo hopped over to his dresser and Sasha assisted him in picking out some clothes for outdoor chores.

"That was a really good lullaby, Timo!" Sasha exclaimed as she buttoned up Timo's overalls.

"You know the stars are still out during the day, right? They don't go away. They don't go to sleep." Acacia sat up and starting brushing her long auburn hair.

"I think they have to sleep sometime!" Timo retorted.

"It's because the sun is so much brighter, you can't see them." Acacia explained.

Sharing a bedroom with her little brat brother was so annoying.

"Well actually the sun is a star too and it sleeps at night, so the stars sleep during the day. They take turns." Timo had it all worked out.

"Sounds fair to me, buddy."

Sasha stood up to inspect Timo's farm boy attire. Timo looked ready for anything, including collecting chicken eggs.

"I bet Rooster Rodney and the hens are hungry and eager to go out into their yard, Timo."

Timo nodded. He had named Rodney and all of the hens when they were chicks, but only he knew all their names.

"And there's cinnamon raisin muffins on the kitchen counter if you want to take one out with you." Sasha loved baking in the evening so the whole house smelled delicious overnight and the freshness was ready to savor in the morning.

Acacia did her outdoor chores in the evenings because she preferred to sleep in. That is, of course, when her precocious little brother wasn't serenading the stars at the crack of dawn. Between Timo and Rodney, Acacia never stood a chance at a late morning rise. At least Rylar could get more shut-eye.

Timo munched on his muffin as he pulled back the chicken wire gate and opened up the yard. The hens scurried out as quickly as they could fit through the door. Rodney strutted around after them. Timo laughed at their syncopated avian movements.

"Four eggs today!" Timo announced as he gathered them from the nesting boxes.

"Great, hopefully they will keep laying this winter" Sasha was always within earshot because they had a small farm and their wooden barn had one room dedicated for chickens and the other for goats. Assembled in their stalls, the goats were ready to be milked before being let out into their yard. Sasha had the best feel for it and the goats seemed best-behaved for her.

Sasha collected two buckets of goat milk while Timo refilled the hopper with chicken pellets, then goat feed. Their annual supplies were dwindling and she hoped against hope that the feed store in Salmon Springs would still carry more.

She knew of at least three country neighbors who would share their stock in a pinch but, ultimately, they all counted on the same inconsistent supply chain for their feed. Since The Long Collapse, the amenities were rarely available. However, essentials were attainable for the right price. Usually.

If not, Sasha had connections at the farmers market. Her network was resilient.

The sun was ascending past the treeline now.

Sasha brought the goat milk in for bottling and cold storage, then watched Timo run around the yard. Her little goat herder.

Three cats bounded through the tall grass and came to rest on the back patio to sun themselves. They were all a mix of white, black, and brown in typical tortoiseshell coats. Likely from the same litter.

Wild pets were a common sight during The Long Collapse as more animals were left to fend for themselves. On balance, they were more successful than their human counterparts.

These cats were mostly feral but Timo insisted on feeding them and naming them, though the names often changed. Bippy, Sippy, Tippy. Then Howdy, Rowdy, and Bowdy. Recently, Timo had been calling them Tres Gatos since he was working on his conversational Spanish.

Whatever their names, they livened up Fenix Farm and kept the rodent population in check, though also downing their share of birds in the process. With so much disruption, it became more difficult to identify which species were endemic or invasive to a given region. Though as far as farm cats went, Tres Gatos were either welcome regular guests or infrequent occupants (no one could decide which).

Sasha sighed. She felt tremendous gratitude for her family and farmstead even amidst so much loss. The grief of losing Emmalyn several years ago never really faded. Just seeing Acacia and Timo together on the farm reminded her of their deceased middle child. The gap in their family that wouldn't heal, the hole in the fabric of their story.

But who was Sasha to dwell on her losses? She couldn't think of anyone she would trade places with or anywhere she would rather be.

Country living was strenuous, but it was a familiar strain, a rewarding strain. It was a slower, more quiet pace of life and it felt consistent and reliable as compared to the squalor of decaying cities and tumultuous suburban sprawl. Those were lifestyles hit hardest by The Long Collapse because they relied so much on outside supplies and external systems to function.

As long as Fenix Farm had the basics, Sasha and Rylar could make do. This was their homestead.

And make do they had. After Sasha graduated from Salmon Springs College, she decided to stay in town and work for a community nonprofit providing supplemental education programs in local schools. She had fallen in love with the cool, verdant greens of the Pacific Northwest and rarely missed the brutal, dry heat of her suburban Arizona childhood.

Sure, more sun would be nice, but it was always a blessing to receive a solar kiss upon her skin even for a few minutes a day.

Sasha looked from end to end, thinking back to when she and Rylar first bought the land. It was trashed beyond recognition. The estate had been condemned by the county for cleanup because it had been used as a methamphetamine lab. Someone had died here.

Sasha tried not to think about it. She and Rylar had bought it on the cheap and put in two years to clean it up and build the foundation of the barn and grow dome. The helpers they hired soon became the neighbors and community connections they kept.

Making new friends during The Long Collapse was easier than Sasha had remembered. Many of the cultural silos broke down – either out of material necessity or the erosion of those specialized echo chambers which relied on technology that no longer reliably worked.

Every catastrophe could be a gift in disguise. Sasha tried to never overlook someone's pain or misfortune, but instead to see the hidden opportunities or overlooked possibilities. The times demanded as much.

With the morning fog rolling over the autumn treeline, Sasha counted her blessings. Timo was happy, Acacia was making new friends at school, Rylar had plenty of work but still made time to go fishing with his buddies. The goats and chickens were producing. The farmers market had been profitable enough this year to get through winter. And soon she would be hosting an exciting Homecoming party.

For living in tough times, Sasha had a great life.

"Are we going to the library today?" Acacia stood in the doorway, fully dressed and chomping on an apple. She inherited her mom's vibrance but also her dad's stubborn impatience.

"Oh yes, and soon. Thanks for reminding me!" Sasha had never been great about scheduling and counted herself lucky to have a daughter who always kept an eye on the clock.

"Do you want to read some short stories or poetry to the little kids today?" Sasha was hoping Acacia would warm up to the idea of being a junior staff volunteer for the Saturday Story Hour. Acacia was already doing it, but without the title. Titles weren't her thing.

"Yeah, sure. But I still have homework to get done first." Acacia was determined to complete all the correspondence assignments online before winter break so she could start the next year a grade ahead. It was a secret for now, but Acacia was planning to finish high school abroad. Get out of Salmon Springs. See the world – or at least any good parts that are still left.

Sasha and Timo finished the outside chores and gathered up their books and lesson materials for the day. It was too expensive to drive into town daily, so Sasha would take Timo and Acacia to the Salmon Springs library every week, sometimes twice a week. In exchange for her reading and writing lessons, Sasha arranged for more tutoring time and online classes for her two kids.

The breakdown of the public education system was a highly disruptive aspect of The Long Collapse. It looked different everywhere, but most communities closed ranks and found internal solutions to the teaching of their children and their developmental needs.

Some segregation occurred and that lead to more tension. Neighborhood schools bore the inequality of neighborhood wealth disparities. State governments tried to bridge those divides as they became more acute, but the demands for more police, more prisons, and basic healthcare funding subsumed public education.

Homeschooling, or something like it, was more common; "learning pods" of a few families or an entire city block was a makeshift solution at scale.

The larger public school model of the previous era had imploded and was unlikely to return anytime soon. Of course, the wealthy elite always had private boarding schools – now with enhanced security to keep everyone else out and to keep their pupils safe from the ravages of civil unrest.

The good news was that Sasha and other involved parents had many opportunities to contribute their knowledge and passions into childhood education and youth development. As fewer and fewer people had traditional full-time jobs, there was more availability to meet the needs created by a diminished public school system.

Most parents were homemakers, educators, and breadwinners to varying degrees. And when parents fell behind, other parents were quick to step up. Everyone who had forgotten that it takes a village to raise a child quickly remembered.

Rylar stood in the doorway, refreshed and rugged in his bathrobe after a hot shower. Hot showers were a luxury. The Fenix family's water heater was the best investment they had made in solar energy appliances. They decided to forgo a dishwasher or microwave, but a hot shower after a muddy toil on the farm was incomparable.

"Off to the library?" Rylar was spooning down a bowl of grits. He usually ate the less glamorous selections from the kitchen so the kids could enjoy something more delicious, like the cinnamon raisin muffins. Goat milk was almost always on the menu and eggs were plentiful. Their grow dome and land plot provided a rainbow of fruits and vegetables, and meat was served several times a week as supplies allowed.

Rylar and Sasha always tried to balance the teaching of frugality and thrifty habits necessitated during The Long Collapse against savoring the delights of the Surplus World they had known growing up. What should a childhood be like in these times? The Fenix household strove to include rigorous work ethic but also magical curiosity and lifelong play.

"Yes babe, anything you need from town?" Sasha kissed Rylar between his spoonfuls.

"A box of two-inch nails if Crosstown Hardware has them. The workshop needs some new roofing supports after that last storm."

"Got it, babe. Timo, can you remember that?" Sasha turned to Timo as he gathered various fallen leaves.

"Yeah. Wait, remember what?" Timo was preoccupied with collecting one of each leaf in an array of autumn colors.

"Two-inch nails!" Rylar and Sasha laughed as they spoke together.

"A box of two-inch nails." Acacia repeated sarcastically as she zipped up her book bag.

"Yeah. I'll remember" Timo remained distracted by his colorful leaf quest.

The Fenix family maintained a passenger van from before The Long Collapse. Two rows of rear seats were removed and Rylar had built and installed a wooden frame with shelving so Sasha could transport products to sell at farmer's markets throughout the region. Everything had to be multipurpose these days, including vehicles.

"Can I ride in the back?" Timo always asked this.

"No Timo, there aren't any seatbelts in the back." Acacia reminded him.

"What if I build one myself?" Timo imagined how that would look.

"That's a good idea, Timo. Why don't you draft a design while we're at the library today and show it to dad tonight?" Sasha was an expert at the affirmative redirect—a vital parenting skill.

"Yeah!" Timo hopped in his usual seat and began to study his seatbelt closely, then looked at the wooden rack in the rear of the van. Surely it could be done!

"Why do you want to sit in the back of the van, anyway?" Acacia had the weirdest little brother.

"I want mom to park by backing in. Then I can jump in and out without touching the dirt. Too many ants. They bite too much. And other reasons. Lots of reasons. Like what if the ground turns to lava?" Timo was under no obligation to explain his genius to anyone, especially his grouchy big sister. She didn't get it.

Sasha started the engine and waved goodbye to Rylar. By the time she returned home, the house would be cleaned and the produce tables would be washed and ready to prep any fruits or veggies ready to harvest—the usual afternoon routine.

Rylar had no formal education beyond sophomore year of high school, but he was quick to pick up a new skill or try to fake it.

This meant Sasha could count on at least one person willing to try her newest innovation or enterprise.

It was just under an hour's drive to reach the Salmon Springs library from Fenix Farm. Unless a rainstorm or flood had washed the road out, it was steady going. Traveling by highway was an unreliable proposition lately, especially during the peak of wildfire season. Sasha knew the best routes to Salmon Springs, but they could change by the year.

Rylar went back inside the house as their van with his wife and kids turned off their unnamed lane. Many years ago, Acacia had painted a rainbow onto a wooden slat with the words WELCOME TO FENIX FARM in big, bold letters.

The van disappeared between the rolling, tree-dotted hills adorned with its autumn color palette. The morning fog had lifted.

Tres Gatos gathered to nap on the front patio, which was lined with potted plants and a string of lights draped from the roof. Were they ready for the upcoming Homecoming party?

[6 – Holt Harbor, Arbitrator]

"They have a one million dollar policy per incident and that's what they're offering you today." Holt Harbor, Arbitrator stood at the front of the room, holding his notepad and glancing down at it to verify the terms of the settlement proposal.

With his trimmed silver beard, Holt was rotund and well-dressed. He adjusted his glasses.

The view of downtown Salmon Springs in the summertime was stunning from their posh high-rise conference room in the business center. Holt continued.

"Industrial Maintenance is the parent company. Their counsel expressed to me that they're most concerned about settling this quickly so you can move on, they can move on, and this doesn't go public. They are ready to sign today. I am here to facilitate the logistics of whatever you decide."

Jill looked over at Sasha, Dugen, and Nate. They were all dressed in their finest business attire. So was she, but she was the only one with a cast on her leg and a set of crutches. The expressions of their faces varied from shock to disbelief.

Jill rolled her eyes.

"So first they hire a perpetual drunk as a company driver, then they stonewall us for months while I'm in the hospital and missing graduation, then they decide they want to bring us into arbitration before we even file a lawsuit, and now they want to give us a million bucks to shut us up?"

Nate smirked. Dugen put his pen to the page and began jotting down furiously on the notepad provided by the business center. Sasha sipped on the complimentary Mandarin Spice tea. Holt removed his glasses and put them in his suit pocket.

"Well, yes. In a sense. They're buying your silence and anticipated closure. Industrial Maintenance isn't in a position to admit wrongdoing because it opens them up to liability, but... well, in strict confidence... they know they were in the wrong."

Holt leaned in. He had grandchildren around their age.

"They hired Mr. Blanton without running a record check. That record check would have shown two priors for driving under the influence. It seems Mr. Blanton was day drinking on the morning of the collision because the officer at the scene recorded a point-one-two blood alcohol level, which is well above the legal limit. His employment was promptly terminated. Nonetheless, their attorneys communicated to me that they believe—again, this is their official position—the circumstances suggest mutual fault or superseding causation by Mr. Magnus."

Nate sat up and cleared his throat. "I signaled. I was changing lanes when the guy pulled into traffic without looking. I was changing lanes and he should have seen that. It's not mutual fault. No way."

"The record reflects that, Mr. Magnus. And the other party knows that, their attorneys know that. They initiated this arbitration proceeding and are offering you and your passengers a million dollar settlement offer because they don't want this to be drawn out further."

"They don't want everyone to know they hired a drunk driver to transport their heavy equipment all around town. That's why they're offering us a million bucks to shut up about it." Jill was indignant. She had suffered the worst, she needed the money for medical bills the most, and so much else that had gone wrong. The last few months had been an excruciatingly painful and disorienting blur.

Dugen held up his notepad, now full of illegible numbers and scribbles.

"Minus arbitration costs and the attorney's fees, we would each get roughly $210,000. Maybe a bit more if we can get the law firm to reduce their percentage since we settled on the first day of arbitration." Dugen underlined **$210,000 each**.

Holt smiled. At least some of the parties in the room were warm to the idea of reaching a settlement. "Industrial Maintenance is covering the costs of arbitration as a gesture of goodwill. They want to get this resolved. Their insurance offered up the most they could under the circumstances."

Nate looked at the other three. The victims of his speedy carpool service. He had wrecked his station wagon on the day of That Crash, but he had also wrecked Jill's running career. Sasha and Dugen had no serious injuries; they missed class that morning and not much else. But Jill was hospitalized for a week and still recovering months later.

"I guess I'm okay with it, but it has to be unanimous, right? We can't each decide separately whether to settle or not today?" Nate looked across the table, trying to read the room.

"That's correct. The settlement offer reflects their desire to sever all potential claims by any of you – driver or passengers – against Industrial Maintenance, Ltd."

Holt had seen these kinds of offers before. Almost to a person, they would settle out of pragmatic considerations... unless there was someone who wanted to litigate on the principal of the matter – someone who wanted to hear a judge or jury tell them that they were in the right and the other party was in the wrong.

Closure looks different for different plaintiffs.

"I say we do it. Think of it as a graduation present." Dugen had no idea what to do with nearly a quarter million dollars. That's too much to contemplate for a guy who was perpetually broke. Maybe he would get his own car since Nate no longer had the station wagon for him to sleep in.

When you lived in the back of a car, a traffic accident makes you homeless.

Sasha was more hesitant. It wasn't about the money. It's about what was fair for all of them. And she felt awful for what Jill had been through. And all because Sasha offered Jill a ride to class.

"Whatever we decide here is fine with me. It was Nate's car that got totaled. His insurance only covered a loaner for him to drive while we work this out. Dugen has been staying at our dorm. And Jill suffered broken bones in both legs... she couldn't compete in the state track meet to qualify for nationals. You all lost something more than I did. I just, got shaken up, a few bruises, and missed class."

Sasha looked at everyone with concern and reassurance. In a strange way, the car crash and ensuing complications had brought a group of oddballs and unlikely compatriots closer together. Nate and Dugen became better friends since they were no longer bickering over who had occupancy rights to the back of Nate's station wagon. Take away their toys and the boys stop fighting.

And in turn, Jill got to know the two guys and her freshman interest group partner. Sasha had been by Jill's side almost the entirety of her hospital stay and cooked up a storm to take care of Jill while she was bedridden. Catastrophes bring out the best in the good-hearted.

It was almost a blessing to have been through that turmoil together as a bonding experience. And now they were being offered a million dollar check on the other side. Almost a blessing. At least that's what Sasha thought.

Nate shrugged.

"It's Jill's decision, as far as I'm concerned. She's had to go through the most. Personally, I am just happy to get this over with. No more meetings with lawyers, no more paperwork asking about all our finances dating back ten years and whether anyone was on drugs at the time. Blah blah blah. I am happy they aren't trying to fight us on every point when they know they were in the wrong."

Jill looked at all three of her newfound friends from Salmon Springs College.

"What they did to us was super shitty. I get the importance of holding them accountable so this doesn't keep happening to other people. I get that buying our silence just enables a scummy company to keep looking the other way when they hire dangerous drivers."

Jill sighed and shuffled her copies of the arbitration guidelines and party position statements. This was just a big homework assignment. It was time to turn it in and move on. She had new goals to set.

"Let's settle it today. It's good money, it can help us all out. But I don't want any charity from you three. I know you mean well. I appreciate all you've done for me." Jill looked at Sasha with newfound gratitude. "Really I do. But we are gonna divide the money four ways, even split, and move on."

Holt looked at the four young adults. This was among the most consequential decisions in their short lives. He whispered aloud. "If I were you, I would take it. This could be in court for 18 months or longer. You all have your whole lives ahead of you. Get a head start. I promise you, Industrial isn't that big of a company. This is going to cost them for years, especially if their insurance carrier drops them for failure to perform due diligence in hiring. I see it all the time. Maybe just as well get on with your business and put this behind you with a good chunk of change in your pocket."

Holt stepped back. "But again, completely your decision. I know it isn't easy."

Jill looked at Nate, baring a smile burdened with chagrin. She wasn't ready to forgive him yet. Or Sasha. Or herself. But she wasn't going to hold anyone up while she worked through it on her own terms.

"I say let's do it."

"Score, baby!" Dugen started giving high fives like they just hit the jackpot at the slots.

Nobody else felt this way, but they were amused that Dugen did.

"Done." Nate wiped his hands in one motion and then puffed his breath across them.

"Feels like the right thing to do." Sasha nodded and drew a sigh of relief.

Holt looked across their faces once more, nodded, and exited the room to inform opposing counsel.

Hours later, the four crash-survivors-turned-arbitration-party stood in front of the entrance of Salmon Springs Office Suites in the city center plaza.

The sun was getting low in the sky. It had been a nail-biter of a day, with the arbitrator going back and forth between a room of injured college students and a room of nervous corporate executives.

"So what are you going to do with your money, Dugen?" Sasha was genuinely curious.
Everyone else would likely make sensible investments in their future careers and personal journeys.

"Establish a portfolio, diversified across high-performing asset classes, and live off the interest, of course." Dugen hoisted his duffle bag over his shoulder. "It's gonna be summer in Antarctica in a few months. Maybe I can live with the local wildlife and bring back some glacial ice before it's gone for good." Dugen began to waddle like a penguin.

Sasha laughed. "I'm sure the penguins will love you!"

Sasha turned, hugging Nate close. "You did great, Nate. You did everything right. I want you to know that."

Nate nodded and blinked hard as his eyes began to well up. "I know you're right. Just doesn't feel like it." Nate worked through the lump in his throat.

Jill straightened her suit jacket. "Anyway folks, it's been... well, it's been something." Her cab arrived and she loaded her crutches and slid in the back.

Dugen smirked. He'd never been with a cripple before. She was still a hot piece of ass.

Sasha and Nate watched as Jill's cab turned the corner into rush hour traffic.

The summer evenings were so serene. The songbirds were chirping in the high tree branches. Vanilla clouds. Warm summer breeze. It was an unlikely sliver of paradise after months of stress and suffering; the promise of good times ahead.

On August 22nd, 2025, Dugen, Sasha, Nate, and Jill were official signatories to a settlement agreement with Industrial Maintenance, Ltd. It effectively extinguished any legal claims they had against the company for hiring a reckless driver and allegedly causing a serious accident on their way to class in the spring of their senior year at Salmon Springs College.

They were not allowed to discuss the terms of the settlement with anyone else.

A few weeks later, each of them would receive a check for $211,400.25 and co-sign a disbursement acknowledgment in front of a notary.

It was the last time they would see each other for over twenty years.

[7 – Welcome to NO Salmon Springs]

The rolling hillsides were getting more lush, more verdant again. The past several days of travel were so dry, so parched. What wasn't brown and dusty was black and ashen.

Ten years of drought, five years of crop failure, and at least five years of mass exodus from these same arid regions... it all took its toll. Soil too thin to hold nutrients, rainfall too sparse to water crops, wildfires too intense to recover.

The world of The Long Collapse was a damaged object and a wounded animal at the same time.

Jill sat up in her reclining chair as the worn, rusted train sped along the steel rail. Seeing days of boarded up towns and burned down buildings made her want to blot the view with her window shade until she got to Salmon Springs.

Would it also be this ravaged, this broken?

Whatever was on the tracks ahead of her, Jill was ready to move on. She was done with Wynhill Heights and Suncoast Management. She was done with the incessant stacks of paperwork, files to manage, client accounts to service, corporate posturing to mimic, groveling for the good grace of whatever empty suit she had to impress for her next quarterly review, her next promotion, her next sales call, her next audit, her next back-flip of bullshit to launder another load of prestige and justify her six-figure salary.

She didn't have to justify anything. She boxed up her condo and put it on the market. It sold within days to a foreign estate management company looking to expand its investment portfolio. Would anyone actually move in? Would anyone want to resume the same rat race Jill just left?

Only a rat can win a rat race.

Jill put up almost everything in an estate sale. She had been ready to purge her life of the possessions which possessed her long ago. That pathetic excuse for a layoff from Suncoast Management was the spark that lit the powder keg, the excuse Jill needed to "peace out" and put the entire lifestyle obsession in her rear view mirror. But without a car. She traveled by rail, instead.

Commuting by train had remained the most reliable and efficient method during The Long Collapse – especially long distances. Volatile fuel prices due to a plummet in global oil production put most commercial airlines out of business. As a result, air travel was prohibitively expensive and reserved for only the very wealthy who could charter private flights above the embattled hinterlands. Some innovations with alternative fuels proved too little, too late for the airline industry. It was now strictly a luxury on demand.

Car travel was common for short distances, but longer treks were too risky, too unpredictable. Road conditions continued to deteriorate, fuel shortages meant frequent delays and the perils of being stranded, and roaming gangs were rumored to setup roadblocks or simply cause travelers to veer off the road in order to rob them, scrap their vehicle for parts, harvest their bodily organs, or worse.

State and federal resources were reinvested into rail travel as the best means of maintaining a supply chain. Trains could haul huge loads of cargo for long distances at a much lower fuel price. The same economics came to bear for passenger travel. What was old became new again, and locomotive transit took on renewed popularity during The Long Collapse.

"Next stop: Salmon Springs station. This will be the terminal destination for this route."

The tracks didn't used to end in Salmon Springs. The tracks previously went on to Porter Hills and Kitwitsch, but the Redwood Complex Fire of 2038 decimated those towns and left the region so barren that subsequent coastal flooding washed nearly everything away. There was talk of rebuilding those locales but the money and interest just weren't there any longer.

"Rebuild Fatigue" had become a common theme – new vocabulary in The Long Collapse lexicon.

At a certain point, it no longer made economic sense to keep reconstructing residences, businesses, commercial, and industrial operations where there was a substantial likelihood of another environmental calamity. The "once in a hundred years" storms, floods, hurricanes, or wildfires seemed to happen "once every other year."

But the prohibitive financial costs became the lesser obstacle to rebuilding during The Long Collapse; Rebuild Fatigue was less a monetary phenomenon than a spiritual one.

Behind the spreadsheets with alarming fiscal projections was deep emotional depletion. It was too crushing to lose everything, summon the resources and willpower to rebuild, only to lose it all again a few years later.

"Oh no, not again."

It was as if the natural world was telling a defiant human enterprise:

"Told you so."

The train approached the outskirts of Salmon Springs.

An old-timey, folksy "Welcome to Salmon Springs" sign adorned a wall mural on the side of the road. It had faded substantially but nonetheless visible. Several abandoned cars and a stack of tires littered the peripheral.

The locale looked all but abandoned, like the era of welcoming travelers had long since passed and the current protocol was haphazard scavenging, slim pickings, and finders-keepers. In large black graffiti, someone had added to the sign.

"Welcome to **NO** Salmon Springs."

What did that even mean? The answer reaches back deep into the history of Salmon Springs. Over the past few days commuting across the ravaged continent, Jill had been on her tablet reading about the town's history – before, during, and after her time in college there.

The municipality of Salmon Springs was originally named after its abundant rivers and streams, recharged by snowmelt runoff from the Timberline mountain range. Like many towns in the mountain west region of the United States, Salmon Springs got its start as a settlement for commodity extraction – mostly timber, fishing, and fur trapping. This process was industrialized in the late 1800's with the railroads.

Salmon Springs was best known for its Chinook "King" Salmon, and the town grew through a combination of tourism and local business activity connected to outdoor recreation. However, the large scale operations from the Titan Corp. paper mill and chemical plants soon eclipsed the small businesses in town as the largest employers. For several decades after World War II, Salmon Springs continued to flourish.

However, Salmon Springs began to fall on hard times during the 1980s.

Titan Corp. began laying off its workforce, favoring increasing automation and outsourcing its manufacturing to China and Mexico. Nonetheless, some professional industries continued to grow, as did Salmon Springs College and healthcare facilities – regarded as some of the best in the region. Jill could personally attest to that.

The town's receding industrial economy more or less transitioned into an informational one, even if many of the workers from the former had been left behind.

The real economic blow to Salmon Springs was also an environmental disaster.

With few regulations and no political will to enforce them, Titan Corp. had been discharging its chemical waste into a nearby creek and wetland area on the edge of its manufacturing complex, which then seeped into the soil and ran downstream into major waterways.

By the time environmental cleanup began in the 1990s,

regulators attempting to hold Titan Corp. accountable discovered it was a shell company and had largely inverted its corporate structure. There was no money to collect.

Cleanup was limited and the area was declared a superfund site filled with hazardous waste. Salmon Springs became known nationally as "No Salmon Springs" because the fish populations, along with smaller invertebrates, had plummeted throughout the region. What fish remained were no longer safe to eat.

As the Johnny Cash song warned, "don't drink the water (because the water isn't water anymore)." That became the cautionary, unauthorized ballad of the town.

The toxins killed the fish, the story killed the tourism.

That's very likely when the "Welcome to **NO** Salmon Springs" graffiti was added to signs around the city. The graffiti was a form of vandalism and environmental activism at the same time; the defacing was a form of truth in advertising as well as a moral indictment of the political and business leaders who allowed the river to be poisoned and the fish to die off.

No doubt many were replaced. The signs, that is; not the salmon. The latter would require a degree of commitment to environmental stewardship that never happened. Replacing the signs was much faster and, from a tourism standpoint, adequately papered over the real problem.

The notional aesthetic of a spring full of salmon was entirely the purpose of the name, fish populations be damned.

Accordingly, Salmon Springs was able to make a limited recovery in the new millennium, but not for environmental tourism. The bad publicity and widespread chemical waste kept tourists away and a generational "brain drain" resulted; most younger people able to move out of the area did so and rarely returned.

Getting out of Salmon Springs became a resume building aspiration.

With all these factors in play, Salmon Springs was able to maintain subsistence levels of commerce through being a perennial college town and attracting tech development and IT training companies. For a little while, it seemed like "better living through chemistry" was supplanted by "technology solves everything." From one naive panacea to another.

Anyone old enough to remember the industrial manufacturing days of Titan Corp. spoke of a "devil's bargain" which promised prosperity but delivered pollution and poverty.

The transition away from toxic chemical production was a welcome one, even if it meant being weaned off the industrial economy which had defined Salmon Springs during its expansion.

Indeed, the small city looked to be on the upswing just before The Long Collapse.

It was under these conditions that Sasha, Nate, Dugen, and Jill met at Salmon Springs College in the early 2020s. Jill remembered the vibrance and prosperity vividly. At the time, it appeared as something of a heyday for the town. Robust economic and cultural activities, optimistic leadership, engaged community, and a sense that the worst times were behind Salmon Springs. But in retrospect, it was the last gasp.

Jill moved to the East Coast for work and mostly forgot about Salmon Springs. Or at least she tried. That Crash her senior year rattled her to the core and deprived her of the ceremonious trajectory she had sought. Only when she was on the train heading back to her alma mater did she learn more about what happened after she graduated and departed.

The 2030s brought unprecedented environmental disasters.

Maybe Jill was fortunate to have gotten out when she did.

As a result of more suburban sprawl from the town center into the mountainous geography around it, the region was more vulnerable to wildfires and flooding. Climate disruption brought extended droughts followed by record-breaking rainfalls. Floods wiped away entire neighborhoods one by one, then droughts would be so severe that the floodplain became a tinderbox. Several years of intensive wildfires burned down large areas of Salmon Springs and the surrounding brushland which used to be old growth forest.

This left Salmon Springs in a state of perpetual stagnation. State and federal government support was entirely inadequate and no combination of private sector forces were able to reproduce the periods of growth the region had enjoyed over the previous century.

Efforts to keep together a small community with limited, basic town supplies was all Salmon Springs could offer its residents. This was why Salmon Springs College no longer held class reunions. This was why Sasha created her own Homecoming invite for lack of an official occasion.

Jill had seen photos of the devastation and efforts to rebuild, only to be destroyed again. She mentally prepared herself to see firsthand.

"Last stop: Salmon Springs. End of the tracks."

Jill gathered her rolling suitcase and her large designer handbag. It was all the cargo limit would allow, but plenty for a long weekend. What she left back in Wynhill Heights she had donated to goodwill or put in a storage unit that she put up for an online auction. No next of kin, no beneficiaries, no close friends. Relentless careerism had become the spouse who never loved her back. In the divorce, she left almost all of it behind.

But what was ahead? Jill shuffled down the aisle as several other professionals and a family of four queued up to exit the train. The Long Collapse had the effect of flattening public transportation such that everyone but the super rich shared the same rides again.

Some called it "Disaster Egalitarianism."

The air was cool and cloudy, as if just after one rainfall, but before the next. Puddles on the cracked sidewalk spilled over into the mud. No fresh sidewalk had been laid in at least fifty years.

Jill stood upon the same squares of concrete which she had done growing up in Salmon Springs so long ago. The visible aging of the city conveyed her own aging, but in an accelerated way. It was as if Salmon Springs was much older now, visibly past its prime.

But as Jill scanned the horizon from the train platform, she saw the resilience of the people she always remembered – the ones who never left.

Though worn, the business district still looked functional. The tracks ended, but surrounding the train station were practical and basic storefronts even as the high rises around them looked empty and disintegrated. The shell of big business in the city was gone, but the artisanal vibe of local entrepreneurs had stepped back in their place.

"There you are!" Sasha exclaimed as she stepped through a crowd loading onto a connecting bus.

To Jill, Sasha hadn't aged a day but for cropped hair with traces of silver. To Sasha, Jill had glammed-up features, frills of metropolitan style, and looked out of place in the practical, low-key granola populace of Salmon Springs.

Sasha was the transplant, Jill was the one returning home. The differences between them were suggestive as much to whom they each once were as how their environments had shaped them.

"Hey, Sasha! So good to see you again." Jill was prepared for a warm, full-bodied hug from Sasha. She expected it. She had been looking forward to it. And true to form, Sasha delivered.

They held each other for a full moment of time. It was the first reunion of its kind either woman had in a very long while.

"Your train ride go okay? You never can tell these days." Sasha helped Jill carry her bags through the wet dirt towards her van.

"Other than seeing how wrecked everything is from coast to coast, it was relaxing." Jill laughed nervously. Sometimes even just knowing how to talk about the erosion of finer civilization gave her anxiety.

Sasha shrugged and hoisted Jill's suitcase under her arm like a full sack of goat feed.

"I know, I know. I try not to think much about it. Can't change everything! I just focus on doing what I can at Fenix Farm and hold things together."

"I'm excited to see it in person! I saw you had a website with pictures of your land. It's gorgeous!" Jill grew up in the exurbs of Salmon Springs but had never spent time on a farm before, other than a field trip in first grade.

Now her estranged Future Women Leaders interest group sister had her own plot of land. All Jill had was a box of meaningless awards and a stack of digital assets from her stock portfolio, savings accounts, ETFs, and a sizable transfer of funds from the sale of her condo. What would Jill do with it all now that she left her old life behind?

"It's a very special place! We're excited to host you!" Sasha warmly announced.

"Oh, I have a hotel booked. I don't want to impose." Jill never took someone's hospitality as a given.

"We can cancel it later. We have a bed and towels ready for you." Sasha smiled with gracious insistence. It was her goal to be a good host and she finally had a longtime friend to keep in her company. What good was owning a large house with land if your guests didn't stay awhile?

As Sasha and Jill loaded up the back of the van, Jill marveled at the improvised shelving built into the rear. It told a story about the resilience and ingenuity it took to succeed during The Long Collapse, the re-tooling and multi-purposing of everyday items. Renewed purpose.

Jill sat in the passenger seat of the Fenix van. As Sasha was about to step into the vehicle with keys in hand, she looked back at the train station with one last impulse of curiosity.

A cargo train had just arrived and the crew was unloading shipping boxes. Just as it came to rest on the tracks, a scruffy-looking man jumped out of one of the freight cars with a duffle bag slung over his shoulder.

Sasha squinted and looked closer.

"Holy shit. He actually came."

It was Dugen.

He had hitched a ride as a stow away.

Because "yeah, of course he did."

[8 – Farm-to-Table]

From the middle seat, Dugen looked back with marvel at the shelving in the Fenix Van. Stacked crates of milk, eggs, and blocks of cheese lined the rear of the vehicle.

"We have all this and more at the farm if you'd like to try some, Dugen. I just might insist!"

Sasha smirked as she glanced back at him from her rear view mirror. Just the prospect of feeding a perpetually-hungry renegade philosopher again was a fond serving of nostalgia.

"Fresh milk is hard to come by these days. I more or less got used to the powdered stuff." Dugen sat forward and looked out the windows from all sides as the vaguely-familiar sights of Salmon Springs whizzed by.

"Powdered milk?!" Sasha exclaimed in an overly-dramatic, feigned disgust.

"More or less. Never the same." Dugen missed being on the receiving end of sarcasm.

"I could never drink powdered milk" Jill muttered from the front passenger seat. "If I'm going to have dairy, I want it to be the real thing."

"Well, it doesn't get more real than at Fenix Farm! You can milk the goats yourself, if you want."

Sasha had given her fair share of farm tours at this point, mostly practical tips for her country neighbors, but sometimes for new arrivals or tourists who wanted to reconnect with the forgotten ways of the old times. The plentiful times.

"That's probably too real for me." Jill laughed. "And don't goats eat trash?"

"If you feed them trash. Garbage in, garbage out. But we feed them high quality ingredients and you can taste it in every drop of their milk."

Dugen couldn't help himself any longer. He reached for a glass bottle, popped off the cap, and started drinking the goat milk. It was the only fresh food he'd had in many days.

"This bottle was about to fall off the shelf! I saved it." Dugen explained as Sasha eyed him from her rearview.

Dugen had long maintained that eating food on the verge of being wasted was never theft. And any container in the back of a moving vehicle was at the precipice of falling and shattering, after all.

"It's... odd. But good." Dugen licked his lips and re-capped the bottle.

"Have you had goat milk before? It can take some getting used to."

Sasha had grown up on cow's milk like most kids during the Era of Plenty. But at the dawn of The Long Collapse, industrial dairy and beef production were the first to be disrupted by extended drought, price shocks, and fossil fuel and petrochemical supply chain breakdowns.

Owning cows proved to be unwieldy for most homesteaders, but a few goats were easy enough to maintain on a small plot of land; they readily produced dairy and meat.

"Here we are." Sasha was finding her voice as Homecoming tour guide.

The Fenix Van pulled up to the remnants of a strip mall parking lot. Only patches of asphalt remained intact; the rest was covered with grass, moss, and shrubs. Mother Nature was always quick to reclaim abandoned parking lots as promptly as they had been paved over.

This particular site was the Evergreen Shopping Plaza, or at least that's what the run-down sign at the entrance indicated. The plaza had fallen into blighted condition well before The Long Collapse as shopping malls across the country succumbed to overvaluation, recession, and online commerce.

Like many such spaces, the plaza was abandoned for at least a decade before being reclaimed by dedicated locals to meet social and humanitarian needs. From the cadaver of disposable capitalism grew community services.

Services such as the Salmon Springs Farm Cooperative. Like most farm co-ops, membership grew quickly during The Long Collapse.

What was previously a niche market for a class of "granola bourgeoisie" opened by necessity to a broader constituency of working class families with empty bellies and a renewed interest in working the land.

After a few generations of gigantic, air-conditioned, sterile grocery stores with virtually no connection to local food production, The Long Collapse broke down the illusion of high-volume commodity produce and restored the previous era of small-scale, regional agriculture.

Most hearty meals were now and again farm-to-table.

Jill was feeling nothing but regret and remorse. She worked so hard to escape Salmon Springs after growing up here only to return as the place looked wrecked and like absolute shit. The drive from the train station was nothing but bad memories and run-down buildings. She must have gotten off at the wrong end of the tracks.

But Sasha intuitively knew Jill was returning to her hometown on different terms than she had left it. And though Salmon Springs was a haggard shell of its former glory, Sasha was determined to show Jill the hidden gems of this new world which homesteaders were dedicated to building.

"I could have done my weekly produce drop-off any day of the week except Sunday because the farm co-op is open almost daily, but I wanted to do it on the day I picked you both up at the train station so you could see what things are like here. Including the good things."

Sasha put the van in park and turned off the engine. She had been preparing to give this speech for weeks because she sensed upon her head rested the dual hats of longtime friend and quasi-apocalypse tour guide.

"I know our official class homecoming was canceled due to the campus fire. I know that Salmon Springs looks rough and has for a long time. And I don't blame either of you for leaving. You had good reasons. You had your own lives to pursue. Well, I mean, you still have them!"

Sasha laughed nervously. Jill and Dugen looked intently at her. The emotional tension in the van began to build.

"But I grew up in generic suburbia and I fell in love with this place the day I stepped off the bus during orientation week. And although Salmon Springs has fallen apart, much like everywhere else, it still has fertile soil to plant the seeds of something really special."

Sasha felt herself getting choked up—a surprising development that was not part of her planned speech. "Literally and figuratively, I mean."

There was a long pause. Jill and Dugen both sensed this was important to Sasha, even if they didn't fully understand why.

Sasha sniffled and laughed again. This was not going as planned, but perhaps better. Seeing her old friends again reminded her of who she was, who she had become, and presented her with the unexpected gift of seeing those two selves merge just by virtue of reuniting with her college buddies.

"Anyway, I wanted to show you a special place that fills me with hope and joy. Not because it's perfect or even because it's as good as things used to be, but because I have membership here in the deepest sense of that word, in the most profound sense. I invited you back here for our twentieth class reunion so you could feel like you still belong."

Dugen nodded. Jill smiled warmly. It was a sweet sentiment, rarely expressed in such sordid times. A sense of belonging was the most one could hope for during The Long Collapse. A sense of membership was even more fundamental, and altogether rare.

"Anyway, anyway... anyways? Anyway." Sasha laughed and dried her eyes.

"I realize that notions of membership are probably more important to me than to either of you... you're both so different, Jill and Dugen, but you are both relentlessly independent. And... I'm just rambling now. But thank you for listening."

Jill smiled back at Sasha in the way only old friends could do. Steeped in business culture and corporate proceedings, Jill had forgotten what it felt like for someone to share something so genuine and personal, to be so courageously open about who they are, and without expecting anything in return. Jill felt like she really saw into Sasha in that moment, precisely because Sasha boldly, effortlessly let her in.

"Thank you for sharing that, Sasha. I really appreciate it. I appreciate everything you did to bring us together." Jill leaned across the center of the van to give Sasha a warm, affirming hug.

"That was a really great pep talk, Sasha. But maybe you should've given it after we stepped out of the van." Dugen had to say something to break up the mushy, Hallmark movie-of-the-week girl talk. Everyone laughed to reset the emotional mood.

"Why, so we could hug it out more easily?" Sasha asked between giggles.

"No because, well... the goat's milk." Dugen ripped a loud, extended flatulence.

"Oh. My. God." Jill was shocked but not surprised. He truly was the same gross guy from college. Everyone quickly evacuated the interior of the van. This was not a drill.

Jill took two steps away from the vehicle and fanned her arms, inhaling fresh air, trying to forget what just happened.

Sasha shook her head. Raising kids of her own and running a small farm, almost nothing grossed her out anymore. The Phoenix suburbs would scarcely recognize Sasha today.

Sasha opened up the rear of the van, pulling out a wheeled cart and loading up the weekly produce to drop off at the farm co-op. As a means of doing penance for his pungent transgression, Dugen helped Sasha transfer the milk bottles onto the cart. Jill thought more about Sasha's remarks.

"I was always proud of myself for not needing to belong, not needing membership. And I thought by not wanting it, that made me stronger and less brittle. I kept putting myself into situations where I could succeed as an outsider, like that was proof that I could really make it."

Jill looked around, seeing other farmers and their families transporting fruits, vegetables, meat, bread, jars of honey, yogurt, soup, jelly, and heads of cheese to the co-op in the center of the grassy pavement.

For the first time since leaving Wynhill Heights by train, Jill felt a desire to belong somewhere.

"But maybe not everything is about strength and competition. Maybe sometimes there is a virtue in being vulnerable and cooperating."

Jill couldn't believe the words coming out of her mouth. It was like 20 years of cutthroat corporate speak was deprogramming inside her mind, one moment at a time.

Sasha smiled, glancing at Jill as she finished loading the cart with Dugen.

"You said that, not me."

Dugen wiped his forehead, having worked up a sweat from all the dairy product power lifting.

"Outsiders become insiders; insiders are cast out. The weak grow to be strong; the strong age into weakness. There is no fixed position, just the illusion of one at any given point along this continuum. If I've learned anything, it's to wake up each day and meet myself for the first time."

Jill nodded. "Yeah. I get that. I just... I guess I don't like change. I mean, I know everything is changing. The leaves are changing, the weather is changing, society is changing. I grew up here and hated how everything seemed like it was always the same, so I moved away to a big, loud, rapidly-paced city full of kinetic energy... then I come back to Salmon Springs and there's been too much change."

Jill shook her head. That sounded so stupid to her.

"Change can be so beautiful, even if it isn't what we wanted. Because sometimes those changes give us something we never knew we needed before." Sasha continued, "Trust me, I was not 'ready' to have kids. Acacia was quite unexpected. Rylar and I had only been dating a few months. But we talked it over, decided to go for it, and everything since has been an amazing adventure. Not because it's been planned and predictable, but precisely because it hasn't been."

Sasha squinted. "Does that make sense?"

Jill nodded. "I think so. I think that's really beautiful."

"If I woke up and noticed nothing had changed," Dugen interjected "I would check my pulse. Maybe I died."

"That's true, Dugen" Sasha concurred with laughter.

"But even dead people change" Dugen continued. "After the first twelve hours..."

"Okay, we get it, thanks." Jill was adapting to Dugen's brand of pontification and body humor.

The three college homecomers wheeled the cart of produce from the Fenix Van to the informal entrance of the Salmon Springs Farm Cooperative. It was late afternoon and some storm clouds were building, but this was typical weather and the moisture was always welcome. No one appeared to be packing up. Covered with tarps and tents, the co-op rarely closed early. As an essential source of sustenance and community connection, it was too valuable to curtail.

Sasha waved at longtime friends and caught up with them about their weekly business. She introduced Jill and Dugen to a fruit vendor named Marvin and a shepherdess named Diane. They seemed so optimistic, despite it all. Jill quickly forgot the details of the conversation, but the underlying feeling of warm, cordial acceptance remained.

Children played games like Pickup Sticks and Knucklebones in the beds of pickup trucks covered in quilts. There were almost no screens in sight except to take orders and check inventory.

An old man with a long, gray beard played a dulcimer from atop a wooden barrel. After a few chords, he broke into a melodic, soothing song.

only need some rich soil
to get where I'm a-goin'
deeply loyal to some rich soil
to get my roots growin'

only need some raindrops
to get where I'm a-goin'
green tops with some raindrops
to get my branches growin'

only need some sunshine
to get where I'm a-goin'
glowin' fine with some sunshine
to get my flowers growin'

ain't askin' much, just askin' for such
as the earth and sky provide
as the earth and sky provide
as the earth and sky provide

Walking the corridor of folding tables, large gazebos, and wide tarps spread like a storefront, Jill was overcome with a sense of possibility, of abundance, of bountiful potential. It was altogether strange to her – at this time in her life, at this place she fled so many years ago.

It was like Sasha knew the nutrients in the food were secondary to the nourishment of Jill's morale from the farmers co-op itself.

Jill noticed almost every transaction was with coins. Given that she had been living in a world of plastic cards and digital account transfers, it was a strangely retrograde practice that brought her back to a childhood of pretend stores and collecting international coins.

Jill had so many bigger questions to ask of Sasha, perhaps it would be suitable to start with this much smaller one.

"Everyone uses... coins?" Jill observed curiously. Sasha and Dugen were offloading the wheeled cart of its milk bottles to the dairy coolers kept on site at the farm co-op. Sasha smiled after reminding herself that what has become so normal to her must be so new to Jill.

"Yeah, it's pretty standard everywhere around here. Probably for the past ten years, or five at least. Paper currency burns and falls apart too easily and there isn't more being printed in circulation anymore. As for plastic, most of the cards stopped working. The readers fail, the networks aren't reliable, and there were some severe bank runs as things started looking bad. Lots of panic at first, but minting coins became more common and everyone remembered how stable they are by comparison."

Dugen loaded the last of the milk crates into the coolers. He had definitely had his fill of goat's milk for the day and stepped away to find an outhouse suitable for his needs.

Jill nodded. "That makes sense. I had heard about all that on the news, but in Wynhill Heights the banking system held together and everyone more or less kept using digital currency. Well, those who had it."

Jill rummaged through her wallet to count the number of credit cards she had, loyalty cards, transit cards, so many plastic rectangles that symbolized something but which had no intrinsic value. Suddenly, a pocketful of coins seemed so much more... useful.

Sasha walked over to the Duncan Farm table nearby. Their spread was covered with an array of apples, pears, cherries, lettuce, spinach, beets, and carrots. She loaded several cloth bags with a rainbow of produce. Jill was getting hungry already.

"She makes the best cheese!" Mrs. Duncan exclaimed as Sasha

introduced her to Dugen and Jill. Sasha handed over two large wedges of goat cheese. This was part of the exchange between the Fenix and Duncan families, which left them both with reliable portions for family meals.

Sasha turned to Jill. "But coins are a last resort around here. For the most part, we try at the co-op to barter for what we need. I bring in milk and cheese, I take back fruits, veggies, and bread. It simplifies everything since we all contribute something."

Dugen chomped down on an especially red apple and offered one to Jill. She accepted.

Sasha continued, "No one here can grow everything on their own, though we come pretty close. Sometimes though, I just like to sample the variety from around our co-op and get new ideas for what to plant next year in the garden plots and the grow dome."

"Food seems like a pretty big deal around here." Dugen observed.

"Everyone has to eat, Dugen!" Jill reminded him.

"Well sure, but look around you. The relationship isn't just a functional one." Dugen gestured as the trio walked with full bags of produce loaded onto their cart.

"These people are friends. They share stories as they swap produce. When you go to a grocery store, you are just another alienated commodity acquiring alienated commodities. Here, you meet the people who grow the food you're taking home to your family. It probably takes more time, not strictly a market efficiency... but it's time spent connecting with the people who bring the meal from their farm to your table."

"Amen." Sasha agreed.

As the three reached the Fenix van, Jill stopped before opening her door. She looked across the parking lot as a rugged, unassuming man loaded a slab of rock into the back of his worn pickup truck. He looked vaguely familiar.

"Is that..." Jill squinted. Sasha and Dugen looked over.

"No fuckin' shit" Dugen walked towards the man at his truck.

"Nate the Great, you still have the truck you bought after the wreck?"

Nate looked up with a glint of wonder in his eyes.

"Wow, I thought I could get rid of you" he laughed.

Dugen pulled Nate in for a rough hug and back pats.

"Never."

Nate looked over at the Fenix van. Jill and Sasha waved.

"Wow... well hi, Nate! I just picked these two up at the train station and we were at the farm co-op."

Sasha was overjoyed. She hadn't seen or heard from Nate in ages. Dugen nudged Nate again as the two walked across the cracked pavement towards Jill and Sasha.

"Oh, that's cool." Nate paused and collected himself. He felt blindsided. He had never anticipated seeing any of them again, and not all at once.

"I was just in town picking up a few things. I come down here maybe once every couple months... Wow, we're all here."

Everyone exchanged hugs with Nate. It felt like they were standing outside the Salmon Springs Office Suites after their arbitration session all over again.

"I looked for you in the class directory but my search went cold, Nate. You are a hard man to find." Sasha looked upon Nate with care and concern.

"Nothing personal, but I kinda like it that way. I've been off the grid for a long time now. My cabin is up near the trailhead to Timberline Bluff."

Nate had always struggled with eye contact, always struggled with sharing about himself, always hesitated for fear of talking out of turn.

"Oh, that's a beautiful area!" Sasha exclaimed.

The re-acquaintance banter continued for a few minutes. Jill watched as Sasha and Dugen were lit up with excitement about seeing their old friend. She felt a touch of envy; Jill hadn't kept in close touch and realized there wasn't anyone who would react to her with such familiar jubilation upon first glance. Not even her own father.

Sasha was so pleased with this chance encounter and incorporated it neatly into her itinerary.

"So we just took care of dairy drop-off for the week and I've got a few extra portions of my weekly pick-up since I was already expecting company. We would love to have you over for dinner at our farm tonight, Nate! It's our class Homecoming, after all."

Sasha wouldn't take 'no' for an answer and Nate knew it.

"Ah yes, who could forget Homecoming?" Nate totally forgot Homecoming.

"That sounds amazing. I used to decline all invites as a matter of habit and tell people I needed to get home by dark to take care of my dog... but she passed recently."

"I'm sorry to hear that. Oh, we're so sorry to hear that." Jill interjected, still wrestling with being back in this oddball of a quad group. Sasha took Nate's hand and nodded to console him.

"I wanna see the school. What's left of it." Dugen barely masked his morbid curiosity. His feelings toward Salmon Springs College were mostly negative after the administration refused to confer the Double Doctorate in Everything he had been pursuing all those years.

Sasha nodded. "We can do that. There's not much to see last I checked, but I'm fascinated as much by the amount of plant regrowth in one season. The campus is on the way back to the farm, anyway."

Sasha got in her van and Jill joined her. Dugen stood by Nate. Sasha rolled down her window.

"Nate, you want to follow me? Maybe Dugen can ride with you so the two of you can catch up?"

Sasha was the master at social nuances; this was how to get Dugen away from Jill after he unexpectedly joined them early. Maybe Jill would get used to him after a few more bad jokes and a drink or two.

"Sure, that sounds... good." Nate had planned for a quiet fall weekend in the mountains, but he realized he was now being sucked into the swirling vortex of a duration-indefinite group activity ripped straight from the social calendar of his college years.

It felt awkward, but it always did. Nate learned to push through the anxiety and go with it. Plus, Sasha's cooking was amazing twenty years ago and was altogether likely better by now.

"That sounds good." Nate reiterated.

And with that, the four college friends from the class of 2025 were reunited in October of 2045.

The Fenix Van and Nate's "Frankentruck" of a light-duty pickup pulled out of the remnants of Evergreen Shopping Plaza. The newly-formed Homecoming caravan took a long side road, running the perimeter northbound.

Heavy, dark clouds were gathering overhead and introduced the possibility of a light rain. The ghostly remains of the Salmon Springs College campus awaited the downpour.

[9 – A Good 150-Year Run]

"This is all from one fire?" Jill was stunned. Sasha parked the Fenix Van at the south end of campus. From here, nearly the entire 36 acre property was visible, end to end, thanks to an almost complete absence of structures.

"Yeah, it was one of those 'once in 500 year fires,' they said." Sasha and Jill stepped out of the van as Nate pulled up next to them.

"Hell of a half -millennium this campus has been through in one year." Jill muttered.

Dugen hopped out of the cab of Nate's truck and immediately climbed into the truck bed, as if he'd wanted to ride in the back the entire time and Nate refused to allow it. That's probably what had happened.

Dugen wasted no time climbing onto the roof of the cab and

surveying the quiet, ashen campus grounds from his perch.

"Looks like the Pearling Science Building is still intact... let's see what else is still standing."

Dugen felt like he arrived at the aftermath of an architecture competition: who could build a structure to survive a blazing wildfire?

Nate stepped out of his truck. He kicked away some charcoal-hardened remains of wood and tried to make a clear path amidst all the debris.

"Your hippy dippy hangout Woodgrove Sunbeams is toast, Sasha." Dugen was almost as bummed as Sasha about this because he couch surfed there most often. It seemed like half the population of that dorm at any given time were officially 'guests' (but more functionally squatters or vagabonds).

"I can give you the official summary if you'd like, at least from what I recall when it happened." Sasha returned to her stint as a quasi-apocalypse tour guide.

She stood before her three guests and prepped what would suffice as a campus welcome for the Homecoming fanfare that never was.

Dugen hopped down from the Frankentruck to join Jill and Nate in giving their host full attention.

"So as you probably heard, there was a massive wildfire in the summer of 2044. Just over a year ago now. It burned close to 200,000 acres... I don't remember how many."

"Around 185,000 acres, I read" Nate added.

"Of course, the forest management expert knows! Thanks,

Nate." Sasha pulled her hair back away from her face and glanced around.

"Anyway, it would've been the largest fire in state history up until the other extreme fires starting in the 2030s. Not long after we graduated, actually, there had always been talk about it like it was inevitable. And sure, we had evacuation drills, and there were efforts to keep the wildfire fuel levels down in terms of deadfall."

Sasha looked off to her right, noting that the hillside running against the perimeter of campus was now barren where trees once stood.

"But none of that made enough of a difference, evidently. The droughts were too severe, the extreme summer temperatures were unrelenting. There had always been fires across the Pacific Northwest, but the dry, hot conditions made this fire unusually severe and widespread."

"Not trying to sound argumentative," Dugen loved a good argument "... but the entire proposition of what is 'usual,' what is 'normal,' has changed. Not overnight. But definitely over our lifetimes. This was one of those 'once in a hundred years fires,' right?"

"One in five hundred, is what the analysts said." Jill recalled from Sasha's earlier statement.

"Right, exactly. But in the past decade or so, how many alleged 'low probability' events have happened, suggesting they have a hidden, higher probability? Countless."

Dugen rubbed the tip of his nose. The soot in the air brought on a sneeze.

"AH-CHOO!"

"And I concede there's some hindsight bias, cognitive bias and all that. We selectively remember the headline-grabbing disasters and ignore all the times they didn't happen and didn't make the news. But still, you know, these wildfires happen more than they used to."

"At least more severe than they used to, that's true." Nate had been quiet among the four homecomers until now. Maybe he was finally warming up to the act of having conversations again, or maybe this topic gave him a sense of authority and self-confidence. Probably both.

"I volunteered for a few fire seasons. It wasn't at all what I wanted, but the need was so great and the crews were struggling to combat the spread, everyone in my office shut things down for a few months just to fight fires. Like if we didn't do it, we wouldn't have our jobs anymore because there would be no wildlife areas to manage. At least not in the same way."

Nate paused. "But I don't want to ramble. I mean, I can talk more about it later. We're here on campus now, and Sasha was telling us about it. Sorry."

Sasha smiled, happy to see Nate coming out of his nearly impenetrable shell even for a moment. "It's okay, Nate. That was important, thank you. Thank you for sharing."

She continued, "...It was called the 44-Cascade Complex Fire. The cause was determined to be a faulty powerline or transistor or something, way far up the Timberline Ridge from Salmon Springs. I don't think I've ever been up there. That's where the sparks erupted. They think it was due to an overwhelming demand on the power grid from the heat, leading to more cooling appliances in demand. Peak AC use is around 4pm they say, with residential and commercial buildings running at the same time. Anyway, that's what probably started it."

Sasha looked around again, noting very little left standing.

"The campus was evacuated as quickly as possible. Thankfully, it was summer session and there were few classes going on. It was almost miraculous that no one on campus died in the fire.

However, the fire spread so rapidly, and beyond the projected burn area... well, quite a few people died in the nearby residential areas. An entire nursing home, a day care facility, off-campus dorms and apartments, some neighborhoods. It was really tragic. I think over 300 dead in total from the fire. Then at least twice as many in the weeks to follow due to smoke inhalation and other respiratory problems."

Sasha paused. She had gotten through the hard part. Everyone remained silent. Solemn. Processing the grief in real time, at the place it happened. It was almost like the cool afternoon air whispered about the tragedy which had transpired over a year ago.

"Anyway, the rest of the semester was canceled. Some classes have moved entirely online. Some classes are still taught in other buildings around town, at the community college, and I think they opened up another campus in Ninebrook Falls, next town over. SSC is no longer enrolling new students. Existing students have all transitioned to completing their degree plans elsewhere."

Jill began walking across the main campus commons, slowly glancing from one old memory to another. That was the bench where she would study between Econ 255 and Accounts Management. There was the walk-up coffee stand where the cute guy worked, wonder what happened to him?

Those tree trunks remained from the grassy field where she would lay out a blanket and sunbathe, listen to podcasts, and attempt a genuine study break. And just beyond the dusty pile of debris where Nichols Hall used to stand was the track and field complex.

"All of it burned down." Jill muttered under her breath, as though she was too stunned to make the sounds her lips were forming.

She had never been back to campus since she graduated, and she had never been on the track since that car wreck. Despite all the devastation, the running track looked almost the same. Slightly ashen and with patches of dirt, but comparatively intact.

"They still use the running track sometimes, I hear." Sasha stepped forward to stand by Jill.

Behind them, Nate and Dugen kicked around debris to see what they could identify.

"I can't believe they didn't restrict access." Nate looked around, as though some valuables remained.

"I bet anyone looking for precious remnants, like copper pipe or other scrap metal, picked through it awhile ago" Dugen spoke with some degree of experience on the matter. "At this point, what's left to access?"

"It's about what I expected, honestly. You see one burned-out town, you've seen them all." Nate shook his head. This was not on his daily to-do list.

"When was Springs founded?" Dugen scratched his scruffy crimson whiskers.

"... The town or the college?" Nate kept his hands tightly in his pockets, as though he didn't want to fully commit his limbs to being here.

"The college. This burned-down college. The one we're stand..."

"—I think around 1895."

"Ah, the 90s." Dugen laughed. "Those were the good ol' days!"

"So I hear." Nate shook his head. After a silent survey of the horizon, Dugen took a deep breath and began to amble along through the debris.

"You know, you don't expect to outlive your college. Especially one this old, you know?" Dugen wasn't talking to anyone in particular, but Nate half-listened as a courtesy and began to slowly meander alongside him. A willing audience for what was sure to be a rousing lecture.

"We intuitively understand that the buildings we construct will outlast us. That's half the point of building them."

"We didn't construct these buildings, Dugen."

"You know what I mean, Nate. The collective 'we.' The eponymous human experiment. The effort of the masses. We build with the expectation of permanence, even in the flagrant defiance of the natural world in which we situate such lofty structures."

Dugen gestured to the barren treeline along the hillside ridge. "The hubris! We built a college right up against the edge of a forest. Forests burn. It's simple fire ecology, right?"

"Sort of. Low intensity burns are common in temperate deciduous forests, but they leave the old growth standing because the larger trees can withstand the heat." Nate was trying to be helpful.

"Exactly!" Dugen pointed back at Nate. "Exactly. We raised the stakes, we pumped the heavens full of petrochemicals and the heat trapped us into this inferno of our own creation. Then the structures of permanence went up in flames. The illusion of a forever campus, of a forever society, burned down, up in smoke. And fueled by what? Our own extractive energy practices, our own gutting the earth of the remains of the dinosaurs, the reptilian masses of the previous era."

"They were probably early avian species, Dugen. Dinosaurs were the ancestors of birds."

Nate shook his head. He'd forgotten what it was like to be linguistically assaulted by Douglas Dugen.

"And the dinosaurs turning into fossil fuels? Yeah, that's a common myth. If you're talking about subterranean oil fields, they had formed long before the Jurassic period. If the dinosaurs knew how to drill for oil, they could have done so."

Nate was trying to be helpful.

"Brother, we can discuss whether dinosaurs would drive gas or electric cars another time." Dugen put his arm around Nate like an overly-chummy drunk after the bars closed.

"But all I'm saying is, these buildings were designed to outlast their occupants. And for like, 150 years? They did, until they didn't. Until the paradigm changed. The age of buildings that last, campuses that are intact forever, that's over now."

"Looks like it." Nate wondered if Dugen was done.

True to form, Dugen was not done.

"The campus of the future is now the campus of the present. And presently, the campus must be mobile, it must be flexible. It must be able to move with the changing seasons, with the waves of climate disruption. It must be portable rather than permanent. Academic in your pocket. And once you understand that about a college, you can understand that about humanity. About all of life."

"All of life. That's a good note to end on. Want some applause?" Nate clapped a few times in mockery mixed with appreciation. Dugen should feel honored that Nate finally pulled his hands from his pockets.

"Thank you, thank you very much." Dugen curled his lip in a long lost Elvis reference.

Up ahead of them, Sasha watched as Jill put her hair in a ponytail, laced up her shoes, and stretched.

"Are you going for a run... now?" This was not on Sasha's planned Homecoming tour.

"I never got to complete my senior year running season. Maybe, maybe this is my time." Jill crouched and took a deep breath.

She looked at the track ahead of her. For a moment, the piles of debris and burned landscape transformed into a green field. Crowds gathered at the sidelines, cheering with anticipation. Jill closed her eyes, taking in the memories as a distillation of the present moment.

She opened her eyes.

She pushed off her back foot.

She leaned into her stride.

She ran.

She ran hard.

Nate and Dugen caught up to Sasha on the side of the running track. It was tarnished by soot and mud, but was otherwise intact.

And perhaps for the first time in over a year, someone was running on it – not to escape a deadly blaze, but to achieve a different kind of escape.

Jill felt her heart race, her muscles burn, the pulse of exertion throughout her body. She remembered every sensation, every nuance of every gait, every curve and every straightaway, every pivot and every lean forward, until her mind was clear and her legs flared.

Her doctors told her that she would be able to sprint again with enough rehab, but Jill didn't trust them. She didn't trust herself. But in this moment, in this burned-out place where once she trained absent any encumbrance, she felt that confidence return.

She was back.

Jill completed her 800 meter dash. No one was timing her. No one ran against her. There was no photo finish. No stats for the scorekeepers. Yet she felt complete victory.

"Damn, I'm... I'm outta shape." Jill breathed hard and furious, trying to control every inhale and exhale, trying to slow down her heart rate.

Tears streamed down her cheeks. Her quadriceps began to tighten and cramp. She wasn't star college athlete material anymore.

"Girl, you make 40s look good!" Sasha exclaimed.

Dugen tossed Jill the water bottle from the front of her van. Sasha rubbed up and down Jill's back as she rehydrated.

"I forgot about the altitude. It's not like I never run. I just never run like this anymore." Jill kept her hands on her hips to catch her breath. She wiped her brow and shook out her ponytail.

"As fine as ever..." Dugen nudged Nate.

"She's probably still single, but way too good for you." Nate replied dismissively.

"So you, uh... wanna race me next?" Dugen was up for anything.

"Fuck no." Nate definitely was not.

The four homecomers collected themselves and continued strolling along the remains of Salmon Springs College.

What might have been rebuilt before was generally just left abandoned in The Long Collapse. In most cases, a rebuild cost more to excavate and construct anew than to simply build elsewhere. In most cases, even a relocated build was too pricey. Insurance policies never covered losses like this anymore; there were too many disaster incidents and insurers were more likely to declare insolvency than to pay for an unprecedented claim.

"Society has always structured itself around anticipation and allocation of risk. If the anticipated risk is smaller, the allocation will also be smaller. No problem, right?" Dugen had been thinking about this more lately.

"If the anticipation is greater and the allocation is smaller, that's ideal for any sustainable model. Anticipated risk must be greater than allocation of actual risk. This campus was probably prepared—financially and psychologically—for a single building to catch fire and have structural damage before the fire department arrived to contain it."

Dugen gestured in many directions, pointing every which way to total destruction. "But the entire campus and surrounding area burning down? The allocation of risk greatly exceeded what was anticipated. There's no leeway for that much loss."

"You know," Nate added, "Building towns and cities right up against the ocean or right up against the forest seemed like a good idea. Most civilizations are founded upon a river, a lake, an ocean, right up against the woods."

Nate continued, "It makes sense; humans require those resources to build and sustain life. There's no escaping those natural forces. We're each part of all that."

Sasha looked up as the storm clouds gathered. A flock of birds crossed the skyline. This would likely conclude their campus catastrophe tour.

Nate concluded, "But it was a good idea premised on a certain threshold of risk tolerance, a certain set of assumptions about the severity of coastal flooding or hurricanes, a certain set of prediction models about drought and dry heat in a forested area."

Nate had studied this in detail, mostly from college textbooks written for an age when forest management was a minimal process of maintaining an existing ecosystem – one conducive to mammalian life.

A cool rainstorm began to fall lightly on the charred campus grounds.

"Can we go now?" Jill looked to Sasha for permission to end their tour.

"Of course, I only thought we would stay for a few minutes, not try to set a lap record in the half mile sprint!" Sasha nudged Jill playfully.

"Yeah, well... 800 meters is basically a half mile." she laughed. Standard versus Metric humor.

The four Homecomers turned back towards their parked vehicles. Dugen kicked around at some debris, hoping to find a useful bit of something – a textbook, a binder full of notes, a computer console, something to claim as a souvenir for his makeshift Homecoming weekend.

And there it was. A small metal plaque from the base of a trophy case that had burned up so fast the rest of the objects melted together. Dugen picked up the plaque and dusted it off, polishing the surface to brush away the ashy residue.

Model United Nations
2038 Championship Team
Salmon Springs College
Honing Diplomacy Among Nations Today
Building a Peaceful World for Tomorrow

Dugen cracked a wry smile and put the plaque in his pocket. "Wonder how that worked out."

As the Homecomers reached their vehicles, the rain began to pour.

"Nate, you wanna follow me to the farm? We'll make something warm and delicious, I promise!" Sasha was already dreaming up the ingredients for a hearty stew with a bit of everything in it.

Fall always yielded the best ingredients for soups and this

evening was the perfect occasion.

Nate and Dugen hopped into the truck. Sasha and Jill got into the van.

Their headlights cast a spotlight on the remains of Salmon Springs College. In the heavy rain, one could almost imagine the trees, the buildings, the walkways all as they were before.

"It was a good 150-year run, Sam!" Dugen wasn't the first to call the campus by this name, but he surely must have popularized it.

As the truck and van continued on the muddy paved road north, the rainfall around campus collected into grooves, forming ditches alongside the edges of collapsed structures. Over time, these grooves would deepen into canals, then eventually converging into a creek that wove its way through the center of campus.

The bifurcation of the watershed would continue for several centuries until it formed a shallow canyon with a flowing river at its bottom. The shrubs would branch out beyond their trimmed forms, the post-wildfire sprouts would become saplings, the saplings would grow into mature trees, and the piles of campus debris would be overgrown entirely.

And just as before the 150 years of Salmon Springs College, this verdant region of the Timberline Valley would again grow wild.

[**10 – Homecoming Festivities**]

Rylar tuned his guitar. It had been awhile and he wanted the sound to be presentable for his guests. The rain was still pouring but the dry front porch served as a hospitable gathering place.

Tres Gatos agreed. Though skeptical of the three human strangers arriving at Fenix Farm, the felines scampered to the edges of the porch with curiosity, having no desire to be out in the soaking downfall.

"Hold on, hold on... I think I got it. Ready?"

Nate and Dugen put down their beers. "Ready."

Sasha and Jill had been inside the house, but stepped out onto the porch with table settings.

"This might be the last weekend of the season to eat dinner

outside, but we've been doing it all summer... I don't want to capitulate to winter just yet" Sasha said of their outdoor dinner venue.

"Hun, would you call the kids for dinner?" Sasha was in multitasking mode and loving it.

Rylar threw his head back and started strumming his guitar rapidly, throwing out a range of loud notes across the scale. He sang in the timbre of a folk ballad with improvised, ruffian origins.

> *now gather 'round for the festive hour*
> *as starlight (maybe later) rises upon you*
> *now gather 'round to break bread together*
> *and that means Acacia and Timo, too!*

Rylar looks around with glee as he continued, inviting his guests to get into the festive vibes of the moment.

> *Hey-o! it's harvest and we've bounty aplenty*
> *all the grains of the world, all the heirloom seeds*
> *Hey-o! it's harvest and we've spared no appetite*
> *for all our guests wants and 'course all their needs*

Nate and Dugen leaned in. This was getting good.

Acacia peeked out the front door to survey the scene and rolled her eyes. Her dad was being embarrassing again. Timo darted from behind her and dove for his favorite bean bag nestled to one side of the porch. Tres Gatos gathered around him and he pet them playfully, promising them dinner scraps.

Rylar cleared his throat and continued. He rarely had dinner guests, thus was inclined to put on a show—if for no other reason than to practice for the eventual reuniting of his local band, The Real Scrapadeerios.

a stew, a stew is what's been brewin'
delicious hodge-podge of autumn embrace
she knew, she knew it's my cravin'
so get in my belly and don't leave a trace!

Dugen and Nate clapped audaciously, then Timo joined in because the adults had established a noise-making permission structure. Timo howled like a wolf and Sasha rolled her eyes as she brought out a big pot of stew.

"I knew it, I'm raising a wolf-child among chickens" Sasha laughed.

Rylar took a jestful bow and set aside his guitar as his attention turned to the spread of dinner delights.

"And cats and goats, mom!" Timo made animal friends with predator and prey alike. When he "grew up," he didn't want to *grow up*; he wanted to be his own Mowgli in his own Jungle Book.

"How many cats, Timo?" Sasha took every occasion to be a teachable moment, as a homeschooling parent's lesson is never complete and class is not only 8 to 3.

"Three cats" Timo looked among them, formerly known as Howdy, Rowdy, and Bowdy.

"Si Timo, ahora en Español" Sasha nudged him.

"Tres gatos" Timo replied.

"Muy buen, Timo!" Sasha started ladling out portions of stew as Jill collected empty bowls and passed around full ones. "Cuántas cabras?"

Timo thought for a moment. "Diez cabras?"

"Doce cabras, no?" Sasha had trouble counting the goats, too. Timo shrugged.

"I only know to ten so far!" Timo paused and stared up at the string of lights draped along the perimeter of the porch. He had it! "Diez cabras y dos cabras!"

Sasha laughed and nodded. "Correctamundo!"

"Improvised linguistics and arithmetic in a second language? Kid's incredible." Dugen looked on with awe.

"Primo Timo!" Dugen shouted. Not to be outdone, Timo bowed like Rylar had moments earlier.

"Alright, now that the boys of the house have impressed our guests, it's time to feast!" Sasha had transitioned effortlessly from tour guide to chef and hostess.

Nate, Dugen, and Jill pulled up their chairs, each an orphan of a different furniture set. The guests took in the array of rich brown stew, bread, chopped and grilled veggies, and a side of goat brie.

"This looks marvelous!" Jill proclaimed.

Sasha joined hands with her two kids on either side, then Rylar beside them, and her guests did the same, forming a connected circle of celebrants around the Fenix family table.

"Sorry, just a second." Nate reached down and fumbled through his backpack, propped up against the siding of the house. He produced his sturdy camera.

"I take this everywhere" Nate admitted bashfully, "even though I don't go many places."

Nate framed up the Fenix family and guests into a jubilant group photo. Timo made a silly face, Sasha beamed with joy, Jill put on her best smile, Dugen pointed at their dinner with anticipation, Rylar and Acacia gave more neutral, dinnertime mugs.

SNAP.

"Thanks, everyone!" Nate raised a hand of timid appreciation.

"What a lovely occasion for a photo!" Sasha exclaimed. She turned to her eldest, her only remaining daughter.

"Acacia, would you like to say grace tonight?" Sasha gently rubbed Acacia's hand.

"Would I *like* to?" Acacia rolled her eyes.

"We rarely have guests over for dinner, right? How does it feel to see new faces around our table? Think of it as a reflection and a greeting." Sasha knew Acacia was going through some things. It was that age.

Acacia fully committed and intended to do so in a manner so thorough as to be retired from this awkward dinner table task from this point forward. She looked up high, as if about to start an extended performance.

"Um, sure. Roman Numeral One: A Reflection." Acacia dramatically cleared her throat. "Today, we stayed home because mom needed the space in the van to pick up our dinner guests. Which was fine because there was lots to do around the farm. Timo forgot to change the water in the hen house again and—"

"Didn't forget. I was gonna after putting in new straw." Timo wanted to set the record straight.

Rylar and Sasha smirked as their guests enjoyed a spicy taste of their colorful family dynamics.

"So anyway, dad thought it would be a great idea to take the tractor motor apart because it was sounding like a dying goose. Or whatever that sound was. Anyways, um, I helped him with that and learned a little about mechanics and also some new swear words. But this is a family meal so I won't repeat—"

"Thank you, Acacia." Sasha interrupted with gratitude.

"Everyone worked hard, got a lot done, yadda yadda. Builds character, free child labor, lovely life in the middle of nowhere, breeze carrying the smell of animal dung." Acacia was testing the limits now.

"Sounds amazing, where do I sign up?" Dugen leaned into Acacia's sarcasm and Timo laughed in response.

Timo slid a fresh napkin over to Dugen. "Oh wow, anyone got a pen?" Timo hopped out of his chair to go look for one.

"After dinner, Timo. It's an open-ended offer." Rylar tried to keep everyone focused on finishing the blessing for this meal so they could finally E-A-T.

Timo returned to his chair and grinned from ear to ear. Jill and Nate were trying to conceal their amusement so as not to encourage more of these mealtime shenanigans.

"I like having guests for dinner." Timo beamed. Acacia laughed.

"Gross, Timo. You make it sound like you're gonna eat them."

Timo laughed, everyone else tried to hold their laughter back.

"Well maybe I am!" Timo rubbed his hands together.

"I am the wolf-boy, after all!" Timo bared his baby teeth and growled, then broke into laughter.

"Any further words for grace tonight, Acacia?" Sasha saw the lingering appetites around the table and wanted to keep everyone on track. Acacia continued.

"Oh yes, Roman Numeral Two: A Greeting. Welcome to our guests, Dugen, Jill, and Ned."

"Nate" Sasha corrected.

"It's fine, nobody remembers me without extensive practice. It's always been like that" Nate blushed.

"And Nate! My apologies." Acacia was ready to wrap things up.

"Fenix Farm invites you to this world class meal of stew and veggies with bread and cheese, made with local, organic, free-range ingredients and prepared with your discerning tastes in mind! May the gods bless our meal for health, wealth, and happiness!" Acacia raised her glass to close out her pronouncement in high celebration.

"Amen to that!" Several voices chimed in at once. Their assortment of glass and plastic cups clinked together in a cacophony of commencement.

"Great job, Acacia." Sasha anticipated some antics but allowed for them. Running a family on the edge of the woods in times like these, a little wilderness slipped into everyone. It was part of what made the experience special.

"Not a day goes by without something crazy and memorable around here," Sasha told her guests.

"And funny!" Timo laughed as he took in spoonfuls of rich, brown stew.

Jill looked around the table between bites of homemade deliciousness and drank in the scene. The illuminating warmth from the string of lights overhead made everyone at the table glow with a serene aura about them.

It felt like a storybook family dinner, one unlike any she experienced growing up. A genuine sense of family, of connectedness. Nate was smiling more. Even Dugen seemed more friendly, less creepy than usual. Rylar was into his second helping.

Something about the Fenix family dinner on their front porch was a slice of magic in a fallen world.

Sasha looked around attentively. "Does everyone have enough of everything?"

"This stew is so good..." Nate wiped his chin with the cloth napkin from the table setting, which looked to have been woven by hand.

"I know the goat's milk takes some getting used to, but the goat cheese is already my favorite." Dugen proclaimed between oversize bites.

"What's for dessert, mom?" Timo was always preparing for the sweet hereafter.

"Your favorite, Mr. Timo. We made them last night, remember?" Sasha replied.

Timo thought a moment. When you're six, yesterday feels like three weeks ago.

"Pudding cups!!!" Timo remembered.

"That's right! I hope everyone saves room. We put a layer of vanilla cake on the bottom." Sasha gave away the buried treasure awaiting guests at the end of each pudding cup.

Acacia collected empty plates off the table. She decided to make this her 'waitress internship' so she had steady work when she was able to leave the farm to stay with Courtney in Seattle, at least for a summer. A girl can always dream.

Sasha surveyed the dinner spread. Her homecoming guests looked satisfied and content. She felt vindicated, having gone through the effort to find her long lost friends from a college which is no longer standing. Amidst the ashes, their friendships were renewed.

Looking out past the porch, Sasha noted that the rain had stopped and the night sky was beginning to clear. In the distance, a set of headlights approached from the dirt road. At this hour?

Sasha kept an eye on the horizon as she refilled drinks. There was only one neighbor past Fenix Farm on their road, known as Gallagher Gardens. But they were already away for the winter.

Sasha set aside the water pitcher and leaned against the porch to keep a closer watch. Rylar glanced over with interest as the dinner guests were lost in casual conversation.

Sasha focused, her pulse beginning to race.

The headlights had stopped moving just in front of the gated entrance to Fenix Farm. While the property was gated and fenced to keep the goats in, it sometimes also kept strangers out. This instance was the latter.

"Babe? Not expecting any more guests, right?" Rylar asked.

Sasha shook her head but kept her attention on the idling vehicle at the end of their driveway. The gate was closed, but not locked.
Rylar looked around the table, then to a long wooden chest in the corner of the porch. It was time to make the call.

"Gate, gate, gate."

Rylar spoke in a loud, clear, but calm tone.

Timo and Acacia knew what to do.

This was not a drill.

Timo turned off the porch lights.

Acacia took Timo by the hand and let him inside the house.

"Please come with us" Acacia said to the guests, her voice trembling but firm. Jill looked to the road, then to Sasha.

"Everyone inside, please, my apologies." Sasha moved back from the edge of the porch and put her hands firmly on Jill and Dugen.

They crouched low as they moved into the house.

Nate looked to Rylar. Rylar looked back, then gestured to the front gate, then gestured "stay low."

Rylar pushed the guitar aside and opened the wooden chest. He lifted up a rifle with a scope. It was infrared. In the low light of the moonless sky, Rylar crouched down upon the floor of the porch with the wooden chest propped up against the slats which formed the porch perimeter. He slid his rifle barrel between the slats and put his eye to the scope.

"I have a pistol in my truck, want me to get it?" Nate whispered.

"Too late, just sit tight. I have more guns inside if we need them." Rylar kept his breath slow and steady as he glassed the front gate and the headlights beyond it. In the stillness of the night, Rylar could hear the distant engine idling.

Inside, Jill and Dugen stayed with Timo and Acacia under the dining room table. Sasha was in Rylar's workshop, gathering a shotgun with shells and two pistols with clips.

It was a modest armory but enough to fortify a farm family.

They hadn't drilled the 'intruder-at-the-gate' scenario in a few months but everyone got to their place in record time. Sasha waited with weapons ready. If she heard a single shot, she would keep the shotgun, give a pistol to Acacia and the other to Rylar.

Timo was told he had to wait until age eight to be armed, but Sasha trusted Timo with it now in a last resort. She didn't want to imagine what that would look like.

Rylar kept drawing slow breaths. The headlights stayed in place.

Rylar couldn't make out the number of inhabitants in the vehicle, but it looked to be a large sedan in good condition.

"C'mon, what's their deal?" Rylar muttered.

"You owe anyone money?" Nate whispered.

"Not enough for this shit" Rylar smirked. He was a skilled

enough marksman to drop two intruders before they were through the gate. Looking for anyone rolling down a window to fire back, Rylar was alert and his adrenaline was flooding his muscles at a steady pulse.

No movement.

It was a long split second.

A flash emergency that dragged on.

Everyone was on edge in their own way.

Jill felt an innate guardian response to keeping Acacia and Timo safe. Sasha felt her mamma bear instincts kick in, ready to do anything necessary to protect her family.

Dugen had a flashback to some retro Chiptune battle music from an obscure Japanese RPG he played as a kid. What a time to be alive!

Nate's mind was flooded with regret. What good was his Ruger going to do him in the glove box of his truck? He prided himself on preparedness and self-sufficiency. Here he was in a deadly situation and completely disarmed, unable to protect his friends. He vowed to always carry concealed from now on, even at a family dinner.

In The Long Collapse, disaster could strike anywhere. And clearly this family was prepared; this family wouldn't have second-guessed Nate keeping a firearm on him around a meal together. Safety was just an illusion, shattered by the first sight of an unfamiliar vehicle on the horizon. Nate always found a way to let everyone down, especially this crew. Especially Jill.

"They're turning around. Probably just lost out-of-towners. It happens." Rylar lifted his eye from the rifle scope to watch as the headlights backed away, then spun around in a three point turn, then the vehicle headed back towards Salmon Springs. Rylar let out a sigh of relief.

"Clear, clear, clear! Thank you, everyone!"

Rylar stood and stretched. The moon began to peek out from behind the dissipating storm clouds, lighting up the tree-dotted hillside. Nothing like an emergency drill to bring out the serene, nocturnal beauty of a peak lunar cycle.

Sasha put away the shotgun and pistols. She had never held a gun before moving to Fenix Farm, and she had never fired a gun until The Long Collapse.

Whatever lifestyle, whatever cultural affiliations one had during plentiful times, the urgent challenges of the present had a way of casting all that aside. It wasn't a political act to stockpile firearms and drill readiness; it was a requirement for survival on this apocalyptic retro-frontier.

Dugen and Jill crawled out from under the table with Timo and Acacia. They felt a bit nonplussed about being assigned the "kid section" during the intruder procedure, but it was their first time and it was just as well they were secluded.

"We do this sometimes at dinner." Timo explained to the guests.

"There are worse things than wolves out there and so we are ready for it. When I get older, I'll be out there with dad. We're ready for anything. We've got guns."

"Ready steady, Freddy!" Dugen gave Timo a high five.

"Who's Freddy?" Timo was curious.

"He's got claws and he comes for you in your dreams!" Dugen

136

wiggled his fingers and then raked his nails down Timo's back. Timo giggled.

"That's unpossible!" Timo then growled like a wolf to scare off any Freddy that would come around. Dugen rolled over onto his back and curled up his arms and legs, playing dead. Timo rolled around and laughed again. Dugen was way more fun that his stuck-up sister.

"Mom, can Mr. Dugen live with us now?" Timo shouted into the next room as Sasha emerged and turned back on the house lights.

"Probably not, but hopefully he can visit more often than once every twenty years." Sasha grinned with relief as everyone seemed to remain in good spirits, despite the emergency.

It was never the moments of fear or paranoia which eroded one's spirit during The Long Collapse; it was the inability to recover from them.

"I am in favor of it. Timo always wanted a big brother, anyway." Acacia stood up and went to the kitchen, preparing a platter of bowls to be filled with cake and pudding.

Jill smiled and shook her head. There was something admirable about Dugen. Even though he was clearly immature and irresponsible, breaking social norms like a hobby, and being generally boorish by nature, Dugen always retained genuine wonder and a playful attitude towards life. It served him well. It kept him from hardening with despair. It kept him young and full of life. Perhaps, Jill thought, she could learn something from such an impish man-child.

Rylar and Nate rearranged the porch. Like most everything else, each space took on many uses. The passenger van was also a farm delivery truck. The front porch was a gathering place for guests but also a fortified lookout to defend the farm. Transitioning seamlessly between each use was the finesse forged from adversity and necessity.

Tres Gatos had scampered away in the darkness, but now returned to the porch as the string of lights illuminated the dinner table once again.

"Welcome back from a brief intermission, everyone." Rylar assumed the role of emcee. He drummed on the table as the Homecomers and kids gathered back around and found their seats.

Sasha smiled with reassurance as her guests settled into the atmosphere of hospitality again.

"Next up: pudding cups!" Timo clapped and howled like a wolf. Dugen joined in. This was the kind of ruckus he could get behind.

Sasha shook her head in delighted disbelief. What did she expect would happen when she introduced her favorite college goofball to her wacky wolf boy for a son?

It was by all accounts the rowdy, near-perfect kickoff to their Homecoming weekend.

[11 – Into The Timberlines]

Rooster Rodney stood atop his perch in the chicken yard.

"Err-err-err-err-errrrrrrrrrrr!"

"Err-err-err-err-errrrrrrrrrrrr!"

"Err-err-err-err-errrrrrrrrrrrrr!"

This had been going on for at least ten minutes. Jill sat up in bed. An uninterrupted, solid sleep. When was the last time that had happened?

No nightmares, no cold sweats, no panting and heart racing. Just a relaxed, rejuvenating slumber. Perhaps it was something in the stew, or those delicious pudding cups the night before – the magic of a four-course, locally-sourced, organic, home-cooked meal. Or maybe coming back to Salmon Springs had already given her a measure of peace and reconciliation.

"Ugh!" Her legs were cramping and acutely sore. She hadn't pushed herself to run like that in a very long time. But running on the old SSC track once again? Worth it. Totally worth it.

Jill looked around the guest bedroom at Fenix Farm. Judging by the pastel colors and design, it used to be a nursery for the little ones, and then it was a little girl's room.

Jill noticed a family photo tucked away behind a lamp atop a corner table. Sasha looked serene as she always did, Rylar with fewer gray whiskers and sun-baked wrinkles, Acacia leaning to one side and years before her growth spurt, Timo as a smirking toddler in diapers, and a bright-eyed little girl with ribbons in her hair.

"They had a third child." Jill whispered to herself.

The door to her bedroom creaked open. Tres Gatos let themselves in, clearly irritated that a new human had moved into their room.

"Well, hi there. Don't mind me!" Jill opened her suitcase and put on a sweatshirt and some running shorts. Maybe a light morning jog would help work through the muscle tension.

Stepping into the living room, it was like Jill walked in on her new instant family captured in their early morning bustle.

Timo and Dugen sat on Timo's blanket in the middle of the floor. Hair unkempt, faces still soggy from sleep, nonetheless driven to succeed at Go Fish. The cards were worn and some were tattered, but it was Timo's favorite find from an abandoned daycare center.

Sasha came by with a hairbrush and attempted to tame Timo's twisted locks as he looked intently at the cards in his hand.

Dugen was a cutthroat Go Fish player and spared Timo no mercy – just the way Timo liked it!

Rylar was frying up some eggs and Nate was chopping veggies. Perhaps they were making omelets? In any case, Nate looked less sullen than Jill had remembered; maybe just feeling included in the culinary tasks of the morning gave Nate an extra dash of pep. Nate had been living in the cabin with his Sheprador for so long, he had forgotten what it felt like to have a guy friend again.

In one corner, Acacia sat in a rocking chair by the window overlooking the front pasture. Towards the driveway, towards the gate, towards the road. She was knitting a wool sweater, its colors fading from a deep blue into sea green.

Jill recognized the look in Acacia's eyes: of longing to escape, to explore, to see the great big world. Jill wished Acacia had inherited a better world to explore, a less broken one. That was something Jill had taken for granted when she fled Salmon Springs twenty years ago.

"Hey, your sweater is really coming along!" Jill approached Acacia with a Thermos mug of coffee in hand. Acacia kept her eyes on each stitch, counting her row.

"Thanks." Acacia knew she was supposed to be more social. And Jill seemed cool enough. Acacia looked over as Jill sipped on her coffee and looked out the window, still negotiating with herself over the prospect of a morning run.

The plumes of thin, wispy mist slowly crept upward in the still morning air, then evaporating into the stratosphere. The rising sun lit up the fall foliage in a mosaic of yellow, red, orange, and brown patches upon the dark thicket of dense forest. Nothing like the industrial landscape of skyscrapers jutting through the smog of Wynhill Heights. This was a sublime, primal, painterly vista.

Acacia glanced over at Jill, standing in her sweatshirt and running shorts. In the morning light, Jill's scars were more visible. "What happened to your legs?"

Jill was unsure how much to say. Usually, it was just "a car accident, a long time ago," so that's what she blurted out.

Almost out of habit. Acacia nodded.

Jill continued, "Did your mom ever tell you about it? I don't want to be the first one to mention it... but yeah, all four of us. Senior year. It's how I met Nate and Dugen. But your mom and I, we go back to freshman year."

"You used to be a runner. I can tell." Acacia put down her half-knit sweater. "Well, seems like you can run again now, right?"

Jill smirked. "Wanna find out?"

Acacia stood up. "I can show you my favorite trail that loops around from the road to the back of the farm near the chicken yard."

"Great, then let's go!" Jill and Acacia headed out the front door.

Sasha watched from the window as her first daughter and her first friend from college ran down the driveway and onto a forest path, disappearing between the trees. Sasha had forgotten how much her kids benefited from the mentorship and attention of other adults. It was a trust she was building back after losing Emmalyn.

Nate and Rylar had finished making omelets and put out plates for a hearty breakfast.

Dugen and Timo were now in the championship round of Go Fish, the winner of which would be known as the Greatest Go Fish Champion King Of All Time. Tres Gatos observed casually, more drawn to the smell of breakfast.

"Breakfast and then morning chores, Timo." Sasha knew that a trio of guests was an exciting disruption to the Fenix Farm routine, but somebody had to restore order around here.

Jill and Acacia returned in time to join the rest for breakfast. They had only run partway; Acacia showed Jill where the blackberries grew and they abandoned their run in favor of gathering the ripest ones. Some eaten, some returned by the handful to add to a fruit salad, or cereal, or pancakes, or baked bread? "The possibilities are endless" Acacia told Jill.

Timo wolfed down his breakfast, intent on completing morning chores and showing Dugen the tree fort he was planning to build once Rylar got the lumber for it. Acacia took her time, but both soon left the table to attend to their usual activities. Of course, Dugen tagged along with Timo for the tour and to make a proper introduction with the farm animals.

Sasha sat around the table with contentment. "That was an amazing omelet, hun!" She praised Rylar's cooking often, even if just a simple breakfast entrée.

"Nate suggested the chopped peppers and onions, and that really livened up the dish." Rylar nudged Nate, who quietly bowed.

Sasha clapped softly and Jill gave the breakfast her 'chef's kiss.'

As Sasha and Rylar cleared the table, Nate spoke up during a lull in conversation. "So I was thinking, if you haven't been up to Timberline Bluff before, I could show you. My cabin is up there. I don't know what all we have planned, I didn't even know about this homecoming thing, but I just thought I would put it out there."

"Oh, I don't..." Sasha looked to Rylar. Rylar nodded with approval.

"You can go, hun. The kids and I have plenty to do here. Have some time with your friends."

"We wouldn't be back until after dark, it would be so late." Sasha wasn't used to staying away from the farm during the night hours. Last night's intruder scare illustrated why.

"If you wanted, I would be happy to host tonight. I know this is a homecoming weekend and you've been such generous hosts already." Nate hadn't offered anyone a place to stay in as long as he could remember. He wasn't entirely confident he could be a good host, but he was certain his guests would make due nonetheless.

"I mean... thank you, Nate. For offering. I'm sure it's beautiful up there this time of year." Sasha was hedging, wrestling with her sense of duty to the farm but recognizing this could be exactly what their homecoming weekend needed next.

"I'm all for it" Jill proclaimed. This entire trip had been a series of envelope-pushing experiences, an exercise in pure comfort zone abandonment.

Sasha looked out the kitchen window to the back pasture. Dugen and Timo were scouring the chicken yard for eggs that hadn't been laid in their nesting boxes. It happened sometimes.

"What would Dugen think, maybe we should ask him?" Sasha paused, she already knew the answer.

"Dugen stole a van to lift some bikes to get a ticket out here, then

144

came up short on funds and was a stowaway in the cargo train the rest of the way. This is the same guy who rented the back of my station wagon as his primary residence for a semester. I'm pretty sure he's fine with staying at the cabin."

Nate was right and everyone knew it.

Sasha looked to everyone around her. "Okay, it's decided. I'm going to prep some snacks for the kids, Rylar can have dinner with them while we're out, and we'll be back mid-morning tomorrow. I can pick up any house chores that are left over after —"

Rylar put his arms around Sasha as he stood behind her in the kitchen.

"—We'll be fine. The kids know the routine better than I do. Enjoy a trip to the mountains, the fall colors and all. Nate can take his camera, get a few good pictures. We'll make a stationary print from them or something." Rylar knew how to convince his partner with a few constructive activities to waylay the impression Sasha would actually be sedentary or docile.

"Right." Sasha took a deep breath. "You're right. This is gonna be great!"

Dugen and Timo returned with a basket full of eggs and a harrowing story about Rooster Rodney chasing after Dugen.

"We had a showdown, that's for sure. Rodney's fierce, but he saw in my eyes that I had taken on biker gangs and methed-up marauders and crooked cops before; the rooster knew he was no match!" Dugen proclaimed.

Timo rolled with laughter. "And I howled at him to remind him who protects the yard at night! Wolf-boy Timo!" Dugen and Timo both howled.

Sasha shook her head in concealed amusement.

Jill blushed and looked away. What the hell did she suddenly see in Dugen?

Acacia watched from the hallway as Sasha packed an overnight bag. "Why don't I ever get to go anywhere fun?"

Acacia crossed her arms. Sasha zipped up her backpack.

"Last weekend you went with Courtney to the hot springs, and next week you said you want to go to the Duncan Farms pumpkin patch and pick one out for carving." Sasha was always ready with a rejoinder like this. It was required for parenting a tweenager.

"Yeah, it's whatever." Acacia sulked off into her room.

Rylar and Timo resumed work on a produce washing table they had been building in their down time. Timo knew all the tools by name and fetched them quickly.

Dugen, Sasha, and Jill gathered their possessions at the front door of Fenix Farm.

Nate pulled up his Frankentruck for a load-in. It reminded him of group field studies he used to lead a very long time ago. Perhaps that's what this really was for him: another biology excursion.

"There's plenty of room here, between the extended cab and the truck box." Nate had bought the truck after the settlement with a small family in mind. He kept it maintained with newish parts of any make and model. Perhaps now, this was the family the Frankentruck was meant for.

Dugen took his duffle bag with him because his working assumption was always that he might never see his last night's stay ever again. Jill left her suitcase and consolidated her travel items into a large backpack. Sasha did the same. They were travel-ready.

Everyone loaded into Nate's truck. Dugen sat up front with Nate and the ladies sat in back. It was a kind of chauffeur chauvinism.

Nate's nerves were already strained just reliving the experience of being a speedy car pool service again. He knew he had to get over it. He knew what happened before wasn't his fault. And he didn't want to bring it up. Maybe nobody else would notice it was Nate behind the wheel with the same three passengers?

In any case, he had a large, robust truck now and any such collision wouldn't result in the same outcome. Besides, almost nobody was on the road these days.

Dugen rolled down his window. "Hey Timo, what are you gonna do now that you're the Greatest Go Fish Champion King Of All Time?"

Timo laughed. "Build a table for washing vegetables, of course!"

Dugen nodded. "Spoken like a true sport." He waved goodbye to Rylar and Timo.

Acacia stood in the front doorway and gave a disgruntled farewell gesture. She never got to do anything fun.

"Be good, have fun, enjoy the day! We'll be back tomorrow morning!" Sasha shouted out from the back seat.

Nate put the transmission into 'Drive' and the four Homecomers left Fenix Farm as the sun broke through the remaining cloud cover, lighting up the back roads which winded up to the

Timberline Bluff trailhead.

"Does this thing have a working radio?" Dugen began scanning across the frequencies as he tweaked the dial. Nate tapped on the dashboard.

"Sometimes you'll catch a music station or news update, but it's pretty inconsistent. Blame that more on the mountain pass than the... well, everything else."

Nate felt a bit more at ease as the drive continued. It's not like he had never had anyone else in his truck before. It's not like he had never driven other people since That Crash. Just not these three.

That's what had amped up his anxiety. He wanted to prove to them—and more importantly himself—that he was a good driver, a safe driver. It wasn't his fault.

"This looks almost exactly like I remember it." Jill looked out her rear passenger window intently. The Timberline Valley countryside fit the mental image she had held onto during all her years away: the same rustic cabins, an aging trailer park, a quaint general store.

Perhaps everything looked more run-down with time, but the difference wasn't nearly so dramatic as with the formerly upscale areas.

"Yeah, when you're already on the edge of civilization, things don't change much as civilization erodes." Dugen observed. "It's like a recession-proof society because the downturn is already built-in. Rustic at first, rustic for always."

"When you're already at the bottom, you never have far to fall!" Nate tapped on the steering wheel to control his nerves.

"I love it out here." Sasha countered. "It's peaceful. It's close to nature. Yeah, it's a little rough out here. But there's beauty in that roughness. Growing up in the Phoenix suburbs, this kind of place always appealed to me. Like out of a postcard or a calendar."

"The Decline of Civilization in 12 Months." Dugen quipped.

The road grew more narrow and rocky. The pavement had ended entirely. Scarcely a human structure. A small wooden sign was posted at a narrow turnoff:

Timberline Bluff Trailhead: 6 mi.

"This is it. Sneeze and you might miss it." Nate signaled for only the most pro forma of reasons; there was no other moving vehicle for miles.

"Good. I'm allergic to well-marked roads, anyway." Dugen preferred navigating spontaneously, or by happenstance, or pure serendipity.

Nate turned the truck onto the side road leading directly up into the Timberline mountain range. The road itself was little more than two sets of dirt tracks and a median of grass and shrubs between them. If it weren't for Nate driving the road on occasion, it likely would have become entirely overgrown by now. A vehicle with a high clearance was a must.

"Can't imagine your station wagon would make this voyage, Nate. Maybe it's a good thing you got this truck." Sasha's positive karma worldview came naturally to her.

"Well sure, it's been a hell of a ride all these years. I try to keep it as well-maintained as one can given the shortage on factory authorized parts. That's why it's basically a Frankentruck by now."

Nate pat the dashboard, making a mental inventory of the number of different vehicle parts under the hood.

"That's a good one! No wonder it's a Frankentruck!" Jill laughed, feeling the charm of an improvised, 'make due' approach to living outside the boundaries of domestic life.

The afternoon sun dappled the road with patches of light and shade. A cool autumn breeze would shake loose the vibrant golden red leaves, casting them aflutter across the sky as they tumbled into a patch of branches and roots upon the overgrowth, turning brown and crisp for winter's bite.

Nate pulled up to his cabin as the other three Homecomers marveled at the cozy forest neighborhood of fir, pine, cedar, and dogwood trees.

Nate scanned the horizon as he put the truck in 'Park.' "Wait here a minute, okay?"

Nate stepped out of the truck, reaching down to verify his pistol was holstered at his hip.

"Everything okay?" Sasha asked from a crack in the cab window.

Nate held his hand up in a flat 'stop' motion. He circled the edge of the cabin, looking down to see several sets of muddy tracks. Adult size boots.

Nate reached the front door and slowly turned it. It was still locked. The windows were intact. Nate looked inside. Through the dirty, spotted glass, he made a cursory inspection of the interior. Everything looked okay.

Nate cautiously patrolled the perimeter of the cabin. Nothing looked out of place. His heart began to settle back in his chest.

He motioned to the Homecomers in his truck.

"We're good, sorry." Nate heaved a sigh of relief.

"What happened?" Jill and Sasha stepped out of the back doors as Dugen looked around.

"Get any squatters up here? Scavengers?" Dugen knew the type. He was the type.

"Looks like two sets of tracks, maybe three. Lost hikers? Not sure. Nothing is broken, the door's locked, everything's still inside." Nate felt a sense of loss: of privacy, of security, of seclusion.

"Maybe they were casing the place. They reached the front steps. Maybe they weren't sure if someone was inside." Dugen thought for a moment.

"Let's wipe away their tracks and make sure the cabin looks maintained and regularly visited. A lot of vacation homes have become fair game for scrappers, scroungers, and squatters."

"There's a difference?" Jill was curious, yet dismissive of such exotic nomenclature for the same creepy behavior.

"Sure." Dugen was prepared to give a longer explanation, then remembered his audience might appreciate a brisk, executive summary.

"Scrappers are willing to pick off pieces of things because they might be building something of their own and just need to lift some odds and ends. A plank of wood, a few nails or bolts, some plumber's tape, you get the idea... but scroungers are looking to take whatever intact objects are presently useful. Like a chair, a broom, some snowshoes or rain boots, a blanket... and of course, squatters just want somewhere to sleep, somewhere out of the weather, maybe somewhere to lay low for awhile if somebody's looking for them."

"Is someone looking for you?" Jill smirked, but was almost afraid to ask.

"Depends who's asking." Dugen grinned. "I'm a very wanted man. But I'm selective in who I give myself to."

"Oh please." Jill rolled her eyes and started unloading the truck.

Sasha pulled out her backpack and supplies, including some delicious eats to leave with Nate. She didn't like the idea of him up here alone, living off canned food and dry goods. She saw the slab of stone laid flat in the bottom of Nate's truck.

"Helps keep weight in the bed for my rear wheel drive." Nate patted the granite. He then lifted it out. "I put it there for the drive back up in case it got too muddy. But today wasn't so bad."

Nate wasn't willing to tell anyone about the real reason for the granite slab.

The Homecomers gathered the rest of their overnight items from the truck and entered Nate's cabin. The sun was getting low in the sky but it looked to be a clear night.

"Maybe we can have a little bonfire tonight? The pit is out back. I haven't done one of those in many years." Nate recalled the many cozy evenings around the fire with Caitlyn. There was something so calming about the sight and sound of flickering flames, so primal and assuring.

The cabin interior felt cozy yet empty at the same time. It was well-decorated, but the furnishings were aged and dusty. It was as if the preparations for a family cabin were complete, but halted and in perpetual wait for a family. Nate's family.

"Nice place! Feels very Nate. Ornate Nate." Dugen gave himself a tour without trying to appear as though he was casing the place. "I've hunkered down in a lot worse, I'll tell you that."

"Dugen's stayed in worse. I'll take it as a compliment." Nate put the tea kettle on and got out his finest ceramic mugs. He hadn't gotten out more than one set of anything for a very long time.

Jill and Sasha put away their overnight bags and noticed the assortment of maps, photos, and paintings hung on the wooden beams for walls. The place still had the traces of a woman's touch.

Sasha searched for the best words to ask what was on her mind. "So how long since... since you've been here on your own?"

Even that felt like prying. But with Nate, if you didn't gently pry you'd get nowhere in his emotional fortress. Nate got the meaning and never tried to force a protracted confessional.

"Oh. Yeah, so..." Nate cleared his throat. He had been mentally preparing to give the history of the cabin for much of the drive up here.

It was the greatest hesitation since offering to host. If he could get past the explanation and to a place where everyone knew but nobody asked about it, that would be ideal.

"My wife Caitlyn and I bought the cabin together in 2034. We took an early leave from the National Park system because they were cutting back, anyway. I still had the settlement money... this place needed a lot of work, but it was definitely what we were looking for. It was previously a ranger station before budget cutbacks, then it fell into disrepair, break-ins, and looting. Almost felt like the Forest Service hired us to fix it up and stay there, off the clock. Hell of a deal."

Sasha and Jill sat down to give Nate their full attention. Nate monologues were few and far between. Dugen leaned up against one wall. Nate gestured to the framed photo on the mantle of him with Caitlyn and Kyla amidst the Timberline Peaks.

"Our Kyla basically came with the place because she was a pup riding along with the realtor and really took to the place. You could say 'Sheprador included' closed the deal for us."

Nate smiled. He had said the easy part. Now the story got harder to tell. He took a deep sigh.

"During the repairs and improvements, I would get a bump or a cut but it was pretty common for me." Nate held up his hands.

"Any carpenter or handyman worth their salt has nine-and-a-half fingers, right? What I had learned from service work through Build-up Together readily applied to this repair and restoration job. But Caitlyn was new to it. And I should've done it myself, kept her away from it... I mean, it was great for our relationship to build something like this, right? Tangible, teamwork."

Nate wrestled with himself as he stood and spoke aloud, working through his own second-guessing and hindsight bias. Sasha walked over and guided Nate to the sofa next to them. She sat with him. Having brought up the subject, Sasha felt an obligation to see this through and support Nate.

He may not have told anyone before.

"I... uh, I had stepped out to organize the materials for reinforcing the loft and roofing. When I came back in, Kyla was barking. Caitlyn had fallen from a stepladder and struck the side of her head on an exposed beam. There was so much blood... anyway, I got her to town for urgent care after dressing her wounds and stopping the bleeding."

Nate sighed, then continued. "She was okay. She was recovering. But the pain was really intense, so she was taking prescription meds. I think it was Oxycontin or something like that. They gave her so many pills. And I didn't question it. I knew she had break-through pain. So she took more pills. And when I realized she had gotten refills and hid them, kept taking more... it was too late."

Nate's eyes welled up with tears. He broke down and buried his head in his lap. Sasha held him close. Jill looked over at them, then at Dugen. Dugen gave a confounding shrug.

"That's rough man. I'm sorry. I didn't know." Dugen walked over and rubbed Nate's back. Even he could appreciate the comforting power of touch.

"Yeah, we didn't know." Jill added. She joined the others by kneeling and taking Nate's hands.

Nate drew deep breaths and raised his head. His eyelashes now soaked and his cheeks wet.

"We had nearly completed the remodel. I had gone into town that day to get some wood varnish and a few other items for finishing touches, I think... I got back in and she was in bed... Caitlyn looked so peaceful. I thought she was taking a nap so I left her there. Kyla was by her side. A couple hours later, I knew something was off. She never napped for that long. It wasn't... it wasn't a nap. It was her final sleep."

Nate looked ahead, deadpan and drained. "Her skin was already cold. It was too late. I tried everything I could. I should've been there for her. I didn't know. I should've known."

Sasha held Nate close. "It's not your fault, Nate. Addiction can be all-consuming. It can happen to anyone. And you didn't know at the time. You were trying to support her recovery. You were trying to be there for her."

"That almost happened to me, Nate." Jill rubbed Nate's hands and looked up at him, drawing his eye contact. She projected every ounce of compassion and understanding she could draw upon and gave it to Nate through her own eyes as they glistened with teardrops.

"After the crash, I had a lot of problems. Physical therapy, academic counseling, psychiatric counseling, financial counseling."

Jill rolled her eyes and laughed. "Counseling for counseling my counselor."

The four Homecomers were connected now, as if in an impromptu sharing circle.

Jill spoke again after a moment.

"Addiction became this, this shadow that covered all the other problems... Addiction to pills, to drinking. And nobody knew. Nobody. I hid it very well. I even tried to hide it from myself, to convince myself I was still in charge... and when it spun out of control, I was lucky enough to have that intervention and get help. Not everyone gets that kind of grace period. Some people who would recover have one overdose and that's it, they don't make it back."

As Jill searched for more calming words, the tea kettle boiled over and began to whistle.

eeeeeeeEEEEEEEEEEEEEEEEEEEEEEEEEEEEEEEEEEEeeeeeee

"Lemme get that." Nate rose and attended to the tea, pouring hot beverages for everyone. The steam rising from the spout bathed his face in warmth and condensed the moisture, as if Nate was sweating off the tears and expunging the anguish.

"Thanks for the talk. And welcome! It's good to have guests visiting." Nate paused. "It's good to have friends."

Out back, Dugen gathered some dry branches and rolled up newspapers. Jill and Sasha unpacked a cooler and set about cooking a makeshift pot of gumbo from whatever ingredients were on hand. Everyone fell into a rhythm of integrated teamwork.

From a storage closet, Nate pulled out four camping chairs and set them upon the grassy flat of ground behind the cabin. It could've been a fancy patio area, or even a more simple, defined backyard. But that was a project Nate and Caitlyn had yet to get around to.

After her death, Nate only completed what was needed for the cabin to be livable for him and Kyla. A single man and his dog have flexible standards for home décor.

Before long, Dugen had the fire pit roasting and Nate brought out bowls of piping hot gumbo stew. The Homecomers gathered around just as the last light of sun was fading from the sky.

"All in a day's work." Dugen put his feet up to warm them by the fire.

"I don't think I've ever done this before." Jill sipped from her bowl and leaned back in her chair.

"Had dinner with friends?" Dugen asked with a serving of sarcasm.

"Yes. That's what I've never done before. Because only you guys have ever been my friends!" Jill laughed and rolled her eyes. "I mean, no. I've never been out to a cabin with an open fire and just eaten dinner under the stars. Here in the mountains. So peaceful."

"It's truly serene up here, Nate. I can see why you moved here." Sasha could almost see herself living up in the mountains, but it would put her too far from the community of people she loved.

"A few regrets in my life. Big ones, small ones. But moving up here was probably the best decision. It feels different without Caitlyn, but in some ways... she never left. And there's a sense of companionship in knowing that."

Nate hadn't opened up this much in many years, certainly not since he buried Kyla. Plus it was far easier to tell your problems to a dog than to a person, or several.

The crackle of the burning wood mixed with the gentle whisper of rustling leaves in the night wind. The Homecomers emptied their bowls and enjoyed the satisfaction of a day together.

"I'm just gonna say, I've known good times and bad times, hard times and easy times, desperate times and satisfied times... this here, this is a satisfied time." Dugen heaved a deep sigh and slid his arms into his jacket, staring into the fire.

"I agree completely. And I know I'm luckier than most." Sasha rubbed her hands together and held them closer to the open flame.

"I thought I had it so good. I did, in some ways." Jill stared into the dancing plumes of the fire pit and allowed it to draw out her thoughts.

"I played by all the rules. I pushed myself as hard as I could. I got plenty of awards, plenty of recognition. But after the big business charade was over, well... I had a few boxes packed with all of it, living in a box within a box, surrounded by other boxes."

"You got something against boxes? A few flattened ones make for a decent night's sleep." Dugen feigned defensiveness.

"Nothing against boxes." Jill smirked. Dugen's grating sense of humor was growing on her.

Jill continued, "It's just that all that compartmentalization, all those structures... they create the illusion of stability, of organization, of predictability and order. But then you see it crashing down all around you. You know it's an illusion. But it's *your* illusion. You helped create it, you bought into it, you perpetuated it. You take so much ownership in the illusion, you convince yourself it's real."

Dugen waved his hand in disapproval. "Speak for yourself! I break down those boxes and re-purpose them. Literally and figuratively. I break those structures because they were made for another time. They don't work for me. I don't think they ever worked very well for anybody, to be honest."

Dugen rolled a joint and lit it with the heat of the open flames. He took a drag and passed it over to Jill. She hesitated, then accepted it.

"Yeah, I get it. I think I'm getting it now, anyway." Jill attempted to inhale and coughed instantly. "What is this shit?"

"It's the good shit, Jill. The good shit." Dugen laughed.

Jill took another puff, successfully this time, and passed it on.

Sasha would usually decline, but this weekend was about an unusual reunion in unusual times. She hadn't smoked anything since college. She puffed several times and passed the joint over to Nate.

"Can't stand the stuff. Makes me paranoid." Nate passed the joint back around to Dugen.

"Nate, paranoid? Never." Dugen grinned.

"At least you're consistently a stiff. Been like that since college." Dugen looked around. "And seems like it's working for you."

Nate nodded.

The four Homecomers settled into a contemplative mood as the stars came out from behind the clouds. The moon began to rise above the outline of the Timberline Peaks.

"Can I ask you guys something?" Jill broke the extended silence.

"Of course." Sasha felt her alertness fading fast. Maybe it was the pot, or maybe she had just been overdoing it the past few days.

"What the hell is going on? Like, really? Is humanity doomed? Is all this coming to an end? Because it feels like we're living in the twilight of civilization or something." Jill barely paused for an answer, feeling the cannabinoids kicking in.

"I mean, I get it. The news is always gonna be bad. The more you listen, the worse you think things are. But it wasn't like this growing up. Not like this. And I was pretty alert, I was pretty informed. Stuff used to work. Used to be reliable. You could trust people, at least sometimes. You could go out without feeling guarded, without seeing decay and destruction everywhere. All the fires and floods, all the danger and paranoia. It's like we all got used to living in a war zone or a... third world shithole. I mean, I'm sorry. I didn't mean that. But you know what I mean."

"I know what you mean." Sasha rescued Jill from her rambling diatribe of genuine distress. "Yeah, I notice all of it. It's impossible not to. There's so much out there we can't control. And that, in and of itself, can feel defeating. You see how lucky Rylar and I have it with our farm, with a small network of people who look after one another. It's all I could ever ask for, and more than most have."

"What you have together is amazing, Sasha." Nate leaned back and took in the night sky as the fire pit smoke billowed up into the stratosphere. "Caitlyn and I wanted something similar here, in our own self-reliant way."

"You definitely have a place away from it all." Jill observed. "I don't know if I could live this far out... but it's tempting."

"The key is testing the outliers, finding an adaptive modality for living." Dugen finished the joint and tossed the roach into the fire pit.

"There's more than one viable solution to these problems. Flexibility is key. Our existing systems are brittle and based on long-held presumptions about climate, economics, politics, and social capital that no longer exist. I've been getting by in urban areas just fine, but you have to adopt a jungle survival mindset. Even in an urban jungle."

"You've been getting by in the urban jungle because you steal stuff, trespass, and hitch rides." Jill giggled but the underlying critique was serious.

"That's... technically true. It's true. I'm not going to qualify those characterizations, those salient observations." Dugen coughed and cleared his throat, waving away some fire pit smoke.

"But I also give back in at least as many ways as I take. I hand out anything extra I have, I clean up whenever I can, I have given CPR and my last ten bucks to the same passed out bum, then turn around to punk a meal and some pocket change. I've never hurt anyone that didn't deserve it. I've helped many people who probably didn't deserve it. I'm not without moral imperfection, but I strive for virtue in an era of desperation. "

"Dugen is uh, basically a knight among raccoons, basically." Nate laughed.

"He'll go through your garbage, but eloquently and with consideration!" Jill laughed harder.

Sasha shook her head. There has never been a group like this, before or since.

Dugen stood and stretched. "I'll take it. I've been called worse."

Nate had setup two small tents on the side of the cabin with the most level ground.

Camping supplies were something he had in excess thanks to overstocked inventory when the National Park Service shuttered operations and closed visitor centers. Now, camping was a common practice almost everywhere. It was barely called 'camping' anymore.

"Alright, delicious dinner. Thanks again, everyone... so glad you came to..." Nate yawned. "... visit the cabin."

Nate gestured, as if being the drowsiest guide to give a camping tour. "Tents here are for the guys, the bed and pullout couch inside are for the ladies."

Nate wearily shuffled his feet to one tent, then looked back. "This one's mine. Sleep wherever you want. Sweet dreams."

"Night, Nate." Sasha looked over as Nate zipped up his tent. "Thanks again for hosting!"

Jill closed up her jacket. She wasn't ready to sleep yet. Just being out in the mountain wild, the sounds and smells of the alpine horizon bathing in moonlight, it was so enchanting.

"I can take the pullout couch, okay Jill?" Sasha collected the remaining dinner dishes and headed towards the cabin door.

"Totally fine. Or the bed, whatever works." Jill took a deep breath and indulged in some long overdue stargazing.

"Night, you two. Don't stay up too late." Sasha smirked and winked at Jill. She noticed the way Jill had started acting differently around Dugen, even if Jill wasn't ready to admit it.

"Oh, you know me! The paragon of curfew enforcement." Dugen saluted to Sasha as she nodded in feigned concurrence.

After a few moments of silence, Jill stood up and walked to the edge of the fire pit. She faced away, letting it warm her backside as she searched for constellations she could recognize.

"They're all made up, you know." Dugen stood next to her and looked up into the night sky. "The constellations. The astrological signs. The horoscopes. The prophesies. Even the meteorology models. It's all meaning synthesis. Maybe it's internally consistent. Maybe it's replicable. But its ultimate purpose? Its ultimate *value*? Just made up."

"I haven't seen a dark, clear night sky in a decade or longer... and you're telling me it's all made up?" Jill kept her gaze upwards. The two spoke only by the sounds they made, no eye contact, as though they were both broadcasting, podcasting into outer space.

"It's all... all made up. Maybe somewhere in another part of the universe, some other beings are looking up at a similar array of stars and planets. Naming them. Charting them. Creating calendars and schedules and structures around them. The rotation of their planet becoming the rhythm of their days and nights, circadian rhythms of their bodies, predatory hunting patterns or exploitative job hunting patterns. We're all meaning-making machines – some more prolific than others. And most of the universe is imperceptible to us because our senses capture only a narrow band of—"

"But it's so beautiful, Dugen. Can't you just see it for what it is? In this moment? Away from all the chaos and, and complexity? Not as we want it to be, but as it truly is." Jill felt her eyes adjusting, almost as though she could see even deeper into the vast darkness of space.

She felt her heartbeat rising. Could this really be happening?

Dugen leaned up against Jill. "Now you're speaking my language. To see what truly is. Away from the social constructs and imposed moral frameworks. We can no longer afford to hide behind the rigid methodology of scientific dogmas, the self-serving tautology of religious dogmas, of dogmatic dogmatism dogmas, of—"

Jill turned her head and grabbed Dugen by the shoulders like an alpha lioness on the prowl. "Shut the fuck up already."

Jill kissed Dugen aggressive, rough – the way one would punch someone in the form of a kiss. Dugen was taken aback, unprepared. Just how Jill wanted him. There was nothing better than shutting up a know-it-all.

"Well that was, um... unexpected." Dugen collected himself as he leaned back and assessed the situationship.

"You finally getting yourself that 'hot piece of ass from Sam-Co?'" Jill mocked Dugen's stoner affect. She was feeling playfully cruel, triumphant, uninhibited. Could've been because she just smoked the good shit. "That unexpected?"

"I never said that. Okay, I might have said that." Dugen was still stunned. But getting used to the idea.

After a few more punched-up kisses, the unlikely star-crossed lovers explored further with their hands. The fire pit was mere glowing embers now, producing just enough light and just enough heat to extend their impromptu passions a few moments longer.

Jill whispered in Dugen's ear. "Here's what's going to happen. We're going to quietly sneak into your tent. You're going to fuck me hard and proper. Then I'm going into the cabin. I will sleep in my bed. You will sleep in your tent. We never talk about it. This goes absolutely nowhere. You understand?"

Jill nipped Dugen's ear between her teeth, just hard enough to let him know she meant it.

"Challenge accepted." Dugen reached down and squeezed Jill's firm, round butt. Jill ran her hands down Dugen's broad shoulders and toned back.

It had been so long for both of them. Of consequence, nothing else seemed to matter now. Urgent desires consumed them. She leaned against him. His tent was already pitched.

Door flap, then pants; unzipping sounds rippled through the crisp night air.

The encompassing forest darkness enveloped every sigh and moan, the trees rustled along the mountain ridges, and the disjointed blend of clumsiness, desperation, playfulness, and ecstasy in a confined tent were lost to the dense thicket along the Timberlines.

[12 – Circling the Cliff's Edge]

Jill awoke before the first light of day. She had slept in a weird position. She hadn't intended to fall asleep in Dugen's tent at all.

He was snoring softly, a tamed oaf of sorts, all bundled in blankets and a half-opened sleeping bag. In her college days, Jill had bedded worse, but probably not much worse.

Did you know that pressing a finger firmly against the zipper as it joins or separates the two sides almost entirely mutes the distinctive sound? Every sly creature of the night learns this eventually.

Slipping out of the tent as covertly as could be, Jill stood in the cool night air. The bitterness of winter was still several weeks away, but the pre-dawn temperature nipped at her fingers, ears, and nostrils nonetheless.

Jill looked back at the tent one last time, as if to reconcile with herself. Did she regret it? No. Would she do it again? Also no.

Maybe it was to prove something to herself, or maybe Jill just wanted to feel in control and boss someone around for a little while. Whatever the case, doing Douglas Dugen did the job.

It was a very short "walk of shame" from the tent to the cabin. Sasha was curled up on the pullout couch. Jill rummaged around in the cooler for a refreshing drink. She guzzled most of a canteen in one gulp, wiped her lips, and put everything back as it was, leaving the scene as though Jill went right to bed hours earlier.

Because that's her story and she was sticking to it. The stillness of night punctuated these Homecoming indiscretions. The forest held all secrets and never let on.

> *In the twilight I might awaken*
> *and unless mistaken in a dream*
> *find you next to me*
> *my sunbeam!*
>
> *Lips and fingertips upon your skin*
> *you awaken*
> *spread and let me in*
> *as we embrace from waist to face*
> *the morning comes as we the same*

Nate was the first to rouse in the daylight, having briefly remembered his admission wrought with pain the evening before. For so long, it was as though not talking about Caitlyn had buried the experience so deep, Nate didn't need to confront it.

Yet now that he had told his friends what happened and visibly grieved in front of them, he wasn't afraid to do it again. He had made it through, he was bruised but still moving forward, and

Caitlyn's memory was slightly less sharp against his conscience as a result.

It was Sunday now. How could they best conclude their Homecoming weekend? Nate thought for a moment as he started cooking a big bowl of porridge. There was just enough brown sugar left to mix into the folds of thickening wheat cereal for flavor.

Sasha awoke to the aroma of a hot breakfast in the works. She stretched and washed up at the small bathroom sink. Nate's cabin had little more than elbow room in any direction, so small steps and turning slowly was advisable.

Dugen crawled out of his tent enveloped in a ball of blankets, sleeping bag ends, and rumpled clothes. He took a deep breath, coughed, and breathed again as the broken sunbeams warmed his face from between breaks in the wooded canopy.

Whether banging it out with a hot blonde the previous night was a dream or a reality, its memory was just as sweet upon waking.

"Morning, everyone!" Sasha emerged from the bathroom looking fresh and eager for the day.

The four Homecomers gathered in the main room of the cabin, which functioned as its entrance, living room, and kitchen. Save for a bedroom and bathroom, along with a small hall closet, that was the entire place. It was a fraction of the real estate of the Fenix Farm, but it suited Nate and gave his guests an intimate vacation experience. Perhaps more intimate than anticipated.

Jill glanced at Dugen as he entered, looking like he rolled out the wrong side of the bed, but happily so. They nodded in a shared moment of recognition, but also one of closure.

"This goes absolutely nowhere." Like a telepathic transmission. Sent and received.

"So I was thinking," Nate offered as he got out bowls for porridge and chopped some fresh apples, "maybe I could show you my favorite hiking trail this morning before we head back. It winds up and over the Timberline Peaks... there's a huge waterfall and great views of the entire valley. If you've never seen it before, you gotta see it."

Jill was already sold. Sipping on a hot cup of fresh-brewed coffee, anything seemed possible. Sasha hesitated for a moment, already missing her family and their morning routine on the farm. But this was their Homecoming weekend, she invited everyone, and now they were bonding and going on adventures together. What better outcome could she expect?

"Sounds great!" Sasha gave her unofficial tour guide endorsement.

Jill set down her empty coffee mug with authority, like a judge banging her gavel. "I'm in. And my legs are finally feeling rejuvenated after my triumphant return to the 800 meters."

"It was legendary!" Dugen proclaimed.

Jill shot him a sharp look of caution: that was too much innuendo.

Dugen continued, looking at Nate and the two ladies with his approval. "And of course, let's finish breakfast and head for the hills! If we're lucky, the world will explode into a bio-terrorism war while we're lost in the wilderness... and we'll return to find civilization overrun with mutant hybrids – half lizard, three-eighths cockroach. We have to battle it out for the survival of our species."

Sasha rolled her eyes. "That sounds terrible and not very likely."

Nate thought a moment. "There is way too much genetic drift for lizards and cockroaches to hybridize, Dugen."

"Not with the right gene edited, aerosol-deployed, bioplasmic compound run amok! You know the Chinese are already in phase-three trials with those experiments. I've read the unredacted intelligence reports. I still have them on a thumb drive somewhere in my bag."

Nobody was particularly interested, but Dugen was clearly committed to his mutant apocalypse hypothesis. "Look up Program 338. It's real."

"Well, sounds like it's settled! Let's gear up and take a hike." Sasha returned the homecomers to the subject at hand.

"The trailhead access is up along this side road, not far from the cabin road we came in on. I'll take us there." Nate was feeling more confident about leading the group.

Yet somehow, he still couldn't shake the unsettling feeling that something was off.

The morning dew still clung to the grasses and moss as the Homecomers loaded into Nate's truck. The air was still and quiet, as the migratory birds had already headed south. More and more each day, the forest was settling in for a long winter slumber.

The road to the trailhead for Timberline Bluff was rough. Anything less than a sturdy truck or SUV wouldn't make it. To one side of the road, an abandoned car and some shopping carts were strewn about. Intermittent evidence of squatters, scavengers, and scrappers.

The Long Collapse created a trail of abandoned structures in urban and rural areas alike. Everything was 'finders-keepers,' catch-as-catch-can.

One of the reasons Nate rarely left his cabin was for intentional solitude, sure. But another reason was certainly more pragmatic: an abandoned structure was sure to be broken into and looted. Perhaps that's what those mud prints indicated. Nate vowed not to spend another night away from the cabin after the signals he had already witnessed.

"Ever been up this way before?" Nate asked in good tour driver fashion.

"Nope." Dugen kept his eye out the passenger window in search of abandoned treasures or mutant lizard cockroach hybrids. "Look up Program 338. It's real."

"Never. It's so beautiful, though." Jill was in a world completely unlike Wynhill Heights.

The concrete sprawl seemed like such a distant memory now. Did she really put in over a decade imprisoned in the metal boxes of Suncoast Management, convinced she was free? She could hardly believe it.

"I think Rylar and I came up here once before we really got the farm going. It's been tough to get away after that." Sasha remembered the carefree days before her routine of milking goats, collecting eggs – whatever seasonal chores the gardens required.

There was a beauty to that rhythm, but it also concealed this illusory sense of exploration and spontaneity. That was the best aspect of this Homecoming weekend for her.

Nate pulled up to the Timberline Bluff trailhead just as the sun reached the top of the treeline. It was a modest, almost hidden entrance to the winding dirt path between the mountains.

First marked by early explorers and no doubt used by indigenous people before that, the Timberline Bluff trail was never a popular tourist destination; it was a hidden gem favored by knowledgeable locals and dedicated hikers in search of a challenge.

"This path branches off around the other side of the Timberline Peaks, but the main trail circles back around and ends right over there." Nate pointed to a clearing in the thick vegetation at the far side of the dirt lot. "It's maybe a three hour hike, at a casual pace."
"Let's do it!" Jill's body was awakening to the daily adventures in the great outdoors, returning to her youthful excursions before subsumed by an adulthood of charts, graphs, spreadsheets, and quarterly earnings statements.

"Looks lovely! Just how I remember it, but maybe with more of these glorious fall colors." Sasha made a mental note to collect some golden red leaves for a crafts project with her students next week.

"As the saying goes: you don't have to be faster than the bear chasing you, just faster than the slowest hiker." Dugen laced up his worn shoes, which he'd scrounged off a dead body a few years ago.

"Oh, you're on, moron." Jill nudged Dugen and started up the trail.

Sasha looked over at Nate as he locked the truck. "What's gotten into those two?"

Nate shook his head and blushed. "Dugen's tent was pretty loud late last night."

Sasha pulled her hair up in a bun and whispered with a smile. "I knew it, I just knew it."

Nate checked his hip. His Ruger was tightly holstered as expected. "In case we do see a bear. Because I'm not a star athlete of a runner," he explained to Sasha.

The trail crested and fell over the grassy hillside. The Homecomers stepped over occasional deadfall. Trail maintenance was low on the list of priorities during The Long Collapse.

With little to no government services in much of the region, fallen timber was likely to be sawed and hauled away by scrappers looking for fuel or raw building materials. Yet this also kept the trails impassible by dirt bike gangs or the bounty hunters mounted on horseback. A trail littered with fallen timber was a measure of safety.

Jill took the lead for the initial hike, claiming the best view as the trail spiraled around the lush forest crowning the elevated Timberline peaks. Dugen followed and appreciated the view, as well.

"Try to keep up back there!" Jill hit her stride and felt her heart pumping, her legs burning. A sprint around the track made different demands of her muscles than a long mountain hike on an incline.

"Yes, you draw out all the hungry animals and we will be right here behind you. Jill Tavana, last seen wearing a wrinkled sweatshirt and yoga pants. A woman of consummate style until the end." Dugen was leaning into his humor more now that Jill seemed to accept him on some level.

"All things considered, this has turned into a lovely weekend."

Sasha told Nate as she pushed herself to keep breathing. "I was hoping to make something worthwhile out of Homecoming since the cancellation. Thanks for opening up your cabin, your hiking spot, your entire world to us."

Nate nodded. "It was a weird coincidence that I was in town getting granite at the same time you were gathering the crew for a homecoming celebration. I mean, if you believe in coincidences."

Sasha looked forward to Jill and Dugen as they stopped at the vista up ahead. "Maybe a coincidence. Maybe you were drawn to our energy. Maybe you didn't consciously remember it was Homecoming, but you were drawn to it anyway. Maybe this is what you needed all along."

Nate and Sasha reached Jill and Dugen. "Oh wow." Sasha was stunned.

"Yeah, it's an incredible view if you look back at the Timberline Valley from here." Nate turned and drew a deep breath. He was getting out of shape from a more sedentary routine since Kyla's passing. No wonder people with dogs are more fit.

"You can really see the extent of the Cascade Complex fire from here." Sasha traced her finger along the horizon, nearly from one end of the mountain valley to the other. "Makes you realize how unprecedented it was."

Sasha pointed to one side, almost entirely blackened with ash. "And that's the college campus right there. Looks almost like the epicenter."

"It had the most to burn. All those books. All that alcohol. A university education is quite flammable, and now all that knowledge is up in smoke!" Dugen inhaled, as though absorbing the remaining wisps of all the degrees he nearly attained.

"But if you look along the perimeter of the fire" Nate gestured "you can see the first year growth from this season." Nate paused and widened his arms. "Imagine the regrowth in ten, twenty years time."

"I can see that." Jill scanned the horizon.

Despite the ravages of fire, the forest already seemed to rebound and remake itself. Green sprouts pushing out from the blackened soil. Verdant vines curling around ashen tree trunks. Mosses gathering across charcoal rocks. Unlike all the abandoned buildings, broken down vehicles, and eroding human infrastructure, the natural landscape was in a state of constant renewal.

"Maybe we'll have to come here for our fortieth homecoming anniversary!" Sasha was already envisioning this.

"I'm sorry, did she say fortieth? Like, four-zero?" Dugen laughed. "Yo, I will be amazed if I make it up here at all in another twenty years."

"Don't say that, Dugen. You're pretty healthy. You can make it." Sasha knew she could make it. She wasn't so sure about Dugen.

"I'm looking forward to it already" Jill smiled. After another moment of taking in the scenery, she turned and continued along the trail.

"Enough of a rest, slowpokes!"

Nate was determined not to lag behind on the hiking trail he knew best, the one he invited everyone else to traverse. He pushed himself until he was alongside Jill.

"This isn't a race, you know? Not everything in life... is a race, or a competition." Nate heaved his words out between winded breaths.

"I've never been in competition with you or anyone else, Nate. I've always pushed myself. I've always measured myself against my personal best. And then tried to top it." Jill kept looking ahead, eager to see what was around the next bend in the trail as it snaked around the side of the mountain.

"Yeah that's... that sounds exhausting. I couldn't do it. At least... at least not without feeling like a failure most of the time." Nate wiped his brow and reached for his water bottle. He drank half of it in one sustained gulp.

"I've felt like a failure more times than I can count. It sucks. And when I was younger, I would dwell on it. It felt permanent. It felt like who I was." Jill paused and looked back.

Sasha and Dugen were far back, casually chatting and singing an old frat house favorite drinking song to one another.

> *when you get older, will you screw up?*
> *when you get older, who's gonna notice?*
> *well I just got a lot older, so what's up?*
> *well I just got a lot older, and it's not us!*
>
> *when you are aged, when you go gray*
> *when you get creaky, at the end of your days*
> *just make more noise to keep death away*
> *just make more noise to keep death at bay*

Dugen began to imitate a trumpet sound as Sasha made beat box noises. To be alone in the woods is to receive the ultimate permission slip for reckless abandon.

Jill stopped at a cliff overlook and saw deep into the next forest canyon. The midday clouds were rolling in, layered and deep with the promise of moisture. A cool breeze whipped around the rock surfaces, creating a light susurration through the trees as they shed their golden leaves.

"You know, I don't blame you for any of it." Jill looked at Nate. Nate looked back, then down and away. He knew what she meant. He wasn't prepared to talk about it.

"Oh, you don't? Well, that's... That's good." Nate adjusted his pack.

"No, Nate. Of course not. Not legally, that was already established. That guy told us as much." Jill kept her eyes on Nate. She wanted him to engage with her.

They had avoided this for twenty years too long.

"Holt Harbor, Arbitrator." Nate laughed. "I'm pretty sure he took out a trademark for his name. If that is his real name."

"He was great" Jill smiled. "He helped us get to all the places we were going. All the places we needed to go in life. And ultimately, it led us all back... to right here."

"Hell of a place, seems like." Nate drew a deep breath.

"It's been hard for me, Jill. If I'm being honest about it. But we've all lost so much, individually... collectively. Who am I to feel sorry for myself? With what's going on, just surviving seems like some monumental achievement."

"I know. I tell myself that all the time." Jill laughed to release pangs of regret.

"I lived in one of the most upscale condos of the richest neighborhood in the city. Wynhill Heights. It's like they named it to sound as elitist as possible, like it was bragging just to say it out loud in your well-manicured social circles. It never felt like me. But I wanted to wash away the stink of Salmon Springs. Nobody wants to be from there. As soon as you say it, everyone thinks about..."

Nate picked up where Jill trailed off. He knew.

"... about Titan Corp. The paper mill and chemical plants. About all the dead fish and the water that you could light on fire. About the black teeth people got. About the deformed babies and all the cancers. It was a bad science experiment and Salmon Springs residents were all test subjects. I know, I know."

Nate sighed. "It's all a tragedy on some level."

"So why am I laughing?" Jill laughed as she began to cry, at first a sob between giggles, then more uncontrollably.

"It's such a weird time to be alive. And like, nothing prepared us for it. All the rules, all the plans, all the career advice and financial counseling... none of it even matters now. That world is slipping away, it's gone for most of us. If you think things are fine, check your email next Tuesday." Jill laughed again as the tears gathered along her cheeks.

Nate pulled her in for a long hug. "I haven't checked my email in many years. I'm sure I will still be getting emails long after I'm dead."

Jill laughed again. "Same."

The two held each other at arm's length. Neither had ever felt something quite like this before.

Nate looked squarely into Jill's misty green eyes. "I'm glad you forgive me. I struggle every day to forgive myself. I feel like I took away your future, the one you had been working towards. The star athlete. All because I was looking out the left side window instead of the right. That's when the black truck hit us. And it was way worse for you than any of us. For no good reason. You didn't deserve any of it. That should've been me."

Nate sighed. Jill sniffled as her tears dried.

"Are you kidding me? I didn't deserve that, but none of us did."

Nate had been overthinking this for twenty years. "If Sasha didn't recognize you walking to class. If you didn't get in. If Dugen wasn't taking up the back seat so you got in front. If I didn't drive so fast..."

Nate looked away. "I know, it could've been different, but maybe not better. Maybe worse. Maybe some other vehicle would've run you over on the way to class. Who knows." Nate shrugged.

Jill exhaled with a chuckle. "Doesn't matter now, Nate. The past twenty years are exactly the ones I have needed to live. Whether I was gonna be a star athlete or not. Which, let's be honest... I was good, like best in my division good... but state championship good? National championship good? Olympic medalist good? Nah, probably not. I was gonna be a runner in college and then move on. And I was a runner in college. And then I moved on."

"And... here we are." Nate looked around once more, stepping back.

"And here we are!" Jill held out her arms and spun around.

"AND HERE WE ARE!" Dugen shouted as he arrived at the cliff's edge. His voice echoed across the forest canyon and back again.

"And heeeeeeere weeeeeeee arrrrrrrrrrre!" Sasha chanted in a lilting, melodious song with hands raised high in the mountain breeze.

The four Homecomers laughed as they surveyed the rugged natural landscape on all sides. This was the celebration they deserved, if not one any of them had anticipated.

Nate looked out across the tranquil vista before them. "This is Timberline Bluff. The trail loops back around from here."

"So we're like, halfway?" Dugen hadn't had a break yet. Hiking in last place meant never taking a break because the leaders would only stop until the lagging company caught up.

"Yeah, halfway or maybe a bit farther." Nate used to hike this trail often, but it had been a few years at this point. The last time was with Caitlyn. Nate wasn't much of a solo hiker—at least not without occasion. Happening upon his Homecoming crew was just such an occasion.

"Well good, because my legs are cooked spaghetti." Dugen groaned and folded his legs under him, then scooted to the edge of the cliff. He dangled his feet down and shook them, knocking them against each other to relieve the tension.

Nate joined him on the cliff's edge, sitting down with his pack and producing some trail mix and a bottled energy drink. "I've been saving these for awhile. Hiker's food. I wouldn't let myself eat it back at the cabin. Didn't feel right."

Dugen nabbed the drink and sipped from it. "Haven't had warm Gatorade in ages."

Dugen growled like he was starring in the latest ad campaign for sub-optimal refreshments. "Ahhhh! The beverage of kings, the king of beverages!"

181

Dugen swilled the liquid around his parched palette before swallowing. Then he thought a moment. "Wait, you sure this isn't just your warmed-over piss from the last hike, bottled and shaken up?"

Nate laughed. "Could be. Might be an improvement, honestly."

Dugen took another vigorous sip. "Could be."

Jill sat down next to them, sandwiching Dugen in the middle. Suddenly, he felt like Mr. Popular. This after years of being a nocturnal nobody.

"You know, that cliff might not hold all three of you." Sasha stood a few paces back, not yet convinced this was a good idea.

"Girl, you calling me fat?" Jill laughed and knocked her feet against Dugen's. Where did he get those shoes? They looked atrocious up close. Jill didn't want to know.

"No, it's just... what if the rock breaks loose?" Sasha was not in a joking mood.

"Then we'll plunge in the same direction as a result of Earth's gravitational pull," Dugen explained.

"We will fall several hundred feet, scraping against jagged rock surfaces and spiny plants the entire way, finally having our fall broken by coniferous tree branches full of pine needles, ultimately contorted in a pile of broken bones and hemorrhaging wounds. The indescribable pain will linger for a few more minutes as we bleed out from severe lacerations, then losing consciousness as our brains are depleted of the oxygen carried from our ruptured circulatory systems. That's my working hypothesis, anyway."

There was an awkward silence.

Was that supposed to be funny?

"This is what happens if you just let him talk, Sasha. You can't let him do that." Jill was catching on.

"Why didn't you interrupt him?" Sasha was warming up to the macabre humor as the cliff's edge didn't appear to be going anywhere. Not for another 20,000 years, at least.

"Why didn't *you* interrupt him? You've known him longer." Jill laughed throughout her retort.

Nate was working out the math.

"Back in college, that was a significant differential. Sasha had known Dugen for four years longer than Jill had at the point Jill met Dugen. But now, Sasha has known Dugen for over twenty-four years and Jill has known Dugen for over twenty years. That's only about... seventeen percent longer."

"So there you have it. I'm seventeen percent less likely to get interrupted now!" Dugen was proud of himself.

"That's not what I was saying." Nate knew that Dugen knew that.

"When Jill met Dugen." Jill laughed. "Worst rom-com ever." Jill knocked her legs against Dugen's legs again.

Everyone was relatively caught up on what happened in the tent last night. More or less.

Sasha came and sat next to Nate. The four Homecomers dangled their legs off the cliff's edge. They were tempting fate after defying it with a homecoming weekend which ravenous wildfires had failed to completely torch.

"I'm sure this rock is fine. It's solid. You just think about risk differently when you're a parent. You aren't just living for yourself anymore." Sasha had been thinking about Acacia and Timo all morning. Rylar, too. And even Emmalyn. They were never far from her thoughts and rarely far from her presence.

"You just think about risk differently when you're a Sasha." Dugen was right.

"I'm not the world's greatest risk-taker, either." Nate reflected on his past. "But honestly, catastrophe just happens. Whatever your risk profile is. You could be the most safety-oriented person and a plane could crash into your house while you sleep."

"Or you could be randomly carpooling to class when a truck sideswipes you, putting you in the hospital for a month and ending your running career. Not that I'm bitter about it."

Jill laughed again, but with less conviction. "Not as much. Not anymore."

"Humans are notoriously bad at risk allocation." Dugen wiped off the remaining drink from his beard of whiskers. Maybe it *was* Nate's piss.

"We talked about that with the purported rarity of floods, earthquakes, hurricanes, and wildfires. All of civilization. Us as individuals. We write off low-probability events as never happening, but also inflate the likelihood of a rare event as being likely. In the end, we will experience at least some rare events in our lives, but also mistake more common events as being unforeseeable."

"Like a car wreck." Nate agreed.

"Like a car wreck." Dugen continued. "So yeah, this rock surface has been slowly wearing down in the wind, in the rain, in the snow and sun, for a few hundred thousand years. It's going to break off and fall into the forest canyon below. That's mathematical certainty. But will it happen today, October 8th, 2045? What is it now, around 11am? Will it happen now? That's an extremely rare event, and also unlikely given the apparent age and structure of the—"

"—Just looking out for you guys. And I have a farm to manage." Sasha did indeed know it was better to interrupt Dugen.

The four Homecomers munched on trail mix, some bread and fruit, sipping on whatever drinks they had packed. Timberline Bluff was always a tranquil place and rarely had visitors lately. These might be the only people to sit on this cliff's edge for years, maybe decades.

Would they be the last four in the history of the human species? Is that the trajectory homo sapiens were set upon? There's a final time for everything, and rarely known at the time.

"Hey Dugen, what do you want on your tombstone? Just curious." Nate had been thinking about falling to his death. About the granite slab he moved from the back of his truck to the workbench alongside his cabin. About what exactly he would write on it.

"Oh, that's easy. I live by the mantra of my epitaph." Dugen held his hands up, as though reading his grave aloud as he waved his fingers across the imaginary lettering:

> "Here lies a man who sought to push the limits.
> And the limits finally pushed back."

Jill clapped in appreciation. Was she mocking or sincere? Could be both.

"Yeah, that's pretty much dead-on." Sasha shook her head to

185

fend off the unintentional pun. "I mean, that's accurate."

"I don't think I want words on my tombstone. Maybe some artistic etchings of objects that are important to me. Running shoes, a coffee cup... maybe a leaf from this forest. You know, that tells the story of who I am with the images from my life..." Jill had never thought about this before, but now she was searching her memories for the most emblematic items to include.

"... Line graphs of quarterly profit margins?" Dugen was mocking her, but possibly sincerely.

"That's not important to me and you know it. Even at my most committed to corporate life, I knew it was just a means to an end."

Jill picked at a tuft of grass borrowing through the rock surface. There were cracks in it. They could widen with centuries of erosion.

"I just forgot sometimes. Sometimes... a few years at a time. All the awards and recognition, the constant pace of the workload. The inbox that never emptied, the jet-setting for conferences and client presentations, the late nights at the office. It was easy to forget it was a means to an end."

Jill paused and looked out across the vast landscape of forest, some green and vibrant, some charred black from wildfires.

"I'm glad this happened. All of it. The horrible things. The great things. The despair and the joy. It was proof I was alive the entire time. I witnessed it. I experienced it. I made it this far. Right here to this cliff, overlooking everything. At the bottom of everything, at the top of the world."

"We all experienced it. Apart and together." Sasha added.

"AND HERE WE ARE!" Dugen loved any excuse to shout into the abyss. And this phrase seemed so perennial, like the flower itself.

"I don't want a tombstone." Sasha stated bluntly. "I want my ashes sprinkled across the Timberlines so my spirit can be set free."

"You really believe that? You'll be a flying spirit after your body dies?" Nate had never believed this.

"Not flying. More like floating. Omnipresent. Spread out across the land. A part of every flower, every tree, every stream and river, and into the ocean. Everywhere." Sasha closed her eyes with serenity.

"Technically, your particles will be everywhere." Nate conceded. "But will you know it? Will it still be you? I don't think so."

"The phenomenon of consciousness does have a very narrow window of occurrence," Dugen added. "It requires highly specific, incredibly rare combinations of brain cell configuration... found in a minuscule, almost non-existent proportion of the sum total of Earth, let alone the universe."

"I know that. We're all made up of suns and comets, volcanoes and oceans, T-Rex and trilobites." Sasha loved imagining this and would tell Timo all about it when they would stargaze together.

"Isn't a trilobite a kind of computer memory?" Jill had been thinking to herself and just snapped back into the conversation.

"That's a terabyte." Nate pointed out.

"But a trilobite could be thought of as a kind of organic

computer with a genetic memory module. Wait, nobody is still high from last night, right? Right?" Dugen was just wondering.

"Let's keep going! We should head back pretty soon." Sasha was already anxious about what she was missing on the farm. Fear Of Missing Out on Farming. But mostly her family.

"Best way back is to keep going forward at this point." Nate stood up and the others followed.

"This cliff marks the turning point before heading back around to the trailhead. Plus it's mostly downhill. Waterfall ahead! We'll be back at my truck within an hour." Nate started to walk.

"That is, unless Sasha and Dugen keep ambling along and straining the greatest hits of their forgotten youth!"

Dugen and Sasha laughed and began to sing again just to spite Nate the music critic.

> *when you get older, will you screw up?*
> *when you get older, who's gonna notice?*
> *well I just got a lot older, so what's up?*
> *well I just got a lot older, and it's not us!*
>
> *when you are aged, when you go gray*
> *when you get creaky, at the end of your days*
> *just make more noise to keep death away*
> *just make more noise to keep death at bay*

"I always thought it was a good drinking song, especially at a busy pub." Dugen was speaking from experience.

"For me, it's just about the only time I say the 'd' word. Maybe it's safer in a song." Sasha had never thought of it before, but that was probably why.

"'D' word? Death?" Nate realized as he was saying it. For everyone, that word carried a general meaning in the abstract, but usually conjured immediate associations. Painful ones.

"Most art is about pain and adversity. Sometimes succumbing to it. Sometimes overcoming it. Songs are no different." Dugen had taken several courses in art history and theory. His 300 credit hours from the now razed Salmon Springs College gave him a reasonable depth of knowledge on almost any topic.

Maybe someday he could put it all to use.

Jill stayed back now, taking in the scenery with a newfound appreciation for solitude. Hiking in a group had many perks, but it did diminish the awe of being one with nature.

Though she grew up in the Timberline Valley, she had never spent time in the mountains or on the hiking trails, save for a few visits to nearby lakes. How embarrassing that she had squandered this access to natural landscapes before, yet how fortuitous now that she was back—awakened for the first time to the solace of the wild.

"Look up ahead! It's not as impressive in the fall as during the spring runoff, but it runs all year and rarely gets cold enough to fully freeze." Nate pointed above to a cascade of water bursting from the top of the mountain rock face, trailing his finger down the contour of jagged rocks and flat stone surfaces as the flow gathered speed until crashing into a pool far below.

"Timberline Falls. There are several of these right in this area because the bowl of the mountain ridges above empty into this crag of rocks. Any snowpack or flooding from above has carved the grooves of that basin into the long, winding series of waterfalls you see here." Nate sounded like a proper tour guide.

Dugen fished into his pockets for a few coins to hand to Nate.

"Anyone ever tip you during your forest ranger days?" He handed Nate the coins.

Nate refused. "We can't accept tips."

Dugen laughed. "Pretty sure you've been off the clock for a decade now." Dugen looked ahead at the Timberline Falls.

"Okay fine, I'm handing out wishes." Dugen handed a coin to each of the Homecomers before him.

"Imagine that, Dugen is giving handouts to other people instead of taking them." Jill took her coin and grinned back at Dugen.

"It's a one time offer. I'm feeling generous. The falls have shaken my pockets loose and my charitable nature along with it." Dugen grinned in return.

"I love it." Sasha fancied any group activity that bound camaraderie with imagination.

"Everyone! Close your eyes and make a wish. Hold it in your mind. Visualize it." Sasha led children in group activities like this all the time.

Without peeking, each of the Homecomers stood before the waterfall holding their coin.

Each piece of metal had traveled thousands of miles across many years, bounced around in Dugen's pocket for a couple days, now tossing in the roaring thunder of a watery pillar before plunging into a cold mountain pool, ultimately settling amidst fine grains of sand and smooth pebbles.

"Open your eyes. Now release your wishes!" Sasha guided the group as they all tossed their coins, which instantly disappeared into the swirling, descending bursts of mountain runoff.

The four stood in a long moment of silence, the rushing water echoing all around them, cold spray coming off the falls, tapping against their bare skin.

Dugen studied the falls from top to bottom. He put one arm around Sasha and the other around Jill, then nudged Nate to join them. In that moment, all four were locked together at the shoulders.

"Up at the top where the basin empties is one contiguous body of water. In its downward trajectory, the water bursts into billions of droplets as they are tossed through the chaos of friction, gravity, solid objects, and air pressure. Then at the bottom, they all collide and are absorbed into an even larger body of water."

Dugen looked up and down, from atop Timberline Falls to its bottom. The others did the same.

"Right here in the middle of the plunge, we navigate the same forces of physics and idealized metaphysics. But we all came from the same collective matter. We will all return to it. Our lifelong waterfall is our illusion of separate consciousness apart from a shared self—one of nearly infinite past and infinite future. Indefinite also, to be sure." Dugen released his friends from his grasp.

"So are you gonna jump down from here?" Nate was joking.

"Are you joking? I'm prepared for an afterlife in the vast cosmic void, but I'm not in a hurry to get there!" Dugen brushed off his shirt before it was soaked with waterfall spray.

"Plus I have too much to enjoy in the meantime." Dugen grinned at Jill. Jill rolled her eyes. It was almost romantic, but she wasn't fooled.

"I've got an idea, hold on." Nate pulled off his pack and rummaged through it.

"Ah-ha!" Nate pulled his beat up old camera from his bag. He held it at arms length and clumsily took a selfie of the four Homecomers.

SNAP.

It was a surprisingly level, well-composed photo. Sasha was looking off to one side, Jill gave a perfect smile, Dugen made a goofy face in the middle of making an obnoxious foghorn sound, and Nate winked like a sailor happily lost at sea.

"Twenty-Year Homecoming! Woo-hoo!" Jill clapped and channeled her best cheerleader impression.

Sasha led the Homecomers in group hugs. Nate found this quite awkward, but it was the price of admission for the cooperation he required for a group photo.

Nate led the group back to the main trail, the roar of Timberline Falls diminishing as they rounded the next corner of the mountain path. Nate was accustomed to leading hikes, but it had been more than a few years.

"Kyla always loved this." Nate reflected. "Part of having an active dog as my daily companion is that I don't just miss her when I come back to an empty house... I miss her everywhere, because she was always with me."

"Pets are very special. All animals are. They have their own spirit, their own life force." Sasha thought back to all the farm animals – past and present – she had raised and cared for over the years. So many of them cared for her in return. But not Tres Gatos. They seemed genuinely indifferent.

"I wouldn't say I've ever had a pet." Dugen kept his eyes down as the trail grew rocky and steep. "But I've definitely taken in a stray dog or two. Fed a litter of raccoon pups when their mom didn't return. Befriended squirrels and rabbits. Always donate my leftovers to ants, does that count?"

"You *are* a stray, Dugen." Jill knew it for a fact.

"No, that's fair. It's true." Dugen agreed. On some level, his lifestyle overlapped with that of a stray animal on most major characteristics.

"All you need is a flea collar." Jill nudged Dugen in the back. Dugen began scratching around his ears and growling.

"Fleas are probably a good source of protein if one collects enough of them." Dugen was imagining how to do this.

Nate reached the clearing first. "We made it! This trail leads right down to the service road we came in on." Nate pointed. "You can see the outskirts of Salmon Springs from here."

Sasha looked ahead. "That's the old business district. It hasn't been active for at least five years now." Sasha paused.

This destination was not on her tour itinerary. "It's mostly encampments now. An entire tent city, really. The locals call it Salmon Stinks."

Dugen laughed. "Sounds like my kind of place! Blackroot has at least three tent cities. We call them the 'Try Harder Cities.'"

The collapse of society had a certain bleak humor to it.

Sasha shook her head. "It's really sad. I have some friends who were social workers and had caseloads there. That's where I first heard the 'Stinky' nickname."

"What happened to them?" Nate regretted asking.

"Ugh, it was awful. Lost, kidnapped, trafficked. I don't even know what."

"Most homeless people are carrying at least $250,000 worth of human organs inside them." Dugen sounded conspiratorial, yet entirely plausible all the same.

"They call them body-grabbers. Hired mercenaries – usually by the ultra-rich or underground labs who don't want to do their own dirty work. They target anyone who looks lost or forgotten. Somebody that nobody would miss. And they disappear them. Sell them for parts."

Nate shook his head. "Horrifying."

Sasha didn't speak. She knew Dugen was probably right on this one.

"That's all everything is these days." Jill walked along, undeterred. "Spare parts. Scraps. Whatever is left over. That's here. That's us."

"I'm not spare parts!" Sasha was adamant about this. "I'm a farmer, a gardener, a teacher, a mother, a wife, a goat momma. I'm a whole person. And so are each of you. And everyone else."

"Guard your identity. You're the only person who can. And in the dark times, it might be all you have." Dugen was rehearsing more succinct, ominous maxims. For substance and effect.

Nate tried to enjoy the last stretch of the hike.

Thinking about Salmon Stinks, about body grabbers and being sold for parts, it reminded him why he remodeled a cabin to get away from it all. He knew he couldn't repair all that was broken with the world, not even with Salmon Springs. Keeping up a cabin in the woods was a task for which he was fit for purpose. And not much else. That was okay with him.

Jill led the way out of the dense forest brush.

Descending the Timberline Ridge mountain range, the vegetation grew thick again. This side of the valley absorbed the most moisture from cloud mist and precipitation. It was nearly a tropical rain forest, but slightly cooler, with air so dense that it felt like taking a drink just by inhaling it.

The visibility diminished as the four Homecomers descended into a thick fog. The sun was blotted out entirely as the storm clouds gathered. One by one, the hikers followed the trail just before them, down towards the base of the mountain.

They would soon reach the trailhead.

They would not be alone.

[13 – Scrappers in the Fog]

The cool, misty air rolled off the mountain and foretold of an oncoming storm. After traversing so much scarred, charred landscape, the torrents of moisture seemed more than welcome for a parched forest.

Jill was in the lead for the last stretch of the hike. The other three Homecomers were not so far behind as to be lost in the fog. Dugen and Sasha continued to reminisce about their favorite songs from college. Nate remained behind to ensure everyone stayed on the winding path through dense brush.

Up ahead, Jill saw two trucks. With low visibility, it looked more like one very long one. But as the two forms separated, Jill saw several figures climbing around and under one of the trucks.

Nate's truck.

Jill froze. She held her arms out to either side, blocking the trail.

196

Dugen and Sasha stopped their chatter at once and looked over Jill's shoulders.

Nate sprinted forward. "What's going on?" He was too loud.

"Shhhh. Nate, there are some guys at your truck." Jill squinted. She had been meaning to get glasses but kept putting it off. "I count four. Maybe five."

Dugen studied their activity. "Scrappers, almost certainly. They would've just stolen the truck if they wanted to. They are stripping it for parts."

Nate reached down for his pistol, still holstered.

"Motherfuckers. You three stay back. I'm gonna handle this."

"Nate, don't. It's not worth it. We'll find another way." Sasha had encountered some scrappers before, but never confronted them.

Nate could barely contain his rage and protective instincts. "That's my truck. Who knows how long they've been pulling it apart. An hour, maybe longer."

"What are they taking? Looks like the wheels are all there." Jill couldn't imagine what someone would want with old truck parts.

Dugen wanted to be informative but not admit to be speaking from experience.

"They take the easily-removed, valuable stuff. The engine battery, catalytic converter, stereo, sometimes even the tailgate. We all have our packs with us or they'd grab those, too. High resale value, or just their own build. Vehicle parts aren't easy to come by. They could be looking for something specific."

"The tracks at the cabin yesterday. I'm betting it's them. They've been following me for awhile." Nate didn't want to sound paranoid, but he was witnessing a group of guys pulling his truck apart. "Maybe they followed us here today. I didn't notice. I should've been looking."

The four Homecomers waited a moment longer, approaching the edge of the treeline on the perimeter of the trailhead. They crouched together in an emergency huddle.

"Anyone got their phone on them? Call the cops?" Jill defaulted to her big city mentality.

"No cell service up here. No cops, either." Nate usually preferred it that way. But now, not so much.

"Four of us, five of them. Not great odds." Dugen could take down two with the element of surprise. He scanned the gnarly brush for a solid beat-down stick.

"I took a close combat class a few years ago. Top student in my class. Wish I still had my can of mace with me, though." Jill felt her adrenaline flood her bloodstream. She was primed.

"I'm not fighting anyone, sorry. I have a farm to run." Sasha imagined bringing a shotgun, but couldn't imagine firing it in this situation. "It's an old truck, right? You have insurance?"

Nate was done bargaining with himself. He made a promise to himself the other night with Rylar that he would be ready the next time there was a threat. This was that time.

"Oh, I've got insurance alright." Nate muttered as he pulled the Ruger from his hip and stood up, walking hastily into the clearing.

The scrappers continued rummaging under the hood of Nate's truck.

"HEY!" Nate fired his pistol into the air. "GET OUTTA HERE!"

The scrappers scrambled away from the engine and took cover on the other side of Nate's truck.

They began shouting, to each other and back to Nate.

A lean, gaunt man—oldest looking of the bunch—darted behind their own faded green truck, complete with a steel wood rack and a roll cage. It looked like a modified, decommissioned military vehicle that had seen wartime.

Nate remained standing, his gun drawn. "I want you to lay out everything you took. Just drop it there. I'll take care of it. Then get off this mountain before I bury you here in unmarked graves."

Nate had been practicing this threat in his head. He hoped it sounded sufficiently menacing.

Dugen shook his head. This was a tense stand off. But he spotted the gaunt man slide into the bed of his truck and open a metal crate. Nate saw the same motion and pointed his gun at the other truck.

"Hey, come out of there! Hands up where I can see them!" Nate took a week of firearms training during a ranger retreat. Muscle memory and fight-or-flight instinct was driving him.

"How 'bout I bury you!" The gaunt man pulled a military rifle from the metal crate.

Nate pointed and fired at him.

The bullet ricocheted off the wood rack.

The gaunt man aimed his rifle.

Nate fired again. It grazed the gaunt man's shoulder. He winced.

Dugen ran towards Nate.

Nate recovered from the recoil and aimed again.

The other scrappers loaded into their truck, throwing some engine parts into the back.

The gaunt man took aim and fired.

Three shot burst, then three more.

The bullets kicked up dirt and grass.

Nate jumped back and knelt down.

Dugen grabbed Nate and pulled on his shoulders.

"Let's go, let's go!" Dugen pulled on Nate's torso as Nate aimed his pistol again.

The scraggly-bearded scrapper started the engine of their truck. It roared and sputtered, heavy exhaust and no muffler.

The gaunt man took aim.

Nate fired into the cab, then again, putting holes in the windshield.

The hooded scrapper jolted back into the passenger seat, splattering blood against the rear window.

The scraggly bearded scrapper put the truck in drive and floored it.

This was going to be another rundown.

Dugen pulled Nate back, pushing him towards a patch of woods.

Dugen knew this was a losing battle.

The gaunt man fired again, three shots in a burst.

Dugen shouted abruptly and fell onto Nate.

He was shot.

Nate fired round after round into the cab of the truck, at the gaunt man, who fired back from atop the wood rack, until his clip was empty.

Jill ran out from the thick brush, waving both arms.

"Stop! Stop! Stop!"

The gaunt man held his rifle steady. He pointed at Jill.

The scraggly bearded scrapper slowed, then stopped the truck.

Nate pulled Dugen into the woods. He was out of bullets. Dugen was shot.

"How bad is it? Talk to me." Nate laid Dugen out.

Dugen was bleeding from his back and from his shoulder.

"Shot twice. I think. Fuck. I can't feel... my legs." Dugen began to fade, his eyes rolling back.

Jill remained standing, her arms out.

Sasha ran up behind her.

They held their arms out together.

"You got what you came for. Just go. Please. Just go!" Sasha pleaded, standing between the scrapper's truck and the patch of woods where Nate and Dugen had fled.

"Check on Nate. Check on Dugen. I think they've been hit."

Jill kept her eyes ahead as she instructed Sasha. Jill advanced towards the truck, her arms up and out. Something powerful inside her was in control and she didn't know what.

Sasha stepped back slowly, keeping her eyes on the scrappers. The gaunt man kept his rifle trained on the brush where Nate and Dugen escaped. Jill stood in the way.

"We're done here. Your guys got shot. Our guys got shot. It's over."

Jill was forceful. She didn't move. She didn't blink. She didn't look away.

"Fuck all a-ya'll." The gaunt man pulled his rifle back to his shoulder.

He slammed on the hood. "Let's 'git!"

The scrappy-bearded driver jerked the wheel and turned the truck around, peeling out and sending clumps of dirt in all directions.

Another scrapper jumped in the back of the truck, as though they had an established formation for fleeing the scene. They were experienced.

Jill stood and watched as the fortified scrapper truck drove off, loud and muddy.

The Timberline Bluff trailhead had become a bloody crime scene.

Sasha reached the patch of low brush where Nate and Dugen had laid out.

She looked them both up and down.

"Where are you hit?" Sasha looked at Nate.

Nate shook his head and turned Dugen over to his side.

"I'm not hit, just some scrapes. I'm fine. He's got two bullet wounds. Both went through, in and out. His right shoulder and his lower back." Nate had pulled off Dugen's shirt and was applying pressure to each wound as the tattered, long-sleeve fabric absorbed the blood.

"Okay. Okay. Hold on. Okay." Sasha collected herself and grabbed her backpack.

"They're gone." Jill reached the patch of brush as Sasha began pulling out supplies from her pack. "Looks like they took a bunch of parts from Nate's truck with them."

"Those bastards have been tailing me for days. I just know it. I should've stopped them when I had the chance. Should've just camped here in the brush and picked them off as they arrived."

Nate was fuming, exasperated, and shocked.

"Don't worry about that now. Keep pressure on those wounds."

Sasha found the first aid kit in the bottom of her pack. She always had one on her. Farm momma essentials.

"How's he doing?" Jill knelt and began elevating Dugen's head as Sasha packed the bullet wounds with gauze and sterilized the perimeter of each hole.

"I don't know yet. Let's stop the bleeding and suture the wounds shut. Keep talking to him."

Sasha was intent and focused now. This was not her first field medic assignment. Living on a farm meant treating many injuries and they all looked about the same, regardless of species.

"Hey buddy, you'll be okay. We're all here." Jill reached down and held Dugen's hand. Dugen looked up, his eyes faded and weary.

"It's easier to dodge bullets at night. That's what I've concluded." Dugen grinned and squeezed Jill's hand. He had never had a dedicated triage team before. Usually he was left to mend his own injuries.

"Now I've got my own NASCAR pit crew. Vroom vroom." Dugen wheezed and coughed.

"Stay with us, Dugen. I'm going to start stitching you up. Jill, give him something to bite down on." Sasha threaded her needle and pulled the blood-soaked gauze from the bullet holes. "Your shoulder was just grazed. I'm more concerned about the lower back."

"Yeah, I can't... can't feel my legs." Dugen winced.

Jill pulled a scarf from her pack and bunched it up. "Bite on this. Maybe it'll shut you up for a change."

"Only because you didn't ask nicely." Dugen clamped down on the scarf as Sasha began to stitch his wounds. He contorted his face and growled into the garment.

Nate collected himself. "I'm going to check the truck." Nate had several boxes of bullets in the back of the cab. He wanted to reload. He wanted to be ready in case the scrappers returned.

Dugen squeezed Jill's hand and grunted again. Sasha covered the stitches with antibiotic ointment. "Almost done. I promise." Sasha bandaged the wounds.

Jill laid Dugen back into a resting position. "Drink some water. Or warm Gatorade. Let's get your fluid levels back up."

Suddenly, everything she learned at Salmon Springs College was useful again, from high-stakes negotiations to nutrition science.

Dugen sipped on fluids from a canteen as Sasha put a spare sweatshirt loosely over him.

"Let's just rest here for now. We need to make a plan." Sasha's Homecoming weekend took a turn for the worse, and at this point, she just wanted everyone home safe.

Nate returned to the group as Dugen breathed heavy but steadily.

"Motherfuckers really stripped the truck. They must've been at it for awhile. I think they were after all the engine parts. The cab is untouched. We can shelter in it, but it's not gonna run again without some major work, if at all. Maybe I can get a mechanic up here sometime this week, or maybe I can get the parts and fix it up myself... but we're not driving out of here today."

Sasha looked down at Dugen, then back up to Nate. "We can't stay here. Dugen has a serious spinal injury and needs medical attention. He's stabilized for now. He won't make it up here on his own."

Jill looked to the dirt road leading away from the trailhead. "How far to the edge of town?"

"Maybe four, five miles." Nate wiped his forehead and noticed the blood. His blood? Dugen's blood? Didn't matter; he wiped it on his pants.

"It's all downhill from here!" Dugen chuckled and gave a thumbs up, then laid back against Jill's lap.

"So let's walk out of here together. Carry Dugen with us. We'll get there by tonight." Jill looked to Sasha and Nate.

"The edge of town, that's no place to get help. That's a tent city." Nate avoided it as much as possible.

"Then we'll keep going. Get a ride from there. We'll figure it out. We can't stay up here. Who knows when those scrappers will be back." Sasha looked to Nate.

"I know. You're right. You're right." Nate looked at Dugen. "We'll carry you into town. I reloaded and will pack out the rest of the ammo, as well."

"How about you keep your pistol in your backpack from now on, not at your hip? We've had enough shooting for one day, already." Sasha didn't have the patience for more diplomatic phrasing.

"Nate can keep his pistol anywhere he wants, but let's go." Jill didn't blame Nate for what happened.

"Whatever, it can stay in my pack. I was just trying... to defend us."

Nate struggled with his rationale. Why didn't he stay in the brush and let the scrappers take what they wanted and leave? Why did he shoot first? Why didn't he anticipate they would also be armed and shoot back? As the emergency triage scramble ended, the regret and second-guessing set in.

"I'm going down, going down to Salmon Stinks..." Dugen started to hum and sing in a faint, raspy voice. "Going down, no matter what anybody thinks."

Jill and Nate hoisted Dugen up to carry him by their sides. Sasha positioned herself to do the same. Dugen was heavier than he looked.

They gathered their supplies and took anything else suitable for travel with them from Nate's stripped truck. He locked the cab again, despite the engine being excavated and hallowed out.

"I'm going down, going down to Salmon Stinks... Going down, after I catch a few more winks." Dugen muttered as he faded in and out of consciousness.

"We'll trade off carrying Dugen as we walk, just let me know when you want to switch." Nate started down the side of the road with Jill behind him, carrying Dugen together. Sasha inventoried their supplies and kept her eyes up ahead.

This was not how their Homecoming weekend was supposed to end.

[14 – Going Down to Salmon Stinks]

The Homecomers hadn't made it more than a mile along the road before they had improvised a stretcher to carry Dugen. Two long, thick tree branches wrapped tightly with a blanket from Nate's pack did the job.

About a mile further, Dugen needed to relieve himself. But for lack of sensation in his lower body, this too became a group effort.

"I'm just an old baby now. A Lao Tzu for our busted times."

Dugen looked down at his intact body. He couldn't wiggle his toes or flex his legs. It was a mind-body duality more profound than any he's experienced on X-Delight.

"Just relax. We'll take care of this. You'll be in a clinic and the doctors will sort this all out."

Sasha wanted to believe this. She knew access to medical care was much more scarce and difficult to obtain since early in The Long Collapse. This was one of the reasons she did as much at-home healthcare as she could on Fenix Farm.

Nate kept a lookout, but put his pistol away in his pack. He felt like a failure. His heroism lead to tragedy. Now, getting Dugen to safety was his only priority. Like Jill's injured legs from That Crash twenty years ago, Dugen's shattered spinal column was on him.

The afternoon had turned into a rainy, dark atmosphere. The Homecomers covered Dugen with a poncho and put on whatever jackets they had to keep dry. It wasn't working. Jill doubled up her layers and made sure Dugen stayed warm and out of the rain. From one moment to the next, it felt like they were carrying a dead body, but then:

"Gimme a pint or gimme a shot, gimme a double of whatever ya got; drowning out today and probably tomorrow, a bottle of glee for a wallop of sorrow!" Dugen mumbled from under the poncho.

"Keep singing, buddy. You're keeping all our spirits up." Jill reached down to squeeze Dugen's hand again. Anything to prove he was still breathing, still awake.

There was enough food to go around, at least for now. But there was also a growing sense that whatever they had to eat should be rationed carefully. Just as a precaution. These days, everything required more precaution. Nothing taken for granted.

No other vehicle drove on the road as the Homecomers descended from the Timberline Peaks down into the valley below. A few streetlights littered the horizon, but far fewer than Jill remembered growing up.

More common were glowing dots from the bonfires and oil drums ignited for light and heat.

Salmon Springs had always had a homeless population, like anywhere else. But as The Long Collapse deepened, the problems vastly outpaced the solutions, or even remedies, which began to mount. Drug addiction and poverty, waves of economic and climate disaster migrants, a collapse in housing programs, untreated mental illness—these were the most common explanations. State and federal officials had no effective resolutions for any of them, so they just worsened.

Nobody quite remembered when "Salmon Stinks" became the unofficial designation for the growing encampment on the west edge of town. At first, it was a row of tents along the block next to the food bank and drug treatment center. But when those services proved insufficient to meet the need, the encampment grew out several more blocks in each direction.

The tent city butted up against a large, unkempt nature preserve called Buckson Park. It was now a wilderness park – no longer a city park – and that proved fit for purpose to many unhoused migrant populations and local squatters alike.

Sasha had been there before to deliver food relief, but it had been many years. Well-meaning community service programs were shut down after they were raided by scavengers.

Absent police enforcement, which had already been strained to the point of abandoning much of Salmon Stinks, aid organizations were no longer willing to risk being robbed, kidnapped, raped, or worse. Like the horrid rumors of body harvesters.

When the police presence receded, a predictable influx of vigilante justice ensued. Everyone was packing heat. Everyone was on a hair-trigger alert with everyone else.

The scrappers who gutted Nate's truck were a common menace in Salmon Stinks and just about everywhere else outside core city centers – which themselves had become fortified government complexes that did little more than administer their own security.

The Long Collapse brought a lawless sense of the great outdoors met with paramilitary warfare to nearly every city and town. At best, there was a wide array of unregulated adventure to be had. But at worst, it was only the freedom to beg, borrow, steal, shoot or be shot. And now, the four Homecomers were all but guaranteed to experience the good, bad, and ugly of Salmon Stinks.

Nate knew enough to know this was a bad situation. They were low on supplies, no vehicle, and carrying one of their own who was in dire need of medical attention. Maybe saving the truck was always a foregone conclusion. Maybe it was going to get ripped apart by scrappers sooner or later. But Dugen didn't need to get gunned down. The burden of his makeshift stretcher weighed heaviest on Nate's shoulders.

The highway overpass used to mark the perimeter of Salmon Stinks. Any structure that provided shelter from the rain and snow was the preferred place to setup camp. But as more people passed through or stayed, the tent city grew with larger tarps which created a canopy for cover. The Homecomers first came upon one as they followed the dirt road onto pavement.

"The paved road starts here, so I guess we're in city limits now." Nate pulled an old phone from his pack and turned it on.

Sasha and Jill lowered Dugen's makeshift stretcher down so everyone could rest.

"So do we know where we are? Specifically?" Jill may have grown up in Salmon Springs, but this derelict slum bore no resemblance to the city she knew as a girl.

Sasha nodded. "I know where we are. Downtown is due east from here, maybe twenty city blocks. Maybe thirty."

"Great, so we just keep heading straight through until we reach a hospital or what?" Jill was feeling weary, hungry, drenched, and sore.

"Yup, that's correct. Not too much farther." Nate held his phone up.

No signal. Never a signal. Cell service had become so unreliable that most people just abandoned their beloved devices. Too many power failures, too many cell towers destroyed or toppled.

Cellular networks have always been volatile entities, conditioned upon so many other forms of technology all working together, all the time. In retrospect, it was a short-lived luxury to be able to call or text anyone, anywhere, on demand. Those days were over.

Jill knelt down and pulled the poncho down to reveal Dugen's face and chest. He looked peaceful. "Hey Dugen, how are you feeling?"

Dugen stirred, giving a mirthless expression.

"Been better. Maybe been worse, not sure. Got more to drink?"

"Of course." Jill pulled the water bottle from her pack and gave Dugen several slow, deliberate sips. "Glad you are drinking more. You had us worried back there."

"My daddy tried to stop drinking, but he's no quitter. And I'm no quitter, either." Dugen sighed with a refreshed glimmer in his eyes. He looked up at Jill. "You know, I've been thinking..."

"Uh-oh." Jill looked up as Sasha and Nate discussed their course ahead. She had some privacy with Dugen now. "What?"

"You're the last woman I will ever sleep with in my life. I'll never walk again. Or anything, you know, down there." Dugen grinned with a solemn melancholy.

"Um, well... first of all, not confirming or denying that happened. And second, you don't know yet. You could recover. I recovered. Well, mostly."

Jill rubbed Dugen's cheek. Being his emergency caretaker had a bonding effect on her, more than she was willing to admit.

"It's okay, Jill. It's okay. I wouldn't have it any other way." Dugen tilted his head to kiss Jill's outstretch hand, but nipped at her fingers instead. "You know we might have to resort to cannibalism."

"Gross, you're so weird! It's like you know how to turn any sentimental moment into a creep show starring you."

Jill laughed and recoiled, wiping her slobbered-on fingers against Dugen's blanket bedding.

Dugen rolled over slightly and closed his eyes. "I'm sure you taste delicious." Jill rolled her eyes and covered Dugen back up.

She didn't want to know if Dugen had eaten human flesh before. It wouldn't surprise her.

Jill stood up as Sasha and Nate returned. Sasha assumed her tour guide role.

"We can try for the city center tonight. The sun set hours ago but you'd never know it with all the cloud cover. Temperatures are going to drop. It'll be cold tonight. If we keep moving, we'll stay warm enough. We need to monitor Dugen's body temperature."

"Any chance we can stop somewhere for supplies?" Jill instantly knew the answer as she asked, but wanted to at least eliminate that possibility. For the sake of her empty stomach.

"Oh yeah? Where, Jill? Where? See any convenience stores open here in Salmon Stinks? A Starbucks, maybe?" Nate was beyond irritated.

None of this should've happened. This was why he stayed at his cabin. Away from the chaos, away from the misery.

"It was worth asking." Sasha defended Jill. She sensed tensions were high. Everyone was on their last nerve. Hunger was setting in. Nobody looked very warm or very happy.

A soggy, shot-up Homecoming disaster.

"I know, I know. It's whatever. Let's go." Jill reached back to hoist her end of the stretcher. There was no point in shouting back at Nate. Each of them were one another's last, best hope at getting someplace warm and safe.

Nate walked back to help carry Dugen.

Sasha gave Dugen a gentle rub. He was still warm under the many layers everyone had piled upon him. The bleeding had stopped. It could be worse. Like any other day of The Long Collapse, they were making due. And this time, they were together.

Jill and Sasha each took one side of the stretcher where Dugen's head rested while Nate led the group carrying both wooden poles of Dugen's feet. This distributed the weight evenly and kept everyone walking at a steady pace. Dugen probably weighed 180 pounds and the blankets added a few more.

This also meant that Dugen would look straight up to see the storm clouds rolling by, breaking in patches to reveal the night sky. The moon began to rise in the east, more full and bright than the two nights before. Dugen whistled softly and recited a dirge for lovers.

> *you look so beautiful*
> *you look so sad*
> *as though what you desire most*
> *just out of reach*
> *without further speech*
>
> *to tuck you away*
> *to make you feel safe*
> *to wrap the night away*
> *in warm embrace*
>
> *may we soon meet*
> *on a distant shore*
> *just beyond the edges of sleep*
> *I'll see you there*
> *our moonlit melancholy*

The glow of the tent city grew brighter and closer. The sides of the road were now littered with abandoned cars—some scrapped for parts, others burned through entirely.

United States car manufacturing peaked around 12 million units annually a few decades ago. All those cars ended up somewhere. Most were in disuse now. Surely some future civilization would study this behavior.

Occasionally, a lone figure would walk along the road in the other direction. Where were they going? It wasn't obvious. One carried a large bundle of branches. Another was pushing a four wheeler with no engine. And there were bodies – of humans, of dogs, of rats and bats and cats.

The broken road to Salmon Stinks was lined with debris and carcasses.

"Are we walking into a zombie apocalypse or something? Just kidding." Jill wanted to lighten the mood, even absent a conducive atmosphere.

"Or something."

Sasha kept thinking about her family. Surely they were worried about her by now. She wanted them to know she was okay. She wanted to be back on Fenix Farm. This was the longest she had been away in many years, certainly by herself.

"Just stick together and keep going."

Nate alternated between worrying about how to fix his truck or getting a new one. He also imagined cooking up a big pot of chili and a fresh loaf of sour dough bread. With real butter. And a dash of red pepper. Nate frequently cooked in his head during a miserable outdoor trek after dark. Just imagining it with enough detail felt almost like eating a warm meal.

Up ahead, Nate saw the entrance to Salmon Stinks.

Rather than merely dotting the perimeter of town with tents, the permanent transients had constructed a veritable wall out of automotive chassis ends, car doors and hoods, metal shopping carts, large rubber tires from farm tractors, entangled bike racks, and anything else sturdy enough to be piled on high to form a barrier.

In the center of the barrier, where the broken pavement road continued on, was a large steel gate wrapped in corroding barbed wire. Several armed men stood watch.

"It's a wall of junk. We literally have to pass through a wall of junk." Nate hadn't been through this way in a very long time for very good reason.

"I'm getting tetanus just looking at that rusty scrap heap. I'm gonna need a booster shot." Jill wasn't kidding this time.

"Stick together, we aren't a threat to anyone here." Sasha really believed it. Surely presenting at the gate with an injured man on a stretcher would grant them safe passage.

Dugen shook his head. "Coins, jewelry, watches, and other valuables. That's what will get us through the gate. Not appealing to some universal human dignity. That got burned out and blown up a long time ago."

Dugen rolled over to one side, alert and ready to be taken hostage at any moment. Surely his organs were worth more than his observations.

Nate reached the gated entrance first. He leaned down to set Dugen's stretcher on the ground as Sasha and Jill did the same. They gathered cautiously, showing their hands.

"We don't accept dead bodies. This ain't a morgue or a funeral home." The oldest man guarding the door spoke first. From the looks of the three of them, he was the only one who spoke at all.

"Our friend was shot. He's not dead." Nate stepped to one side so the guards could look upon Dugen. Dugen lifted an arm enough to give a thumbs up.

"Pew pew pew! Living my best life. Rock star status. Going to

217

Disneyland after this." Dugen softly wheezed and rested again. That took all the strength he could summon.

"We're trying to get to downtown and put him in Salmon Springs General or something. We were hiking around Timberline Bluff." Nate paused.

He didn't know if these guys were among the scrappers who ripped apart his truck. They looked like it. Rough men with rifles tended to look the same after awhile.

"Oh I bet that was real pretty this time of year. The leaves changing colors. Real pretty. Right, Stanley?" The eldest gatekeeper turned to his portly guard with a braided beard.

"Real pretty, Marvin." Stanley seemed more sincere than sarcastic. But they were both so deadpan and unamused that it was difficult to know for certain.

Jill was less patient and dispensed with the formalities. "Please let us through. We need to rest and get our friend to safety."

Marvin smirked. "Safety? You won't hardly find that here or anywhere else. You got guns?"

Nate paused. He was glad his gun was in his pack. After the trouble his shooting from the hip had gotten them into, he wasn't about to repeat that mistake. This was not a situation he could blast his way through.

"No. Just hiking supplies."

"No guns? Well that's your first mistake." Marvin looked the worn out Homecomers up and down. "Are you with the Reddard Faction?"

"We're not with anybody." Sasha had heard of the Reddards,

which were a formed as a militia when police forces collapsed in the greater Timberline Valley.

"We're just back from our Homecoming weekend at Salmon Springs College. It burned down, you know. So we just got together and then... this all happened."

Marvin sighed and stepped to one side. "Well you should've said that before! I'm class of 2004!"

Marvin was delighted. Meeting a fellow alum was rare these days. He grinned and bared all eight remaining teeth, slung his rifle around his shoulder, and stretched his hand out to Sasha.

They shook hands with vigor as Marvin always gave a proper handshake to those who earned one.

"I knew I liked you. So you're all Salmon Springs grads?"

"Yep, class of 2025. This is our 20 year reunion!" Sasha felt her kind nature emerge without hesitation.

"I knew I liked her." Marvin turned to Stanley as he spoke.

"We're cooking up baked beans and rice tonight. It's nothing fancy but it's piping hot and served by the bowl full." Marvin motioned for Stanley and his compatriot to open the gate.

Nate felt a deep sense of relief. They were finally catching a break.

Sasha leaned in and hugged Marvin, who went from being a gruff armed guard to a congenial grandpa in the time it took to swing the gate open.

Nate and Jill hoisted up Dugen in his stretcher. "Hear that, Dugen? Baked beans and rice for dinner. Hot food!" Jill's stomach was doing the thinking and the talking now.

"With over 300 credit hours, I really should be able to say I graduated" Dugen muttered from beneath his pile of blankets.

The Homecomers collected themselves, carried Dugen on his stretcher, and entered the tent city. The guards closed the gate behind them, keeping the wall of junk contiguous and fortified.

In a distance spanning the Timberline mountain range, military helicopters made their approach to Salmon Springs under the cover of night. The Reddard Faction had claimed Salmon Stinks as one of their tent city compounds many years ago, but the Homecomers arrived just as the Reddard's claim to sovereignty was to be challenged.

[15 – From Upon Cotter's Corner]

The portions weren't generous, but they were sufficient.

Sasha and Jill had spare coins to empty into a large brass bowl at the entrance to the chow tent and happily deposited them. Nate donated a spare multi-tool and a headlamp from his pack.

Living in a tent city meant almost any exchange was fair game, and it was the effort that counted more than a numerical value. Those consumer math calculations were for the old days.

Jill held Dugen's bowl for him and Sasha helped him sit upright. "You don't have to spoon-feed me, but I wouldn't complain being waited on by the two most gorgeous gals I know," Dugen proclaimed.

"Yeah well, enjoy it while it lasts." Jill was happy everyone was dry and safe, warming up and slurping down nourishment by the spoonful.

"I dunno how long any of it lasts. But... seems like if I still can't wiggle my toes or feel sensation in my thighs, this could last forever."

Dugen had spent the hours being carried in the stretcher to contemplate his new life as a paraplegic. He decided it was better than being paralyzed from the neck up, like most people.

The four Homecomers were huddled in one end of a large tent suitable for serving meals to dozens of residents. As Marvin had promised, rice and beans were served piping hot thanks to a cooking stove that worked surprisingly well for its worn appearance. Perhaps it was stolen. Indeed, the rice and beans were very soupy and a bit bland, but Nate found a bottle of hot sauce in the back of an abandoned refrigerator. A dash or two really livened up the dish. At this point, simply being filled with a hot liquid was enough.

For being known as a cesspool of squalor, Salmon Stinks was surprisingly organized. The equivalent of a business district lined one side of the junk wall, with wares resembling a pawn shop or the bargain bin at a flea market.

Everything was either gently used or usable only for parts. There were no prices marked on anything, just a bartering merchant with a lazy eye and a starter pistol for inventory security.

Along the other side of the junk wall were dozens—perhaps hundreds—of smaller tents housing individuals and families. The structures were worn and flimsy, but being staked close enough together did create some resilience from the elements.

The entire ambiance was a tribute to 'strength in numbers' fortification.

A cursory stroll with an open ear would catch many languages and many dialects from native speakers and immigrants alike. This was because, as The Long Collapse deepened in severity to all ends of the Earth, the effects of climate disruption caused mass migration away from coastal flooding, drought-stricken heat, and the ravages of hurricanes and wildfires.

The Timberline Valley region was far from perfect, but it was the 'least worst' option for climate refugees and those fleeing failed states with collapsed economies. Almost everyone was an immigrant, or soon to be one, and the notion of borders hardly mattered any longer. Political boundaries were too expensive to enforce and too porous to seal up, too many armed gangs claimed passages—above ground and beneath it—to keep migration centrally controlled.

Buckson Park formed the perimeter of Salmon Stinks and buffered against the downtown business district of the Salmon Springs city center. Since it had fallen out of maintenance from being a city park, rumor had it that the park remained full of wild animals.

Such places thrived as The Long Collapse depopulated much of the surrounding city. As the pendulum of habitat swung away from human populations, it swung back towards the biodiversity of wildlife and ecology.

"They were here first!" as Timo once said.

Nate looked out between the poles of the chow tent to see several families show up in time for dinner. They looked like they had arrived several days ago because their attire was settled and dusty. It was difficult to tell one family unit from another as a cohort of adults and children alike were gathered for their meal.

Jill and Sasha alternated between eating and helping Dugen to eat, thrilled he was alert and with his characteristically large appetite.

One of the smaller children, spotted with mud but adorned with a bright orange bow in her dark hair, looked over with curiosity. Sasha waved and smiled. She missed her own kids.

Jill finished feeding the last of Dugen's supper to him. She looked over and noticed the way Sasha's smiled concealed a deeper pain. She had an inclination as to why.

"You had a third child, didn't you? Timo, Acacia, and a middle one?"

Sasha nodded, still entranced by the girl at the next table in the chow tent. Sasha was weary, but relaxed and composed.

"Emmalyn. That was her name. And she loved wearing ribbons and bows in her hair just like that little girl. She would insist on wearing them to sleep most nights."

Jill looked over at the girl with the bright orange bow as she turned back to eat with her family, still looking in all directions, taking in the entire scene.

Jill looked over to Sasha. After all they had been through by now, Jill was still hesitant to ask.

Sasha continued, anyway. She knew Jill wanted to know more.

"We lost her about five years ago now. Most people would just say she 'died' or 'passed away.' But that never... that never felt honest to me whenever I said it. Too passive, too neutral. Maybe it's why I never talk about her... even though I always carry her in my heart. Our Emmalyn. Forever five. Timo is older than her now, which is almost, almost... incomprehensible to me."

Sasha's face remained still and calm, even as her eyes began to shimmer.

"I'm so sorry." Jill took Sasha hands in hers. "May I ask, what happened?"

"It was in the local news at the time. But you weren't around so you probably didn't hear about it. There was a shooting at the daycare center, the preschool building. I think at least fifteen kids and three adults died. All ages. Terrifying."

"Oh god, oh no." Jill was stunned. Not because these kinds of tragedies weren't in the news weekly, but because she hadn't known anyone personally affected until now. This is what it felt like.

"It was horrible, so horrible for most of us that it became unspeakable. That's why I say we 'lost' Emmalyn. Rylar confirmed it was her body at the morgue. I refused to look. To me, Emmalyn just disappeared that day. As crazy as it sounds, it helps me to believe I will still see her again."

"Another deranged psychopath with guns?"

Jill lost track of how many headlines like that she had read growing up. Post-Columbine, post-Sandy Hook. School shootings were somewhere on the list of reasons Jill never wanted to have kids.

And now, Jill was bearing witness to the impact of losing a child to gun violence.

"No, actually. There was this big investigation, took a year or two. It was several guys in some kind of militia cult, they were shot and killed on site when police arrived. They wanted hostages to execute for some takeover, I don't even remember at this point. I'm not sure I even paid attention at the time. It didn't

225

help my family to know more about it."

"Were Timo and Acacia—"

"Timo was with me at the market. Acacia was in a different part of the building. Thankfully, she didn't see anything. She hid in a storage closet, a bunch of kids did."

Sasha shook off the sorrow. She hadn't thought about this in years; she discussed it even less often.

"Thank you for telling me. I understand why you never mentioned that before. I'm glad you told me. Emmalyn sounds wonderful. I'm so sorry."

Jill pulled Sasha in for a long hug.

The two women inhaled together, exhaled together. It was like the grief was dispersing slightly, from one body into two. The girl with the bright orange bow looked over at them and grinned. Jill smiled back at her while holding onto Sasha. This wasn't quite reincarnation, but it felt about as close as scientifically possible.

Dugen slunk back down onto his makeshift stretcher. With more alertness came more discomfort. His shoulder stung but the wound was manageable. Everything below his chest was either in searing pain or there was no sensation at all. He was still deciding which was worse.

As Nate finished his bowl of soupy beans and rice, he looked over to Dugen, struggling to sit upright.

"I'm going to look for a wheelchair around here. If we get one, it will make getting Dugen to the city center much easier."

Jill and Sasha released their embrace and looked over at Dugen, still looking agitated and restless.

"Okay, are we getting ready to leave soon?" Sasha was determined to get Dugen to the hospital in the city center once the group was rested enough to keep going. Surely it wasn't far once they passed through Buckson Park.

"That's the plan. Let me see what I can get to make traveling easier for Dugen."

Nate looked down as Dugen grinned and folded his arms behind his head.

"Oh, it's simple as an instant cookie recipe for me. You're the ones hauling my crippled ass through the rain and mud." Dugen chuckled, then coughed, then cleared his throat and groaned. Laughing hurt. The Long Collapse turned every comedy into a tragedy and every tragedy into a comedy.

Nate walked out of the chow tent and began to scan the perimeter of Salmon Stinks. There were no business hours posted, of course, so anywhere with an open tent had the potential to point Nate in the right direction.

A short walking distance brought Nate in front of a grizzled old man in a thick winter jacket. The man leaned up against his lawn chair, nestled against the wall of a large tent.

By the looks of it, he had been living there awhile.

"Hey man, I'm looking for a wheelchair or something like that. You know where I could find one?" Nate stood at the tent's entrance, fairly certain he was speaking loud enough.

After a moment of deliberation, the grizzled old man spoke in a raspy, forced whisper.

"Check the far corner of camp in the junk heap. I seen one or another an' mayhap it ended up there."

Nate looked around with confusion. There were so many junk heaps.

"The biggest junk heap. We call it Cotter's Corner. Cotter founded it, kept adding to it, made it free for everyone. Biggest Lost 'n Found in Salmon Springs proper."

Nate nodded. "Thanks, appreciate the help." Nate got the distinct sense that the grizzled old man hadn't had someone stop and talk to him for a very long time. "I'm Nate, by the way."

"Nate the Great. Can't relate." The old man coughed and laughed, laughed and coughed, then leaned forward in his lawn chair.

"I'm Larry. Larry Blanton."

Nate knelt to meet Larry at eye level. His eyes were shrouded in cloudy patches, lit by a small oil lamp hanging at the entrance of his tent. His teeth were worn and rotted. Yet somehow, Larry radiated a kind of solemn serenity.

"I don't know Cotter, by the by. He might just be a junk heap legend. Apocryphal, like. But Cotter's Corner is real. People travel from all over to dump or scavenge there. Everyone should do it once in their lifetime... lifetime. Ha! Lifetimes are too long, if you ask me."

The old man pulled out a pipe and packed it with something flaky and stinky. Nate pulled a lighter from his pack and sparked the pipe as Larry puffed out plumes of smoke.

"We are in some strange days to call a lifetime, that's for sure." Nate looked around to see another group moving in and out of

228

the chow tent in the distance.

Several armed men patrolled the perimeter. Nate kept his head down. He didn't want to stand out with bad company.

"So uh, what were you doing before you came here?" Nate asked with a kind of charitable curiosity. Larry slapped his leg and cleared his throat with another raspy chuckle.

"Oh, ya know... a bit of working, a bit of drinking... then more working, more drinking. Driving trucks long distance, short distance. Big rigs. Small jobs. Then too much drinking, not enough working. Got in a bad wreck on the job. Lost my job. Out of work, then out of drink."

Nate began to realize who he was talking to.

Larry Blanton.

"Mr. Blanton." That's all Holt Harbor, Arbitrator had ever said about the driver of the black truck.

Now, Nate was lighting his pipe twenty years later.

Of all the tents to stop at on this soggy, sordid excuse of a night.

Larry leaned back with his pipe, sputtering smoke, starting to nod off.

"As it goes, so it went. Been skimming and scraping ever since. Driving for smugglers. Guns and drugs and body parts and don't tell me what... I just drive, okay? All under the table, off the books. Then my eyes went bad. Lost track of time. Or maybe time lost track of Larry. What'n the fuck? In the end, it's Salmon Springs for thee, Salmon Stinks for me!"

Larry grunted and guffawed as he set his pipe down.

"I've... I never knew you, but I've always wondered who you were." Nate tested his capacity for resentment but felt none.

In Larry Blanton, Nate Magnus saw someone too degraded by the decades of his own suffering to further disparage; Larry was too burdened by these dark times to begrudge. Nate and his passengers had made it through That Crash.

At the point of impact between their vehicles and their fates, Larry already had less... and had lost more every day since.

Nate rummaged through his pack and found a wad of 'just in case' cash. Some fraction of the car wreck settlement, no doubt.

He set it in Larry's gnarled hands. "I want you to do something nice for yourself, whatever you want. Thanks for pointing me to Cotter's Corner."

Larry sorted the bills between his fingers. He had no way of knowing how much Nate had just given him. But it was still a lucky break in lean times.

"Bless you, Nate the Great. May you find what you're looking for, a wheelchair or just peace of mind from the great junk heap in the clouds."

Nate patted Larry on the shoulders as he stood and turned to leave.

"Death finds us all" Larry muttered, "but what first we find is what sets us apart. Remember Larry Blanton told you!"

"I'll never forget, my friend." Nate turned to leave as Larry set down his pipe and drifted off.

Nate continued along the perimeter of Salmon Stinks in search of the great junk heap. Surely it was too grand to overlook.

Passing by many tattered tents and ripped tarps, cars and trucks stripped for parts and left as makeshift shelters, wooden pallets and metal roofing stacked up into forts, Nate saw any number of old world items repurposed into housing materials fit for The Long Collapse. It was like a graveyard of objects and people, assembled in preparation for an exodus that never happened.

This tent city was a place of lingering survival, apparently established solely for survival's sake.

The occasional flaming trash barrel or campfire dotted the muddy path with enough light to see ahead. Without any vehicle traffic, the atmosphere was quiet and still. Nate had been born long after the proliferation of machines which generated a constant hum—an aggregate roar at any remote distance.

Though not as whisper quiet as his cabin nestled in the Timberlines, the reposeful reverie of Salmon Stinks did have a certain solemnity to it.

Up ahead, the wall of junk grew higher. Nate wondered if the tent city cropped up first and its inhabitants built a barrier of debris around it, or whether the outskirts of Salmon Springs became the inevitable dumping ground for a collapsing civilization and campers found the reservoir of discard objects to be a useful neighborhood resource. Perhaps a feedback loop of both.

Walking discretely with his backpack on, Nate felt like a disaster tourist. Was he blending in? Was he an obvious outsider? Not one to draw attention to himself, Nate pulled up the hood of his jacket and kept his head down.

The intermittent chatter, laughter, or shouting from the camp created a dull murmur of late night habitation and libations. Without solid walls of insulation between each household, the tent city felt like one big communal space. There was little privacy, but also few secrets.

Nate considered how different it would be to move back into civilization. Surely the negatives outweighed the positives for him, but without Caitlyn or Kyla, his cabin felt more like a tomb in waiting than a cozy den of hospitality.

As he contemplated the finer points of living arrangements, Nate was taken by surprise as a dark figure stepped out from between two overturned boxcars.

"Hey man, what's happening?" The man's lips were cracked and chapped, his eyes glassy, his skin blackened by dirt.

"Taking the usual night walk, you know, heading to Cotter's Corner." Nate tried to sound like a tent city resident of established pedigree.

"Yeah man, nice night." The dirty man looked away and then back to Nate. He seemed twitchy and skittish. "You got any spare socks? I'm planning on walking to Cleveland."

Nate shook his head. "Sorry, just the ones I've got on me."

"You a backpacker? You got a backpack."

"Yeah, I suppose that makes me a backpacker. Easier to carry things around, you know." Nate was about ready to wrap this charming exchange, so he stepped away. "Anyway, have a good night."

The dirty man sniffled and scratched his chin. "If I leave now, how long do you think it would take to walk to Cleveland?"

Nate shook his head. "Buddy, that's over 2,000 miles. It would take you months. And winter is setting in. Even with a change of socks, you wouldn't make it on foot."

'Buddy' paused to collect his thoughts. Nate continued to back away.

"Do you think there are any bridges between here and Cleveland?" Buddy asked with genuine curiosity, like the answer could go either way.

"Yes, probably." Nate knew this was absurd. "Anyway, take care." Nate turned to leave.

"Because I hate walking on bridges. You never know if they're gonna fall down." Buddy the dirty man muttered as he wandered off into the encampment. "Everything falls down sometimes."

Nate felt the soreness in his feet become more acute. He was used to a day hike, but not the marathon of stress and strain he had been under all day. Despite the weariness, he pressed on.

Up ahead, the dim light of moonglow clouds cast a large pile in full relief. It must be Cotter's Corner.

It was the largest garbage pile Nate had ever seen. In no particular order, he spotted spare parts, scraps, rubble, debris, and junk coming in all shapes, sizes, and textures.

If one were to compile all the materials humans had ever invented—sheet metal, rubber fittings, particle board, insulation, fiberglass, concrete, hard plastic, soft plastic, crinkled plastic, formed plastic molding, and yet more plastic— all of it shaped for some single-use purpose or another, then piled it upon itself... it would be the stuff of Cotter's Corner.

"A discarded civilization's greatest shits." Nate muttered as he approached the mountain of junk.

Likely it was the result of municipal landfills overflowing, or simply the expense of concealing them grew too great. Now, simply setting aside the rubbish of the past was all an impoverished society could afford. Yet in doing so, there remained an embarrassment of riches in the junk itself. One declining civilization's trash is another surviving encampment's treasure.

But where to start? Nate pulled his headlamp from a side pocket in his backpack. Fully charged, bright blue light. In the context of Salmon Stinks, a new headlamp beamed with almost futuristic flare. Nate arrived as an astronaut seeking buried artifacts from an ancient planet.

As Nate sifted and circumnavigated the hillside of scrap that formed Cotter's Corner, he began to see anthropological stories emerge: the remnants of a baby's crib alongside a heap of dirty diapers and discarded maternity wear, a deflated basketball and frayed high-tops, the entire suite of filing cabinets and computer equipment of a defunct business.

These were the items in particular sequence of lives lost and times forgotten.

Climbing higher onto the pile, Nate looked back over Salmon Stinks. Stippled with small lanterns, oil drum flames, and bonfire pits, the encampment had an odd sense of home about it. The Reddard Faction had secured and maintained the space for years and, as a result, the tent city was as much an autonomous city as any other. It had to be; the remaining world had forgotten about its inhabitants.

Surely then, Nate reasoned to himself, there was a wheelchair amidst similar items. Rehab equipment, perhaps? Hospital furniture or medical equipment? It was tempting to set aside or pack away the many other promising finds from the heap, but Nate had a singular purpose and never forgot Dugen laying in pain, urgently awaiting transport to proper medical care.

As he sorted and sifted, moved and removed, Nate felt the guilt of his errors weigh upon him again. He knew himself to be his toughest critic, but that did nothing to invalidate the criticism. It was hard not to place himself at the center of blame for all that had gone wrong—even for a poor, shriveled-up sap like Larry Blanton.

Nate saw himself as the fulcrum of his own destiny and all the consequences that rippled outward from that. Maybe there was more he could've done to prevent That Crash. Maybe he could've intervened sooner to save Caitlyn from her overdose. Maybe if he had remained shrouded in the bushes at the Timberline Bluff trailhead, Dugen would still be upright and mobile.

Maybe if...

Just then, Nate's headlamp illuminated the rubberized tire of a metal rim. He tugged on it, shaking the wheel loose from a cluster of tubing and thatched fence materials.

It was a wheelchair! Of all the bad luck in the world, Nate truly struck a measure of treasure from the great garbage pile. Was it improbable? Sure. But sometimes, found objects just happen to fit the demands of the moment. Sometimes, fortuitous happenings happen.

As Nate freed the remaining wheel and frame, he noticed the inevitable defects that precipitated its disposal. The collapsing wheelchair had worn material which formed the seat and backing. Nonetheless, the frame was intact and the wheels remained circular and weight-supporting.

Nate lifted and carried the wheelchair out from the heap. It was near the top, implying it was also fairly recently-discarded. As Nate strapped the wheelchair to his backpack and prepared to climb back down the junk heap, he heard a distinctive noise echo through the Timberline Valley.

A dull rumble at first, then more acute and sharp: it was the fluttering chopper noise of helicopters. Fast approaching.

As Nate looked towards the incoming direction of the sound, he spotted at least six military helicopters on the horizon, their lights almost entirely dampened.

This was no rescue operation. It was a stealth assault.

From a middle distance, a loud air horn began to sound.

RRRRREEEEEEEEEEEEEEEEEEEEEE-EEEEEE-EEEEEE!

Salmon Stinks had an alert system?

"Oh, fuck me."

However bad this was for the transients and residents of the tent city, it was worse for Nate and his friends. They were about to be caught up in something ugly. The lead helicopter blared over a speaker system with an automated announcement:

"ATTENTION: under the authority of the National Defense Force, this encampment has been declared an illegal occupation by the Department of Homeland Security. All persons in the area have sixty seconds to commence evacuation. Enforcement measures up to and including deadly force will be used against any resistance. This is your final warning."

Nate half-slid, half-hopped down the bottom slope of junk forming the base of Cotter's Corner.

As he met the soft dirt soil, he saw frantic activity all over the camp. Small children and grown women rushed inside tents, campfires were doused, flaming trash barrels were capped, a ragtag militia of armed men began assembling with all makes of pistols, rifles and shotguns at the ready.

"Reddards forever!"

The men chanted and hollered. They had trained for this, drilled for this, and likely experienced similar raids in the past.

Staying on the path and in a hurry, Nate hauled the folded wheelchair on his pack and moved with stealth and unwavering determination.

Something overtook him. He did not want more harm to come to his friends. He couldn't bear any more of the guilt.

As though channeling Jill's champion spirit and ambition, Nate pushed his legs until they burned, his lungs heaving, his vision tunneled only on the path back to the chow tent. Back to Dugen as Jill and Sasha cared for him.

"Reddards! Open fire!" One command led to another.

BANG! BANG! BANG-BANG-BANG!

Shots fired.

Nate glanced over to see several gruff militia men take a position on the junk wall, with more strafing and firing wildly. Overhead, the helicopters were lowering, taking an attack formation. One appeared to be pointing straight at the junk wall.

PFFFFFfffffffffttt...

BOOM! BOOM! BOOM!

Nate fell to one side, thrown by the force of an explosion.

The heat on his face burned, he tapped his cheeks. Singed, perhaps. Nothing more.

Nate was panting. His body was in overdrive. He looked back to the perimeter of the junk wall. It was blown apart. Metal debris strewn about. Wooden beams lit ablaze. Plastics melting and simmering. The lead artillery chopper had punched through the junk wall with a cluster of small munitions designed specifically for this purpose.

Blowing up a wall of junk was dirty business.

Some of the shrapnel had slammed into tents, severing one of the militia men in half.

Injured inhabitants, bleeding from shrapnel, fled in all directions. Some wailed in pain. Some were engulfed in flames.

The militia returned fire, to no great effect, as the helicopters landed along the outside of the junk wall. The NDF soldiers exiting the grounded choppers were fully suited in riot gear, shielded and carrying electrified batons. Shocking shock troops.

Nate's mind raced with a flurry of analytical thoughts and historical recollections.

How did we get here? He knew the answers.

For a decade now, the NDF was always mentioned in the daily headline news, as omnipresent a threat in the psyche as ever in the ravaged landscape. Maybe longer. When you're neck-deep in

238

fascism, it feels like forever.

As a propaganda tool for extracting coercion and control, the NDF was oppressively potent. And as a convergence of military and police forces during The Long Collapse, the NDF seemed almost inevitable in retrospect.

As America faced more internal strife and domestic unrest, local police were so frequently overwhelmed that a regular military presence became all but necessary. The militarization of police gear and tactics merged with the regular deployment of National Guard forces.

But "keeping the peace" proved too broad an objective given the constant state of chaos from climate disruption, economic collapse, mass migration of native and foreign-born communities, shortages of food and housing, failing power grids, and the widespread availability of military-style weaponry coupled with growing militant sentiments among the angry populace.

A National Defense Force (NDF) initiative was the result.

Sure, its passage through Congress and signing into law generated controversy from fringe groups to the left and right alike, but most people were too busy struggling to survive. Some even welcomed the prospect of "law and order" to "clean up the streets" with a consolidated military presence.

And at first, that outcome seemed feasible, if not inevitable. However, as at least two eccentric political economists predicted in the mid 2030s, no country's economic output was great enough to fund a 24/7/365 military presence from sea to polluted sea.

The NDF became favored by political leaders for two things: fortifying government centers and launching a strike force at designated targets.

Tonight's raid was the latter. Nate had heard of the NDF before but had never seen their warcraft up close until now. And they were brutally efficient.

Taking a position on the outer junk wall to either side of the freshly-smoldering opening, the NDF soldiers fired Triple Gas into the camp. This formed a drifting cloud of three particulate compounds: concentrated tear gas, pungent stink gas, and a crippling nerve agent.

Triple Gas was formulated to disrupt, disperse, and ultimately disable crowds. It's legality was questionable, but its efficacy was absolute.

Nate gathered himself and fled. The gunfire continued to rip close behind him, some shots rapid and others intermittent. It was an instant war zone.

By the time Nate reached the chow tent, Salmon Stinks was engulfed in complete pandemonium. Some locals had stocked improvised explosives and they were going off in all directions. Even commercial fireworks were flashing and flying fast.

The shanty town was now an ignited powder keg. Detonation imminent.

Scanning the interior end to end, Nate saw no sign of his friends. Of course not. It has been several minutes since the air horn sounded and the initial explosions.

They must have taken cover. But with Dugen in his present condition, they couldn't have gone far.

Nate dropped to his knees, heaving for each breath, crawling for safety.

The Reddard Faction had clearly trained for this as everyone seemed prepared for an intruder and drilled for it, much like at Fenix Farm. Survival wasn't an abstraction during The Long Collapse; it was part of the regular routine.

The families which had been dining in the chow tent earlier were gone. The cooking pot was emptied of beans and rice but still warm. Wherever everyone had fled, they did so in a hurry.

"Nate!" Jill shouted over the constant commotion and gunfire.

Nate looked over to see Jill squatted down behind an overturned table propped up by shipping crates. He crawled over to her, lugging his backpack and the folding wheelchair strapped to it.

"Hey, everyone okay?" Nate looked behind the table to see Sasha leaned against it, Dugen in her arms. They both looked rattled but level-headed.

"So far. What's going on out there?" Jill instantly snapped back into crisis management mode, this time over a calamity of explosions instead of tanking quarterly earnings.

"It's an NDF raid." Nate looked to Jill and Sasha, who seemed wanting for more explanation.

"NDF sucks! Fascist fucks, all of them." Dugen muttered. He had evaded their wrath before.

"NDF is military police. They take no prisoners, trained for sweeping out encampments like this. Seems like the Reddards were prepping for a fight and now they have one."

Nate continued catching his breath. He hadn't sprinted like that in years. Jill should be proud.

"Not our fight. You got that wheelchair? Begged, borrowed, or stolen, I don't care." Jill was prepping her team for an extraction.

No one was coming to save them, and certainly not a battalion of shock troopers. They might still be Salmon Springs College Homecomers, but they looked like Reddard sympathizers to the NDF.

"Let's fix up these wheels and roll Dugen out of here, fast. We can head outta this tent and straight for the gate at the far end of the camp, right into Buckson Park. Once we're in the woods, we should be clear of the crossfire."

Nate looked over at the blankets wrapped around the makeshift stretcher.

"We need the blankets to patch up this wheelchair and secure Dugen in it, then we can use the wooden branches to fight our way out of here if we have to."

"We're glad you came back." Sasha smiled through the pain of their present circumstance.

"Speak for yourself." Dugen grinned. He managed to push off the wooden crate with his arms.

"Now make like a good NASCAR pit crew and prep my wheels for victory."

Nate shook his head and rolled his eyes. It was almost offensive how casually Dugen responded in a crisis. He was lucky to have them. They were lucky to have Dugen.

Unfolding the wheelchair, Nate and Jill bound the blankets around the frame to cover the frayed vinyl material and make the seat sturdy enough to sit in again.

"Good as new." Sasha helped Dugen into the chair, now cushioned with blankets. Jill and Nate quickly wrapped Dugen in another blanket, securing him into the chair.

"We're going to race you out of here, that's for sure. Strapping you in because it could be a bumpy ride and there's no seat belt." Nate was explaining this to himself as much as to Dugen.

There was a lull in the gunfire. Jill stood up and looked in all directions. This was their getaway window. "Got everything? Let's move."

"Hang on, brother." Nate grabbed the handles of Dugen's wheelchair and pushed off, heading towards the exit of the chow tent.

Jill took the lead, checking the exit for hazards, then looking back with a motion to continue. Sasha stayed with Nate, spotting Dugen just in case they needed support. She gathered any remaining packs she could carry for whatever lie ahead.

As the NDF troops advanced block by decrepit block through the tent city, Reddard militia battalions grouped in flanking positions. They were locked and reloaded. This was going to be a brutal episode of urban warfare.

"How I spent my homecoming weekend!" Dugen mixed severity with sarcasm.

Jill advanced out of the tent as Nate wheeled Dugen right behind her. Sasha followed closely, never wanting them separated again until everyone was safe and sound.

Jill pulled her hair back into a messy bun and peered around the next corner. She was scouting their escape route one row of tents at a time. A straight line through was the preferable course in the interest of minimizing distance, but a dangerous path could result in an untimely end to their escape.

Up ahead Reddard militia forces took position against a concrete barrier originally marking a freeway exit. Now it served as cover for taking fire and returning it.

A steady stream of elderly and young people in ragged clothes fled in the other direction. Some were limping. A woman carried a child's limp body. The screams were a mix of fright and exhaustion.

"Let's turn here. This way is bad news." Jill grabbed Dugen's hand.

Nate gripped Dugen's wheelchair handles. Sasha held onto Nate's belt loop. The Homecomers formed a tight line to stay together no matter what.

As the NDF troops advanced, they fired another barrage of Triple Gas canisters towards the Reddard's concrete barrier position. Prepared for this, the Reddards quickly donned gas masks from an army surplus crate tucked away in their outpost. They returned fire.

BANG-BANG-BANG!

BANG-BANG-BANG!

BANG-BANG-BANG!

Jill led her friends around the back of the tent cluster and sprinted as fast as the Homecomers caravan would allow. If they were hit with Triple Gas, there was no chance they would escape intact and in due time.

"INCOMING!"

244

The Reddards returned fire on the NDF and lobbed a claymore bomb in their direction. Covered in tar, nails, bolts, and screws, it exploded in an array of hot metal shrapnel. The NDF retreated behind a barrier of riot shields, then fired upon the Reddard position.

BANG-BANG-BANG!

BANG-BANG-BANG!

BANG-BANG-BANG!

This was a familiar destructive dance to both sides. The Reddards had driven the NDF out of Salmon Stinks initially and maintained their hold on the tent city for years now. When the Reddards pushed towards the city center, the NDF pushed back. Months could pass with little change in their territory. The embattled region had become a modern day No Man's Land of urbanized trench warfare.

But now, the federal government had consolidated its resources and prioritized breaking up the Reddards and other militia groups.

There was an active military draft and in The Long Collapse, it seemed like a lottery ticket to be called up to fight for the cause of the state... as long as it came with 'three hots and a cot.'

While the Reddards could not recruit on the basis of such niceties, many militia members were themselves disillusioned ex-military or police. "The old cops at war with new cops" was a common reference these days.

And so the bloody ballet of bullets and bombs continued. There wasn't much infrastructure left in Salmon Stinks anyway, so it was a veritable war zone just waiting for the requisite war.

Jill crouched against wooden pallets piled high with collapsed cardboard. She looked back to see Nate catching his breath, Dugen crouched low, and Sasha keeping pace with backpacks in tow.

"Gimme that." Jill reached for one of Sasha's bags. "You don't have to carry all that. Besides, I'm thirsty. We're all exhausted. This is one marathon I didn't sign up for."

Jill passed around a full bottle of water as the booms and snaps of warfare reverberated in all directions.

"Maybe I brought all this on us." Nate muttered. "I deserve to be stuck here. But none of you do." Nate fell to his knees and groaned as he rolled onto his back. It was too much.

"None of us asked for this. But whatever we think we deserve, we are going to get through it." Sasha was determined.

"I have a family to get back to and a farm to run. We all have lives to lead. Maybe we will all laugh it off after we survive this, but for now... this is just another car wreck for us to get through."

Sasha paused and looked each of her friends in the eyes. "What? That's it. That's the whole pep talk."

Everyone grinned, with their eyes if not with their lips. "Now let's go!"

Jill led the group around the pallet and a quick dash through an open clearing onto the perimeter of the junk wall.

"Okay, we've reached the far side of the camp. The gate to Buckson Park should be just ahead, maybe a 100 meter dash at most!"

Just as the Homecomers edged closer to the city-side exit of Salmon Stinks, a pair of attack choppers flew overhead. The cacophony of motors and gunfire was overwhelming.

The Reddards opened fire on the helicopters, white streaks of the bullet barrage cutting through the night sky as rapid comets with a death wish.

BANG-BANG-BANG! BANG-BANG-BANG!

The helicopters circled around and unleashed machine gun fire from mounted turrets.

The Reddards retreated behind their concrete barriers, then fled along dug-in trenches which looped back around through tent encampments. This was par for the course of urban warfare.

Dugen looked up into the night sky as white-hot bullets whizzed by and the fires of battle spread across the tent encampment.

"The human experience is highly flammable. The vastness of space is a flame retardant. This is why we were never meant to leave this rock."

"Save it for your next sermon." Nate pushed Dugen along as the wheelchair bumped and rocked over the uneven ground. It was a good suggestion, perhaps for another time.

"This used to be the park entrance to Buckson. See the gravel and painted rocks?"

Jill followed along the markings of what was once a large parking area before the tent city had covered the region entirely.

Sasha reached down and picked up a painted rock from the gravel spread. A souvenir for Rylar and the kids from her unspeakable Homecoming travels.

The Reddards had stockpiled heavy armament, as well.

As the NDF attack choppers circled back for another hail of bullets, one of the militants—positioned behind a chunk of freeway overpass—loaded a rocket launcher.

Aim. Fire. The sharp hiss pierced the night air.

Fffffffffffffffffffffffffffft...

BOOM.

One of the helicopters careened into the encampment, set ablaze from the impact of the rocket. As the flames spread, more of the tent city caught fire in waves of roaring combustion.

The Reddards cheered.

The NDF troops opened fire.

The remaining attack chopper took position for more machine gun rounds. Another militant readied his rocketfire from behind a hallowed-out 18-wheeler.

"Let's go, let's go!" Nate pushed Dugen faster, with Jill and Sasha staying in tight formation.

The crowds of fleeing tent city occupants intensified as the raging flames and jarring explosions rocked the encampment. Some appeared practiced, as though they had trained for this, as though this was not their first evacuation from a war zone.

The NDF troops continued to advance even as more rocket fire exploded in the sky above them.

Firing their Triple Gas rounds, pitch black riot gear with night vision goggles and sealed helmets, these were the anonymous servants of unquestioned authority.

Under the pale moon's glow, over half the slums of Salmon Stinks were burned, emptied, or both.

This was standard protocol. For a decade now, the NDF had become quite experienced with sweeping encampments, kettling dissidents, and taking no one into custody.

They were "tough on crime." The NDF had no medical support or secondary units to provide aid. They were trained only to disrupt and disperse areas under militia control or unauthorized occupancy. They were the lethal eviction squad.

No one remembered how the NDF acquired such sweeping military authority, but everyone knew it was too late to revoke it.

As the four Homecomers reached the entrance to Buckson Park, the desperate crowds all but stampeded over the flimsy fenced gate.

A simple pair of wire cutters made short work of the mesh fencing, followed by arms and legs pushing open the widening hole in all directions. A few drops of blood dripped here and there from the hasty escape, but the raging flames behind the fleeing occupants presented a far worse fate.

Jill stood at the makeshift entryway as the last of a large group squeezed through the fencing. She prepared Dugen's legs as Nate hoisted him up by the shoulders.

"Never knew how it felt to be wrapped for mummification, but now I do!" Dugen looked around as Jill and Nate carried him through the hole in the fence, careful not to get caught on any jagged metal edges. The scrapes, bruises, and gunshots they had endured thus far were injuries enough for one weekend.

"Achievement unlocked."

As Sasha pushed the folded wheelchair through the hole in the fencing, she looked back once more. The flames had spread across the entire perimeter of Salmon Stinks, buttressed only by the towering wall of junk from the Timberline Bluff road to Cotter's Corner.

This was the night Salmon Stinks burned to the ground.

The Reddard militia battalions had disbanded. A few holdouts still took a position to return fire, but then fled nonetheless. They were determined to fight another day.

The NDF troops had cleared the encampment. A large military truck mounted with an industrial-sized plow pushed through the tents, cardboard, and wooden shelters. The high beams and spot lights scoured the horizon for any remaining resistance.

Sasha sighed. She knew the residents of this and many other tent cities had nowhere else to go. Any possessions they had were burned up or crushed down. There was never any relief or respite for the least fortunate, the least affluent, the least able to survive.

The Long Collapse had pulled the thin veneer of civilization off the vast expanse of chaos beneath it.

"Lady... lady... please..." Sasha heard a voice from behind a pile of debris and mangled tarps. She looked to Nate as he situated Dugen back in his wheelchair.

Jill wrapped Dugen's blanket around the mangled wheelchair seat.

Sasha stepped over the loose fencing to see a frail, writhing figure trapped under a heavy chunk of bricks and wood scraps.

"Nate, can you help me with this? There's a guy trapped under there." Jill stayed with Dugen as Nate crawled back through the hole in the fence to assist Sasha.

"We gotta get outta here now, Sasha." Nate looked ahead as the NDF troops continued to advance through the blazing encampment, the rack of lights from the armored truck nearly blinding.

"Just help me lift this for him, then we'll go."

Sasha began to pull off the smaller debris and Nate hoisted a large section of brick and mortar. He looked down to see the injured man turn towards them with newfound mobility.

It was the lean, gaunt man from the Timberline Bluff parking lot. He looked dazed, fazed, and on the verge of death.

"No fucking way. Really?" Nate muttered to himself. The gaunt man looked up and recognized Nate. A mix of fear and relief washed over his tarnished features.

"Hey listen, hey listen, man... I screwed up. It's all fucked up. It's all over, man. I was just selling scrap to provide for me and mine. But now... but now..."

The gaunt man wheezed. Nate looked down to survey his injuries. He had been shot in the gut and was slowly bleeding out.

"I don't know if we can take him." Nate turned to Sasha, betraying a confluence of emotions in his eyes. In a dire moment of crisis, vengeance is a luxury few can afford.

"We can't just leave him, Nate." Sasha said it, but she didn't fully mean it. She knew their circumstances were already beyond boundless charity, whatever her ideals. She saw the gaunt man was mere moments from death.

"No, no." The gaunt man hoisted himself up slightly as his mangled legs emerged from beneath a tattered tarp and splinters of wood.

"I'm done for. Finito. Over. But... my daughter, my Cassie... she's hiding where I told her to."

The gaunt man pointed to a small tool shed along the junk heap wall. Nate looked over, then to Sasha. "Please, she don't deserve none of this. Take her with you."

Sasha didn't hesitate. She sprinted to the run-down shed structure and knocked on the broadest side.

"Hey, hey... Cassie?"

A small door opened, almost as a crawlspace entrance. From it emerged a small set of hands, then the blackened cheeks and bright eyes of a cherubic little girl's face. She still wore a bright orange bow in her hair, though it was dulled considerably from all the dust.

She recognized Sasha from the chow tent.

"Hey Cassie, I'm Sasha. Your dad is hurt and he needs you to come with us now. But we have to hurry, okay?"

Cassie looked frightened but determined. She nodded and held out her hands.

Sasha leaned down and set her eyes upon Cassie with a reflection of the girl's own resolve.

"Are you ready to run fast? Can you show me how you run fast?"

Cassie nodded again.

Sasha took Cassie's hand as they stood. Cassie was alert but in shock, compliant but without full comprehension of the chaos.

Nate turned and stepped away.

"Can't let her see me like this." The gaunt man coughed up blood and slunk back against the pile of bricks. "She's a great kid. She never knew what I did, what I had to do. Just knew to hide from danger until it was safe." The gaunt man closed his eyes. "Until it was safe."

Nate motioned for Sasha to go, so she quickly guided Cassie along the junk wall until they reached the hole in the fencing leading to Buckson Park.

Nate looked back at the gaunt man as he looked upon Cassie one last time. Sasha helped Cassie through the break in the fence and they disappeared into the darkness of dense brush and foliage along with Jill and Dugen. They had escaped. They were going to be safe.

"We will take care of her for you." Nate turned to leave.

"Hey man, what's... what's your name?" The gaunt man was fading fast now.

"Nate." Nate didn't want to know the gaunt man's name. He wanted to leave all these memories behind as much as possible. He felt his inner core actively resisting any influx of empathy, any showering of sorrow. He was emotionally spent. He was rationing any last feelings for his own crew and that was it.

"Sorry about your truck, Nate. Nothing personal."

"Yeah... sorry I shot at you, nothing personal. But you did return fire and hit my friend pretty bad. We're headed to city center for his treatment now."

"This world wrecks us all, Nate. Is there any good left in it?" The gaunt man ran his hands along the rubble, painting it with fresh blood. It was a work of memorial art for a destroyed encampment.

Nate sighed. He didn't know the answer to that question.

"Still looking for it." Nate looked up as the NDF troops brandished their shock batons. They were too close. The flames were too close.

Nate turned and ran as fast as his sore feet would carry him, through the hole in the fence and into the woodland outskirts of Buckson Park. At a quick pace, he would catch up to the other Homecomers in short order.

The gaunt man let out a final sigh as the NDF troops surrounded him and drew their sidearms. He looked up at them with a disinterested defiance, his eyes glazed over.

"I ain't arguing with you. I'm arguing with God. You're just in the way."

Black armor from head to toe, these anonymous executioners did not hesitate, especially with a known Reddard loyalist.

> BANG.
> > BANG-BANG-BANG.
> > > BANG.

The fury of pistol fire was muted amidst the roar of the ensuing tent city fire. The fresh blood dried upon the rubble, as all blood does.

After their defeat at Salmon Stinks, the Reddard Faction disbanded... but would regroup in the next town over, the next tent city, the next underground resistance.

No doubt the brutal NDF purge of Salmon Stinks would radicalize many more transients to join the cause, taking up arms against an oppressive police state; no doubt such uprisings would escalate NDF crack-downs against Reddard Faction cells as the insurgents rebelled.

Military versus militia. Each a pretext for the other, one as the justification for the other's actions. Everyone lost count as to who started it. Both sides remained intent to deliver the final blow.

After tonight, Salmon Stinks would be come to be known as the Salmon Scrapyard. Hundreds of people could not evacuate in time and were consumed by the flames. Those who did escape vowed to move on.

From upon Cotter's Corner, it was plain to see why few would ever return to such a charred, haunted human graveyard of a place.

Yet as with the charred skeleton of Salmon Springs College, so too would the Salmon Scrapyard flourish with a verdant, lush undergrowth in the decades to come.

In the blink of geological time, all this unspeakable suffering would be plowed under; a civilization's corpse into a cadaverous bloom.

[16 – Through Buckson By Dawn]

The cool October night air concealed the crisp bite of winter. This alone was a remarkable occurrence as global temperatures continued to rise. The cooling of the Earth's surface by nightfall was the only remaining respite to the unrelenting heat in an expanding climate band from the equator outward in either direction. The Pacific Northwest had become a popular refuge for this reason – for humans and animals alike.

Each toad, cicada, and cricket chirped and cooed as the first light of dawn staged its arrival upon the horizon. Cassie had grown up in one encampment after another and had never been in a natural landscape overnight. With her orange bow swaying back and forth, she focused upon every noise in the darkness, finding it to be new; a curiosity made fascinating by its suggestion of a deeper pattern. The expansive synchronicity of nature.

"When's my dad coming?" Cassie looked up at Sasha with open

inquisitiveness. Sasha looked to Nate but the pale morning light concealed his somber glance.

"Hold up a minute" Sasha spoke in a loud whisper. She didn't want to give away their location to any NDF troops or Reddard soldiers who could be scouring the area for the second pickings of a firefight.

She knelt down and took Cassie's hands in hers. At a short distance, their eyes met in the low visibility of forest twilight.

"Your dad didn't make it out, Cassie. His last wish was for us to take you with us. So you're one of us now." Sasha looked up at Nate.

Jill stood behind Dugen in his wheelchair. They remained still and tried to convey a unified front of hospitality. Of family.

"... One of you?" Cassie looked across the four adults like it was an altogether silly proposition.

"One of the Homecomers!" Dugen raised an imaginary glass of the finest party wine.

"We're going home?" Cassie was puzzled yet delighted.

"That's right" Sasha spoke with a soothing reassurance. She parted Cassie's long, dark hair and untangled it.

"You've never been to this home, but it can be..." Sasha stopped, then finished the sentence she knew to be in her heart. "... your forever home. With chickens, and goats, and cats, and a new brother and sister."

Sasha's eyes became misty. She missed Fenix Farm. And from the moment she helped Cassie through the broken fence on the edge of Salmon Stinks, she knew that Cassie would fit right in with her raucous, resourceful survivorship of a family.

The trees rustled.

"Shh, shhh. Get down." Jill had remained on the alert and heard movement. She pulled Dugen's wheelchair back into a secluded patch off their trail.

Nate helped Sasha and Cassie into the same alcove of foliage. He reached down and gripped his pocket knife. His heart raced as what felt like the last ounce of burning adrenaline rushed through his muscles.

The sound of plodding feet upon the trail. Some dull murmurs. Clanking metal. Nate readied his knife. In the darkness, he drew up his imaginary foe. A Reddard faction? An NDF battalion?

No. It was another group of fleeing encampment refugees.

Nate stayed in a low crouching position his blade ready. There was no telling who was out there, what they wanted, or if they posed a danger.

Jill crouched low with Sasha and Cassie by her side. She had covered Dugen's face and upper body in a blanket. That finally shut him up.

After a moment, the tromping upon the dirt path faded into the distance. Better to have these escapees pioneer the path forward before the Homecomers met an unpleasant fate before them.

Nate heaved a sigh of relief and sheathed his knife. Once the sounds of the woodland twilight in Buckson Park returned, Nate stood.

"I think we're clear," he whispered to Jill. Their trek resumed.

Sasha held her by the hand as Cassie walked along, eyes glancing up at the forest canopy and down into the thick vegetation and pond formations.

Initially designed as a city pond and garden, the outskirts of Buckson Park had grown completely, unrecognizably wild. Having been built as an artificial wetland of sorts, human neglect had given way to a vibrant flourish of nature.

Jill steadily pushed Dugen along as he muttered something resembling a morose lullaby.

> *the deepest sleep*
> *of miles and millennia*
> *to slumber into*
> *a lifetime of wakeful rest*
> *elate enlightened eyelids*
> *putting sullen dreamscape to the test*
>
> *better a sailor lost*
> *in the ocean wide*
> *than an ocean lost*
> *to a sailor's pride*
>
> *the mumble corps it fumbles more*
> *blighted seacoast foam ashore*
> *ignore, adore, it matters not*
> *across oceanic temporal waves*
> *capsizing consciousness*
> *daybreak knight awash the more it saves*

Other than Dugen's dour poetics, no one spoke for a very long time.

The Homecomers kept a slow but steady pace, as though methodically wringing out their last reserves of energy. Sasha had been to Buckson Park during her college years for an annual food and music festival called Summer Buckson Bash, but it was shuttered and all but forgotten by now.

The path through the park was ceremoniously winding by design. It was never intended to be an overgrown obstacle while making a beeline for urgent medical care at Salmon Springs General in the city center. So when the path would curve around, the weary group would try to head straight through. Problem being, Dugen's rickety wheelchair provided little traction through thick, overgrown grass and shrubs. Thus, it was a meandering route along the paved path.

Sasha released Cassie's hand from hers as they plodded along. Cassie proved to be a resilient and stalwart little hiker. Nate had assumed he would be carrying her by piggyback at this point. He looked ahead as the glow of twilight cast more detail upon the contours of the forestry around them.

The sound of a trickling brook? Nate turned his head to one side.

Why yes, off to one side of the trail was a cracked and ruined park fountain structure. The pipe beneath it was still pumping a steady stream.

"Thirsty?" Nate motioned for the group to join him. He refilled his canteen and took a sip. It was cold, it was wet, it tasted clean. Even a belly full of water could feel filling for a few minutes.

Cassie splashed and giggled as she cupped her hands and drank from the fountainhead. The soggy ground was covered in peat moss and the entire area had transformed into a micro-swamp. No wonder the frogs were croaking so profusely.

Jill refilled her water bottle and shared with Sasha and Dugen. None had drank since their dinner in the chow tent, before the horrors of the night raid. Before the burning of Salmon Stinks.

For this moment, every thirst was quenched.

Pressing further on the trail, the thick undergrowth had claimed a wooden walkway and a gazebo. Now half caved in, the underside was covered with dried mud, branches, and dead leaves to form a dozen bird nests.

Suitably situated, the former picnic area had become an open aviary—a shrine to thrushes, swallows, and shrikes.

Nate looked ahead to see movement between the tree limbs.

"Stop, stop." He whispered. Nate crouched and pulled a pair of binoculars from his pack. Once on a nature hike, always on a nature hike. Nate the Great.

"Holy fuck!" he exclaimed in a raspy intonation beneath his breath.

"Oh, sorry." Nate winced at Sasha, but Cassie looked onward without any offense. Growing up in encampments had desensitized her to casual swearing.

"What's that?" Sasha saw it, too.

Several small deer moved along the treeline, more as silhouettes in the twilight than fully revealed figures. Jill stopped pushing Dugen as he looked in the same direction.

"Good eye, Nate. And woah... are those..." Dugen squinted.

"Spotted red deer. Thought to be extinct decades ago." Nate looked closely at their gait, the nape and shoulders. Had to be.

"Definitely spotted reds. Wow. I never thought I would see them in my lifetime." Nate knelt to hand Cassie the binoculars. She rubbed her eyes and held them to her face with Nate's guidance.

"So pretty." Cassie smiled and shrieked. The deer stiffened with alertness. Cassie looked to Nate as he put his finger to her lips.

"They are very shy, Cassie." Nate whispered, channeling his days as a park ranger and wildlife interpreter. "These deer may have never seen people before. They are very new to this area. This used to be a city park. Now, it is their home."

Nate looked back up as the deer relaxed and returned to foraging. "It's their forest home."

"Wonder what they taste like" Dugen snickered.

Jill jabbed him in the shoulder. "What? I'm getting hungry."

"We're about halfway through the park, I think" Sasha whispered. It had been so long. She was trying to remember where the statue was. That marked the center of Buckson Park.

Nate kept low, savoring what felt like a historic wildlife safari. Was he the first to rediscover a species once thought extinct? He slid his camera out of his bag and took the best photos he could under poor lighting conditions.

SNAP. SNAP.

SNAP. SNAP.

The images captured the red spotted deer well enough. "Surely these will be at least as convincing as those grainy, blurry Sasquatch sightings." Nate thought aloud.

The deer slowly moved along. Nate pulled out the last energy bar from the bottom of his pack. It likely expired years ago, but with some kneading and heat from cupped hands, it was edible nonetheless. Nate divided it into more or less equal chunks and offered them to his companions.

Cassie gladly accepted.

So did Dugen.

Sasha courteously received the thoughtful gesture.

"Gross, no." Jill was not *that* hungry. She donated her portion to Cassie, a gesture met with exuberance.

It was a modest breakfast, to be sure, but one that marked a sense of respite, of sanctuary. The weary Homecomers and their mighty little plus one drew in more relaxed breaths. The sounds of explosions behind them had subsided. There were no more helicopters buzzing overhead, no more overbearing trucks, no ricochet of gunfire, no blazing flames, no chaotic screams and shrieks.

The morning dew glistened as the new dawn illuminated the overgrown park, itself a reclamation of undergrowth into its former undisturbed terrain. With tranquility came the luxury of taking in their surroundings – one inhale, one exhale at a time.

"Hey, you doing okay?" Jill nudged Dugen as he finished his stale energy bar.

"I'm doing better than ole Reginald Buckson over there." Dugen snickered.

"What?" Jill found Dugen impossible. Even a simple wellness check invited some random, jocular response.

"Look just beyond the treeline up ahead, where the overgrown sidewalk slabs all converge."

Dugen pointed. Sasha and Nate looked, as well.

"I remember that statue now." Sasha took several steps forward. Cassie had stuffed her face full and was crawling under the bushes to get a better view.

"Reginald 'Reggie' Buckson." Nate approached the clearing in the forest to see the center of Buckson Park, a monument and series of placards in honor of the park's namesake.

Sasha looked around to see no danger, no other presence in the park's center. That sensation brought about a minor epiphany which had been nagging at her for some time now.

In these run-down locales so common in The Long Collapse, any potential human presence was a sign of danger, but also one of potential salvation. They could be attacked, mugged, shot, or kidnapped... yet also could be guided, fed, sheltered, or protected.

Humans were the variable; nature was the constant.

The danger of strangers, the kindness of the Good Samaritan... both inextricably bound up in the same unknown potential. In a zero trust, emaciated hull of a society, each left to 'fend for themselves' required an instant reading of every situation, a snap judgment about each individual, because it was always feast or famine, fight or flight, collaboration or rivalry; a high risk, low reward duality.

And at this point, it was too mentally exhausting. It was too physically taxing. Even for the most sociable among the Homecomers, an abandoned city park was now an ideal city park. Surely the spotted red deer agreed.

Nate arrived at the base of the monument first, studying how the statue had been ripped from its base and dragged across the lawn. Now wildly overgrown, the gargantuan statue of Reginald

Buckson was consumed in vines, weeds, and a coat of moss and lichens.

Jill forcefully wheeled Dugen through the thick bed of grass to the monument.

Sasha joined them. She remembered the monument intact, the statue in stark relief with a gaze outward with Salmon Springs directly ahead.

Cassie showed little interest as she foraged a nearby patch of brambles for ripe blackberries.

Jill looked over at the fallen statue. "I see what you mean, Dugen. You *are* looking better than Reginald Buckson."

"Yeah, I'm still partially upright." Dugen concurred.

"And not covered in slime." Jill added.

"Moss." Dugen knew the difference.

Jill did, as well, but anything green and slippery was probably also a type of slime.

Nate brushed away the vines and dirt covering the plaque mounted at the base of the statue. The full illumination of sunrise was still an hour from now. He pulled a flashlight from his pack and pointed it at the bronze lettering embossed on the plaque.

"GREATNESS STARTS WITH VISION"

– REGINALD 'REGGIE' BUCKSON

BORN JULY 11, 1918 | DIED NOVEMBER 3, 1996

REGINALD 'REGGIE' BUCKSON WAS BORN IN SALMON SPRINGS TO TAGGART AND IDA BUCKSON. QUICK TO STUDY AND PICK UP ANY SPORT, REGINALD ENTERED THE MAJOR LEAGUES OF THE GREAT AMERICAN GAME OF BASEBALL IN 1937, WHERE HE PLAYED FOR THE BROOKLYN DODGERS UNTIL HE WAS DRAFTED IN OCTOBER 1940.

FIGHTING IN THE ARMY'S 29TH INFANTRY DIVISION, BUCKSON LANDED ON OMAHA BEACH DURING THE HISTORIC D-DAY ALLIED INVASION TO DEFEAT THE NAZI FORCES IN OCCUPIED FRANCE. BUCKSON WAS HONORABLY DISCHARGED IN 1948, HAVING ATTAINED THE RANK OF SERGEANT FIRST CLASS.

HE RESUMED PLAYING FOR THE BROOKLYN DODGERS AND WON THE 1955 WORLD SERIES, THEN RETIRED FROM HIS FAVORITE GAME TO RETURN TO SALMON SPRINGS AND STARTED A SUCCESSFUL AUTO DEALERSHIP, A THRIVING CONSTRUCTION COMPANY, AND A REKNOWNED EQUITY CONSULTING FIRM.

BUCKSON WAS MARRIED TWICE, RAISING THREE SONS AND FIVE DAUGHTERS, ALL IN SALMON SPRINGS. HE IS NOW SURVIVED BY

OVER TWENTY GRANDCHILDREN AND GREAT GRANDCHILDREN.

BUCKSON PIONEERED HIS OWN BRAND OF GREATNESS AND EMBODIED THE CAN-DO DYNAMISM OF THE AMERICAN SPIRIT! HE BELIEVED IN THE POTENTIAL OF EACH INDIVIDUAL TO MAKE A DIFFERENCE AND BE A FORCE FOR GOOD IN THE WORLD.

WE DEDICATE THIS PARK IN HIS MEMORY TO INSPIRE FUTURE GENERATIONS OF SALMON SPRINGS DREAMERS OF ALL AGES!

- Erected by the Friends of Reginald Buckson, July 11, 2018

Nate read the plaque aloud as a good field guide should. "Well, good for him. A shame what happened to his statue, and his park."

Nate put his flashlight away and looked around. "Although... I wonder if Buckson was a conservationist. Maybe what he really wanted was to maintain a wildlife sanctuary for the spotted red deer."

"Fuck that guy." Dugen laughed, almost gleeful at his opportunity to speak ill of the dead. But it was a social transgression with a purpose. Dugen glanced over to see Cassie gathering berries at a good distance from the Homecomers. He continued his anti-eulogy.

"Reginald Buckson was a wife-beater and child abuser, a raging alcoholic, an avowed racist, and his construction company bulldozed the land sacred to indigenous tribes to build this park. But you'll never see that printed on any plaque because history is written by the victors. And this guy was a 'winner' by the dominant culture's standards, so he is lionized on this plaque and with this monument. Not surprised it was torn down and dragged through the mud, like his reputation."

"Do you remember when the statue was torn down?" Sasha had heard about it, but never visited the park once it became overgrown and rampant with wild animals.

"I dunno, 2030 maybe... maybe later. Kind of a dividing line for the beginning of The Long Collapse if you ask me." Dugen was feeling rested and talkative again, whether or not the other three approved.

"The falling of the statue represented the delegitimation of Salmon Springs as a culmination of Western Expansionism, of its ethos and civic mandate. Buckson was seen as a national hero who lived the American dream. He was mythologized to represent the best of Salmon Springs... And I'm sure all of that effusive praise on the monument is true. But it ain't the whole truth. Probably ain't half of it."

Jill sat in the grass and stretched. The ligaments in her knees were flaring up again. Maybe she needed to be hospitalized more than the loudmouth she was pushing around.

"Because what I know came from student protesters on campus when we were at SSC. Even back then, they wanted the monument removed. They wanted the park renamed. They called Buckson a colonizer... which in the strict historical sense isn't true, but arguably Buckson was a paragon of a kind of ideological colonialism. This is what America is, this is who a real American is."

Dugen looked over at the monument, a metallic casualty of conflicting histories.

"Honestly, I feel sorry for the guy. He got 'shell shocked' resulting in PTSD from the war. Nobody treated that shit effectively back then. He self-medicated with drinking. He took it out on his wife and kids. Blamed America's problems on integration of schools and interracial marriage. Rumor has it that several of his kids went to SSC before we did... but changed their names so nobody would know. Even better rumor was that he raped a black house servant and had an interracial bastard child but never acknowledged it happened, just paid her off to be silent."

"Yeah, I can see that." Nate brushed the mossy covering from the statue's face, revealing a stoic conviction set in bronze, now rusted and disfigured.

Sasha sighed. This wasn't on her Homecoming tour itinerary for a reason.

"Well, we all want permission to dream. We all want those permission structures. Monuments uplifting historical figures can provide that. But imagine who else could have stood here. What would their story have been? Whose dreams could they have inspired?"

Sasha mused openly, remembering the feminist icons and peace activists she studied and wrote about in college. "Show me your monuments and I will tell you what your society professes to value."

Dugen interjected. "I just wish I was here to watch them wrap a chain around his neck and tow him off his soap box with a light-duty pickup truck!"

"VROOOM VROOOOM VROOOOOOOOOM!"

Dugen laughed and made revving noises.

"The statue, I mean. Not the guy. Fuck that guy." Dugen chuckled again.

"Do you think this park un-names itself eventually?" Nate couldn't get the spotted red deer out of his mind. They looked so calm, without fear, even without knowledge they were thought to be extinct.

"Maybe... maybe the statue and monument will become completely covered by vegetation and the park ceases to exist. The guy will go down in the history books, but the land never belonged to him. The wild is already reclaiming it."

"I'm sure Buckson is pushing up daisies... just like his monument." Jill stood and looked around. She was not amused.

"Can we go now? Everyone rested? Shared enough of their feelings? Do we need to sing a rousing eulogy in honor of the baseball legend and war hero, or keep kicking him while he's down? Or something else?"

Jill was probably 'hangry' after skipping their breakfast of dubious quality and not sleeping much the last few nights. But she wasn't done venting. She pointed at Sasha and Nate.

"And you two are in charge of pushing this charming paraplegic sociopath from here on out, okay? I've carried more than my weight thus far. And we aren't stopping again until we reach the hospital in city center... unless, unless it's for a hot shower and a double mocha latte."

Dugen liked when Jill would get short-tempered. It made her even cuter. If he could still get one, he would have a hard-on for hangry Jill.

Sasha nodded and deescalated with her body language. She knew everyone was at their wit's end. Fatigue and hunger never brought out the best in anyone. "Okay, totally fine."

Nate tapped the fallen Buckson statue on the shoulder.

"Thanks for the park, bud." He stood to leave.

Sasha looked around. "Where's Cassie?"

She traced her eyes along the edge of the forest, following the berry brush, and spotted the orange bow snagged on a bramble.

"Oh no." Sasha's heart sank and she ran with panic flooding through her veins.

Jill stood, alert and adroit.

Nate took on the Dugen wheelchair duties.

As Sasha reached the orange bow swaying in the berry bush, she looked ahead to see the remnants of a playground. The slide had fallen, much like the statue of Reginald Buckson. The swing sets were a mangled mess of rusted chains and overgrown vines. A series of climbing bars were almost unrecognizable as climbing vegetation had covered them.

And yet there was still a simple merry-go-round, slowly spinning, with Cassie atop it.

The equipment was rusty and bent, yet it spun in an uncanny, near-perfect rotation. She was happily lost in a moment of pure play, of childhood innocence, of exploration.

Sasha watched with relief, having extinguished all the frightening alternative explanations for an abandoned orange bow. She lifted the bow from the brambles and put it in her own hair.

In that moment, Sasha began to cry. To laugh. To heave deep breaths, overwhelmed in emotion.

Sasha instantly recognized the trauma of having lost her own daughter Emmalyn, yet her maternal subconscious remained looking for her in the face of every young girl about the same age. It was a liability Sasha recognized in taking care of Cassie, but also an unyielding asset.

Superpowers. Empathy and interpersonal bonding were Sasha's superpowers.

As Sasha watched Cassie swing contentedly, whimsically about the merry-go-round, she saw the faint outlines of other children who had played here before.

Down the slide. Across the climbing bars. Rocking back and forth on the swings. It was an uncanny, fleeting visage. The ghosts of many children—long since grown, long since gone from this decrepit remains of a playground.

A curious, ancestral memory held intact by a hallowed place even as it was slowly consumed by the wilds of time and primal forces. Perhaps Cassie was the last child on the last playground on Earth. That is how it felt to Sasha in that sublime moment.

"You gonna keep her?" Jill approached Sasha from behind as they watched Cassie play.

"I haven't thought about it." Sasha cleared her throat and dried her misty eyes.

"You're gonna keep her, Sasha. She will have such a good home with you." Jill wrapped her arms around Sasha from behind and rested her head against Sasha's neck.

"You both deserve each other, after what you've been through. After Emmalyn."

"I am trying not to think that way. It's not fair to little Cassie. She's not a replacement."

Sasha sighed. She imagined Rylar, Timo, and Acacia reacting as Cassie arrived at Fenix Farm. They would be overjoyed. They would be happy together. And in that moment, Sasha missed her family and worried about them all over again.

"No one will think that. You'd take Cassie in under these circumstances no matter how many of your own you still had. Cassie will be one of your own. I know that about you. Your family has so much love to give. I can tell. Cassie will fit right in."

Jill squeezed Sasha extra tight and then released.

"Anyway, sorry about earlier. This has all been a little overwhelming."

Sasha rolled her eyes and gave a huff. "A little overwhelming, huh?"

Nate pushed Dugen through the bumpy terrain to join the ladies.

They rested on the hillside with one of Dugen's blankets laid neath them.

The four Homecomers sat in silence together as Cassie skipped from the merry-go-round to a balance beam nearly concealed by patches of flowering weeds.

The rising sun cracked through the morning clouds and lit the tapered slopes of Buckson Park with a golden luminescence. After a 94 million mile journey, each ray of light was golden and serene, catching every glistening dew drop upon every blade of arching wild grass.

Beyond the forgotten playground was the path across Buckson Park into the city center. Salmon Springs General Hospital was mere blocks away now. While The Long Collapse had reduced the quality of medical care overall, triage medicine for emergency procedures like bullet wounds was maintained as a baseline standard of care, even in these desperate times.

Cassie laughed and mounted a toy horse affixed to a creaky spring. She rocked back and forth, back and forth, then waved at the Homecomers overlooking the playground.

Sasha reached over to hold Jill's hand, then reached down to take Dugen's hand.

Dugen followed by taking Nate's hand.

Nate looked down, then over to take Jill's hand.

They were all bound up together. There were no words left.

Together, the four Homecomers watched the sun rising over the wilds of Buckson Park as Cassie glanced back at them, her newfound Long Collapse family.

Cassie grinned and resumed galloping on her trusty, rusty old steed.

[17 – Saturday Story Hour]

Acacia cleared her throat and turned the page. Reading aloud sideways while holding a picture book upright was a skill unto itself, one which she was still mastering.

Surrounded by attentive children spread out on blankets on the floor of the library, some distracted by their own sketchpads or crafts projects, Acacia continued:

> *After the rainfall, the three tree frogs looked out, out, out upon the grass and they jumped up, up, up upon the three big lily pads.*
>
> *"Ribbit, ribbit!" said the yellow frog.*
>
> *"Croak, croak!" said the green frog.*
>
> *"Meep-meep, meep-meep!" said the red frog.*

The children laughed.

Acacia was really improving on her frog impressions this week!

> *The three tree frogs hopped over, over, over, the edge of the pond so they could see what they could see.*

> *Do you know what they saw?*

Acacia paused and looked to the group of eager faces.

"What do you think they saw?" she asked with excitement and curiosity.

"Another frog!" said Davey.

"A tree!" said Shiloh.

"A blue frog!" said Mindy.

"The sun came out!" said Valencia.

"A magic cherry tree that grants wishes!" said Timo.

Acacia shot her little brother a dirty look.

"Hmmm. I'm thinking maybe somebody has heard this story before."

Timo laughed and rolled around on his blanket. Cassie looked over at her adopted brother and laughed along with him. She had never heard of a magic cherry tree that grants wishes.

"What would a frog wish for? More bugs to eat?"

Cassie put herself in the frame of mind which she imagined a frog would be. She began to hop around and stick out her tongue, looking for crickets to eat.

Davey laughed and began to follow. Then Shiloh. Then Mindy. Valencia looked at Acacia in complete skepticism.

Timo giggled and clapped his hands with delight. He loved having Cassie around because she raised the bar on his own antics and gave him more leeway to get away with them.

Acacia pulled out her harmonica and began to play a few discordant notes. Even without much skill, the sounds were oddly soothing and, more importantly, cut through the noise of jubilant clamor.

The children halted their amphibian antics and scrambled back to their respective blankets. They knew it was time to return their focus to Saturday Story Hour.

Sasha watched with pride from the back of the library. She had passed her harmonica to Acacia for situations just like this. There was something about the sound that always enchanted children and recaptured their attention.

"Thank you, let's find out what the frogs saw..."

Sasha smiled as Acacia continued reading *Tree Frogs, Three Frogs*.

Over the winter months, Acacia had been honing her reading aloud skills for their weekly Saturday Story Hour. Now in mid-April, Acacia had really come into her own as a captivating storyteller.

It didn't hurt that Acacia had a 'big sister/little sister' role to fill again.

Although Acacia didn't often talk about losing Emmalyn, she

felt it every day. Timo was very young when Emmalyn died, but Acacia was her older sister and close in age when tragedy struck.

Cassie didn't so much as change what was inside Acacia, but more holistically restored it. Having a little sister again gave Acacia a grounded sense of leadership, of mentorship, for the Fenix family.

Rylar and Sasha noticed this about their eldest daughter. Acacia had less often talked about wanting to leave and never come back. Acacia found something worth sticking around to do: be a 'big' for Cassie.

As Cassie told it, she had lost her mother shortly after she was born. Because her father was a scrapper for the Reddards, she had rarely known him other than as a patriarch placeholder.

Cassie had been raised by a group of traveling women in several tent cities, the last of which being known as Salmon Stinks. For Cassie, the transition to being a Fenix was a smooth one; just as her brain had a high degree of neuroplasticity, her socialization and demeanor were equally as flexible.

Sasha reflected back on the past six months since their monumental Homecoming weekend. As much as those events were impactful, they were more clarifying than consequential. Sasha had kept up her journal and sometimes jotted down a few observational sentences here and there.

As Acacia read to her jubilant audience to claim their rapt attention, Sasha wrote in her journal:

> *The nightmares are less frequent now. That's the first thing I have noticed this spring. Maybe the darkness of winter combined with all the horrors we witnessed last October were manifesting all those bad dreams. With the rebirth of the sun and the flowering of the plants, the budding growth in the*

garden, comes a purge of those negative energies and the nightmares that went with them.

Of course there's no way to know for sure. But I think seeing Cassie continue to blossom in her personality and confidence is part of it. Sometimes I struggle with how much attachment to form with her, not because she isn't a special, bright light deserving so much love, but because I never want her to "replace" Emmalyn in my heart.

And she never will. I know that. I tell myself that all the time

Most parents never lose a young child like we did with Emmalyn. But even fewer parents happen upon a makeshift adoption situation like we did with Cassie. Taken together, those events have really revealed the contours of my heart and forced me to confront how I process loss and grief, then blessings and joy respectively. And all of this within a few years! No wonder my head is sometimes spinning and my heart is often overflowing.

Sasha paused and looked up as Acacia set down their story book.

"Now who wants to hear the adventures of a square who just wanted to be helpful to all the other shapes?" Acacia looked out across the room of enthusiastic faces.

"I know all about shapes!" said Valencia.

"I wanna know!" said Mindy.

"Squares are boring." said Shiloh.

"Read the one about the frogs again!" said Davey.

Acacia nodded and rolled her eyes. "Mixed reaction. Got it."

She looked to Cassie, who had been diligently coloring on scrap paper this entire story hour. "Want to hear about the square helping all the other shapes, Cassie?"

Cassie looked up briefly from her own world.

She made no effort to mask her ambivalence. "Go for it."

Acacia raised her eyebrows from the underwhelming response.

It's okay. The gathering and socializing was the real point here. Acacia had been coming to Saturday Story Hour since she was Cassie's age and knew the underlying learning outcomes.

"Great! And Mindy, would you like to be my reading assistant for this one?" Acacia looked over as Mindy gleefully accepted, stood, then walked over to help Acacia turn each page and point out the illustrations as Acacia read.

Sasha was so proud of Acacia. She had grown so much this past year and it was starting to show in the way Acacia flexed her mother hen skills, her confidence, and sense of responsibility.

Sasha turned her attention back to her journal.

> *I have been journaling since we lost Emmalyn.*
>
> *Initially, it was to cope with such tremendous loss and sorrow. I didn't know what else to do. I had so much overwhelming despair. Or at least that's what I told myself.*
>
> *But what we tell ourselves can be as deceptive as what we tell others. Sometimes moreso because we know that no one else is likely to call us out on it. And I discovered that, as I would journal, the sheer act of rereading what I wrote and reflecting on it, that's a powerful tool to inoculate against self-deception.*

Anyway, I have realized this last winter that losing Emmalyn had become a placeholder for me. That grief and loss subsumed every other one. It was a proxy for all of it. A stand-in for it. More important, a permission structure for not confronting it.

That is what is changing for me. I'm not fully arrived yet, and maybe I never will be, but it is a skill I am building.

Confronting the darkness. Allowing it to pass over me. Even welcoming it.

I have always been an optimistic person. And in these times, people see that as lunacy. And maybe it is a bit fanatical. But the sun keeps rising, the crops keep growing, Rooster Rodney keeps crowing. It doesn't take a supreme amount of effort to see the bright side of things when such things are supremely bright already.

So that's me. That's the Sasha Fenix Supreme Sunshine Style. Maybe I should patent it.

This past winter, though, ever since Homecoming, I realized I was trying to avoid the darkness. The darkness inside me, the darkness of night beyond the edge of the farm. Maybe out of fear, maybe out of a well-meaning impulse of self-preservation. But I had internalized it so thoroughly that it became an impassible obstacle.

I really believe it was seeing how Jill worked through her losses, or how Dugen and Nate did the same... Whatever it was, I began to broaden my emotional tool set because I saw my best friends from college doing the same. In their own time. In their own ways.

That darkness, that loss, it's part of who we are — just as the night follows the setting sun. To love, to lose, and to love again. Bringing Cassie into our own family, after the tragedies which befell us all, forced that issue for me in ways I could have never predicted.

And am still actively discovering.

Sasha turned the page, glanced at the schoolhouse clock mounted high on the wall and realized Saturday Story Hour was nearly finished.

Gotta go now but I've promised myself to write more soon!

Acacia thanked Mindy as they closed the picture book. "So do you think the other shapes appreciate what the square did for them?"

"Yes." Shiloh knew right away.

"Definitely" said Davey.

"Yeah." Valencia thought so, too.

"I dunno." Timo could be quite the contrarian during story hours. Likely it was just to antagonize his older sister in a group setting, or maybe he wanted to refine his rhetorical skills.

"Maybe the other shapes are taking him for granted, like next time around they will just expect it."

Acacia welcomed the dialog and took Timo's objections in good faith, even if he was being deliberately vituperative. She leaned forward and addressed her youthful audience.

"What if all the shapes expect generosity of one another, because that's how they get along?" Acacia paused and smiled as the children lit up with inquisitive contemplation.

"But the definition is, um... of generosity, it's more than what's already expected. Right? That's how we know it's generous." Timo was working through this as he said it.

"You might be right, Timo." Sasha stood from the back of the room and walked forward. "But imagine if all the shapes worked together to redefine generosity. Redefine it upwards. So what is expected for them might seem like generosity to us, but for them it is normal to help out the other shapes like the square did."

Sasha paused as the children thought about theories of acculturation. She smiled at Acacia in a 'got your back, sister' sort of way.

"That's culture. How we create culture. How we shape culture. The culture of the shapes to help each other because they all offer something different..." Sasha looked to Acacia.

"But they solve their problems together," Acacia continued, "and that's the lesson of the square helping the other shapes."

Sasha walked around the room to survey what needed cleaning. "It's about time to go. So let's pick up our spaces, please."

Cassie was nearly complete with her coloring project. Sasha noticed and knelt down.

"And what did you draw today?" Sasha looked as Cassie spread out several pages she had completed.

"The farm." Cassie showed off a bright green landscape with simple drawings for each of the animals. "Here are the hens with Rooster Rodney. All our goats. Tres Gatos here in the grass."

Sasha laughed. "That's right, they love sneaking around in the grass like that! Very nice... and this one?" Sasha pointed to the next drawing in Cassie's pile.

Cassie shuffled her pages to reveal a dark scene of tents and wooden shacks at night. To one side, a plume of smoke and flames filled the page. "This one is sad and scary. I don't know why I drew it."

Sasha paused and took a deep breath. This was surely a manifestation of her journal. This was a moment to put her reflection into practice.

"It's okay to draw something sad and scary. It's okay to feel sad. It's okay to feel scared. I feel those things, too." Cassie looked up at Sasha, meeting her kind eyes with curiosity.

"Yeah. I still think about it sometimes." Cassie looked down.

Sasha put her arm on Cassie's shoulder. "I do, too. It was sad and scary. But it's over... and you know what? That's how we found each other, right?"

Cassie nodded and smiled. "We are a good find."

Sasha felt a geyser of sorrow and joy well up inside her.

"I think so, too." She nodded as her throat tightened.

Cassie held up another sheet of paper, this one colored with stick figures for each member of the Fenix Family. "And here we are!"

"That's right! And here we are! I love the way you put us all in the drawing together. Maybe we can find a place at home to hang it up?" Sasha was already thinking of just the right spot.

The rain was finally letting up outside.

It had been a wet, soggy morning without a ray of sunshine. This was typical spring weather and precisely what Fenix Farm needed. A dry spring would mean a summer drought and a dismal fall harvest. In its own dualistic natural order, such darkness in the sky was the precursor for brilliant blossoms sprouting from the soil.

Rylar pulled up to the broken concrete driveway in the Fenix Van—freshly painted in silver with purple racing stripes and big, bright sunflowers painted along the side panels. As a winter project, Timo assisted Rylar with the base coat of paint, Sasha helped Timo add the racing stripes, then Cassie and Acacia painted on the sunflowers together.

"What did you read together in story hour today, Cassie?" Rylar opened the side door to reveal three rows of child-size seats, secured in for now but easily removable to re-install the shelving for produce deliveries. Today, the Fenix Van was a child carpool service.

"Shapes that help each other and frogs that sing when they are on the silly pads." Cassie was excited to tell anyone, and Rylar made it a habit to get summaries of her daily activities.

"The *silly* pads? Lily pads?" Rylar laughed.

"Silly pads!" Cassie laughed harder.

"Who's coming with us today? Shiloh, Mindy. Davey? Valencia?" Sasha gave a quick head count and held her arms out like velvet rope to guide the children from one place to another. They were always the VIPs of Saturday Story Hour.

"I wanted to take my bike today but it was raining." Davey loved biking in the mud. His mom was less enthusiastic about it.

"Yeah, it's that time of year. Lots of rain." Sasha helped each kid find their usual seat.

"Can we paint the seats, too?" Shiloh refused to sit down and climbed around on his knees, imagining the best art for his seat in the van. "But no flowers. I like turtles."

"I just want to paint mine silver on one side, purple on the other. To match the van!" Timo picked out the colors and was quite partial to them.

"Sounds good to me!" Sasha welcomed the prospect of a community van and all its trappings. With fewer people driving during The Long Collapse, each vehicle became much more multi-purposed, so why not cultivate the aesthetics which reflected as much?

The kids loaded up in the van, one by one, and settled into their seats. Acacia preferred to sit in the far back to get some peace and quiet. Maybe even a nap. Fenix Farm was the last stop on their schedule because each of the other kids would get dropped off first.

"Anything else we need in town this week?" Sasha looked to Rylar as he started up the van.

"I don't think so," Rylar replied.

"Marshmallows! I wanna roast 'em!" Timo had been in his 'cook it over the fire pit' phase lately.

"We have them at home, remember? We got that big package. I just put it on the top shelf so you wouldn't see them every day." Sasha half-regretted giving away their location.

"Oh yeah! Thanks for telling me, mom. Now I won't forget!" Timo laughed and vowed to place them somewhere more accessible from now on.

Rylar pulled the van out of the library parking lot. For being an older municipal structure, it was still in great shape. Likely due to regular and varied uses, the library was kept in good working condition.

The van started along its weekly drop-off route to deliver each child back home. After that was the return to Fenix Farm, where hungry animals awaited their evening feed.

If the April showers let up tomorrow morning, Sasha would start preparing the fields for planting season. Jill made a habit of coming over on Sunday mornings, so this would be an ideal project for a city gal learning to be a farm hand.

[18 – The First Unchurch of Anarcho-Pantheism]

Dugen's hair had grown long enough to pull back in a ponytail, so that's what he did. His beard had grown long enough to braid, but he was still contemplating it.

Putting together a priest's cassock out of found clothing was no easy task. Nor was it entirely necessary. But Dugen understood the semiotics of attire well enough to make an effort. The importance was not to replicate some other church's formal wear, but to assemble something of his own to set the clergy apart from the parishioner.

The cloudy skies broke just enough to let in the morning light. The upper story of the abandoned Salmon Springs firehouse had made for a good winter home and provided Dugen with shelter well into 2046. He had placed the souvenir from Homecoming weekend on the tattered wall of the former firehouse office, now his sleeping quarters.

Truth be told, with cobwebs cleared and dust swept away, this reclaimed place was growing on Dugen—perhaps enough to finally settle in and call somewhere "home."

"The h-word. The motherfucking h-word." Dugen laughed aloud as he wheeled himself across the room. It was a concept he still circled with caution, hesitant to accept it as his own.

After six months of practice, Dugen had finally gotten down the time it took for him to dress himself back to pre-paraplegic levels.

As difficult as the adjustments were, Dugen learned to lean into the benefits of such disruptive changes to his life. In actuality, no one more than Dugen was mentally equipped for such abrupt breaks in life circumstances such as when a 45mm bullet shattered the L3 and L4 vertebrae.

"To paraphrase the late, great Iron Mike, everyone has a plan until they get shot in the spinal column." Dugen mumbled as he hoisted up his pants. Still no wiggling of the toes. The doctors said that if ever he would regain movement, it would be in the first year after the injury.

"You still got six months, little toe. Don't let me down!"

Living alone, Dugen talked to himself more than he did when he lived on the streets. He found it was a helpful way to prep for a sermon.

"What are we gonna bloviate on about this week, Douglas?"

Dugen cinched up his tie—a glorious combination of green polka dots with pink and fuchsia laser beams behind it. It really completed the look of a black robe with white trim. The getup communicated 'I am fully aware of how respectable people dress, but boldly choose not to.'

Just what Dugen was going for.

"The transient nature of physical attenuation? The duality of the experiential mind and the sensory simulations of memory? Maybe the global return to asynchronicity?" Dugen was brainstorming now.

KNOCK! KNOCK! KNOCK!

"Asynchronicity it is, then!" The knock on the door had stopped the spinning wheel of sermon topics. It was as effective a method as any other.

From the loft, Dugen could hear his eager flock waiting at the front door of his church-converted-from-firehouse, surely eager to receive spiritual nourishment from the fount of post-apocalyptic philosophies. Or at least for the free coffee.

He knew it was his loyal parishioners and not the Salmon Springs code enforcement at the door because the latter had given up months ago. They conceded that while Dugen was technically squatting without title to the land, he had satisfied the legal requirements for adverse possession of an abandoned property. Additionally, the city had no other housing suitable for his wheelchair-bound needs and, indeed, faced many more pressing issues around the dilapidated city.

Dugen rolled his favorite psychoactive crushed blend and sparked up, took a drag, and rested the smoldering blunt between his lips as he wheeled his cart to the edge of the loft. For being lifted from a grocery store loading dock across town, this cart was fit for purpose. Hoisting it up to the loft on his own was certainly no small feat without working feet, but partial paralysis is the mother of innovation.

Leaving the cart by the hole in the floor, Dugen firmly gripped the fireman's pole and slid down, lowering himself hand-over-fist. He was getting good at this, and a flawless descent was frequently his favorite part of the day.

But not today. It was Saturday, and that meant his delivery of the weekly sermon for The First Unchurch of Anarcho-Pantheism. The sign out front read, "First unlearn what you know, forget what you thought you knew, then fuck around and fly out."

Dugen's other code enforcement controversy stemmed from the use of the "f-word" on the sign. But Dugen responded by saying "flight" was a longstanding human tradition and also aspirational in nature. He attached a long treatise on the history of aerial technology and the economic stratification of commercial airline industries, subsequent elite access to space travel denied to all others, and the prospect of genetic modifications necessary for biologically-propelled human flight.

The code enforcers gave up after insisting *that* wasn't the "f-word" at issue and Dugen countering that perhaps it should be.

An upgraded wheelchair was parked at the bottom of the fireman's pole. The rickety model Nate had procured from Cotter's Corner gave out within weeks of Dugen's release from the hospital (on mostly good behavior). Nate gifted him a more robust model with all-weather tires.

Nowadays, Dugen could get around by wheelchair on even the roughest streets of Salmon Springs.

Wheeling himself across the spacious former firehouse, Dugen cut a path through the piles of folding chairs left askew from last week's rousing sermon on the parallels between positive nihilism and optimistic whimsy. He aimed to outdo himself every week, setting a high bar for his freewheeling psychedelic preaching.

Dugen unlocked all four deadbolts he had secured to the front door. As a former scrapper, scrounger, and squatter himself, Dugen knew the incomparable value of home security.

But mostly, all the locks were for effect; by fortifying his unchurch with many locks, it created a heightened perception of value as to the kernels of timeless truth to be revealed inside. Or at least that's what Dugen's incomplete bachelors degree in marketing would suggest.

Dugen cracked open the door and wheeled himself to one side as it swung open, letting in the morning light.

Mac and Madison were always the first in the door. They were dripping wet from the morning rain and slung their jackets against some nearby chairs. Dugen took a drag and welcomed his unchurchgoers with a grand gesture.

"Hey Pester Dugen. You really allowed to smoke in here?"

"Of course" Dugen grinned. "It's the fire house."

Mac laughed as Madison helped take jackets of other unchurchgoers as they entered. Dugen wheeled himself to the dingy kitchen sink affixed to one wall.

He turned on an old coffeemaker which worked well enough to be the first miracle on the premises. Was it donated? Was it found? At some point, all re-homed objects attain an ambiguous chain of custody.

"Alright, let's get everyone inside, dried off, and warmed up. Your mind cannot be open if your body is pissed off at you, am I right?" Dugen poured a few cups of piping hot, black brew for the first to claim them.

"Yay, donuts! The breakfast of champions, the sustenance of emperors, the fuel of philosopher kings." Someone had brought in what passed at the nearest gas station for a morning meal. Dugen would never skimp on coffee and donuts to jump start his sermon.

Wiping the crumbs from his bushy red beard, Dugen looked across the room to see the main hall filling up, chairs being arranged, a spontaneous organization of the unchurched. The oddball community he was building served as a metaphor as well as a manifestation of the ideology he espoused. That was validation enough for him.

"Alright my hungry children of the ever-expanding galaxy, locate the metaphysical buckles to your cosmological seat belts and strap in! We're gonna get started."

Dugen kept a wireless microphone and headset slung from a pouch on his wheelchair. He put it on and tapped a small transmitting device affixed to his arm rest. It was a whole setup, really.

Wheeling himself up a ramp adorned with an assortment of found objects ranging from power tools and action figures to glass beakers and potted plants, Dugen centered himself at the head of his unchurch. The overall look was that of any modest mantle of worship, but specifically for an eclectic assortment of polished junk presented as a duality of the sacred and the sacrosanct. The visual motif conveyed a sincere parody of religious tradition, as well as a subtle reverence for it.

"Today's sermon is being broadcast out to anyone who picks up what I'm throwing down. This is Pester Douglas Dugen, your guide and fellow passenger through all things known and unknown, forgotten and remembered, gluten-free or doused in hot sauce."

Dugen paused and grinned with a delirious glimmer in his eye.

"Welcome to the The First Unchurch of Anarcho-Pantheism!"

Dugen pressed a button on his half-sized pulpit, prompting a few bars of aggressive electric guitar to play from a dusty, old speaker mounted in the corner ceiling of the abandoned firehouse. The vibrations jettisoned the dust into a fine cloud that settled back onto the speaker moments later.

"Now I see some new faces, and many old faces. Some pretty faces and some ugly ones. You know who you are." Dugen grinned as his audience chuckled.

He knew that if nothing else, people wanted to laugh during these dark times. And he also knew that whatever else he had to say would be more palatable if mixed in with his effortless, sardonic humor.

"Which means that many of you might wonder why I want you to call me your 'Pester' instead of your 'Pastor.' And the reason is this... and it's simple, really: I do not profess to lead you. I do not have all the answers. Rather, I seek out all the questions. I am not ordained, I have no authority over any theological, spiritual, or religious experience—certainly not yours, my friends."

Dugen wheeled to one side of the stage. He liked to work the room and rarely sat still during his sermons. With his headset on, he projected through the mounted speaker in all directions as his voice streamed and broadcast out on any frequency or bandwidth one could still pick up.

It was more like a deep space transmission in search of extraterrestrial life than a commercial radio station serving regular listeners.

"So I do not Pastor you. Is that a verb? It is now. I do not Pastor you. I Pester you. I bug your brain and I gnaw at your foundation of morality. I prod your ego and I annoy your self-concept. I might even facefuck your cognitive superstructure. Pester Dugen, that's me. And truthfully, I used to do this to myself. I still do. But as long as you keep showing up and bringing me donuts, I will do the same for you. That's our deal."

Dugen coasted across the stage with a few pushing motions to his all-terrain wheels.

"And that's why I could never lead a church. That's why this is the unchurch. We are here to unchurch each other. That's a group effort, by the way. We have so much deprogramming to do, so much ideological garbage and faulty mental software to throw out. We all know that many hands make light work, so let's light up this work together."

Dugen popped a wheelie (his latest handicapped stunt) and clapped above his head. The audience cheered and clapped along.

"Now, when you like what you hear, or when it hits you deep, or when you get real ticked off and wanna let me know, just say it along with me: FU-AP! F-U-A-P! First Unchurch of Anarcho-Pantheism! FUUUUUU-AAAAAAAP!"

"FUUUUUUUUUUU
AAAAAAAAAAAP!"

The crowd responded, then chanted as Dugen pumped his fist in the air each time.

"FU-AP! FU-AP! FU-AP! FU-AP!"

"I founded this unchurch because I found no other system of thinking, no other relational theory of humankind to the universe, which fits our current predicament." Dugen pointed to the crowd as one young woman nodded.

"You know what I mean. Those old paradigms, those ancient mythologies, those outdated faith packages all neat and bundled up to ship to you for the low, low price of $39.95 plus shipping and handling... they no longer work, my friends!"

Dugen began to whip himself into a frenzy. His audience loved it. There was no way they were switching to decaf.

"If you squint and look hard enough, you can see that pile of dead gods stretching from the ground up to the sky. The sun gods, the war gods, the rain gods, the elephant god, the monkey god, the thunder god, the One God, the True God, My God, Your God, Our God, the God Damn, Motherfucking, Genocidal, Homicidal, Narcissistic, Anthropomorphic, No God Before Your God God! The OHHHHHHHHHH MYYYYYY GOOOOOOOD! Those gods, that God. Yeah? You know?"

"YES, WE KNOW!" The crowd chanted.

Dugen held a dramatic silence in the air and looked across the room.

"What happened? All those books. All those rules. The commitments, the commandments, the covenants, the sacraments, the hats and the beads and the scarves and the cloth bags with a slit in them and the magical underpants beneath the three piece suit. We tried all that. What happened?"

Dugen paused. The room grew quiet. Even mournful.

Everyone knew what happened. Their towns burned down. They fled drought, pestilence, fires, floods, wars, food and water shortages, fuel shortages, economic collapse. And they were the lucky ones. They ran out of fingers to count on before they ran out of loved ones lost or left behind.

"What happened? What happened was everything fell apart. And the End Times came and went. There was no rapture up to the heavens above or casting down of the reprobates to the fires below. We sowed the flames across our lands, we reaped the wrath from the heavens... there was no great salvation. All those books with all those rules... turns out they were for a made-up human game that this inhuman universe was never playing. Right?"

"FU-AP." The crowd nodded along.

"Some of us figured this out sooner than others. And that's okay. It's not a race. We're all going to the same destination. But how are we getting there? What are we doing along the way?"

Dugen paused and collected himself. He closed his eyes.

"I founded this unchurch because we have so much still to unlearn before we can understand what is upon us now. This great reawakening. This grand reimagining of our place in the world."

Dugen open his eyes. He wheeled along one side of the room, slowly zig-zagged down the center, and back across again. He was among his parishioners now.

"Whatever sets of rules we invent, the universe beats those rules back down and explodes them like a dying star until they collapse in on themselves. We are all involuntary anarchists no matter what system of rules we invent."

Dugen continued looking across each face, making a point to stare down each unchurchgoer at least once per sermon.

"But there are rules." Dugen grabbed an empty cup from one parishioner's hand. He tossed it across the room, where it bounced on the ground before coming to rest.

"Rules like physics. Entropy. Thermodynamics. Energy systems. Chemical systems. Biological systems. Ecological systems. Right?"

"FU-AP." The crowd nodded.

Dugen wheeled himself towards the front of the room again. He downed the rest of his coffee and chomped on a donut.

"We are obligated to recognize that the chaos all around us is nonetheless bound up in a natural order beyond our contemporary religious preferences or malleable ethical intuitions. We invented the gods that suited us, but this chaos reveals itself as an omnipresent, all-encompassing force more powerful than any of the gods we conjured up. That's anarcho-pantheism. This is our unchurch."

"FUUUU-AAAAAP!" The crowd cheered.

Dugen nodded and clapped. This was a good theological pep rally. He was getting somewhere. But where? Oh, yes. "Now, today's talk is on the global shift to asynchronicity."

Dugen parked himself on the edge of the stage. He learned the hard way that it was always best to clamp down the wheelchair brakes before getting too involved with his weekly sermon.

"For centuries, arguably for millennia, the human species has sought to synchronize itself. Calendars, clocks, currencies, schedules, stop lights, speed limits, Internet protocols, codes of conduct, terms of service, community guidelines... You know what I mean. And so on and so forth, et cetera, ad infinitum, ad nauseam. Latin for 'blah blah blah.'"

Dugen scratched his beard and emitted a donut-flavored belch.

BUUUUUUUURRRRP.

"That seemed to be the trajectory of civilization for thousands of years. And for good reasons. Economic reasons, social reasons, psychological reasons, political reasons. Lining up every man, woman, and child into categorical imperatives."

Dugen paused. The audience clung onto his every word.

"What for? Group cohesion. Collective outcomes. Building stuff. Making money. Getting the trains to run on time. Making two thousand hamburgers for two thousand hungry sports fans on a Friday night. Putting you and everyone from your eighth grade history class on a plane from Austin to Boston on a Tuesday afternoon. Hello? Calling Beijing. Ring, ring, ring!"

Dugen held his hand up in the shape of a phone. He pointed at a face in the crowd.

"You gonna get that? It's for you. Ring, ring, ring... hello?"

Dugen leaned forward and gave an unceasing glare at the slightly embarrassed audience member. She put her hand in the shape of a phone.

"Hello?" she said meekly.

"Hi, who is this?" Dugen grinned.

"I'm Christina. Um, my friends call my Starlight."

"Well a rowdy howdy to you, Christina Starlight. This your Pester, Douglas Dugen speaking. Do you have a moment?"

"Um... sure." The crowd laughed awkwardly.

"I'm calling to tell you... that time's up." Dugen leaned forward even further, zeroing in on Christina in the middle section of the lively former firehouse. He put down his imaginary phone and pointed at his imaginary watch.

"Okay." Christina blushed.

"Time's up." Dugen put his hand phone down and covered the imaginary receiver. "Should I tell her? Should I tell her the truth, the whole truth, and nothing by the truth, so help me anarcho-pantheism?"

"YES!" The crowd cheered.

Dugen picked up his hand phone again.

"Ms. Christina Starlight, I'm going to ask you to put me on speaker so everyone can hear me, okay?"

"Okay." Christina blushed as she pretended to press down on the speakerphone 'button' on her hand.

"Great, thanks! I'll do the same."

Dugen pressed on his hand phone and then set his hand face up on his wheelchair arm rest. He always tried to make his sermons interactive, endlessly pushing the limits of disbelief. By getting his audience to play along, they became active participants in his pontification. They helped to reimagine what is real, what is possible.

"Time's up, folks. The age of synchronicity is ending. Mid 21st century. Some pinheads in a faculty lounge somewhere decided to call this 'The Long Collapse.' That's what they said and it seems to have stuck. But what's collapsing? The infrastructure, the stock market, the implementation of man-made law, the legitimacy of political authority? Yes, sure. But what else is collapsing?"

Dugen paused again. The room fell silent. Dugen gave his parishioners a hint.

        tick
            tick
               tick
                  tick

"Synchronized time. Collective organization of the temporal plane."

Dugen looked out across the impressive gathering of FUAP fans. Just waiting to be pestered.

"We are entering into an era of asynchronicity. And I'm calling Christina Starlight and anyone else who is listening to tell them the good news!"

Dugen turned to one side and assumed a folksy drawl. *"The good news? Pester Dugen says that the collapse of society is good news! He must be a classical nihilist. He needs to switch to decaf."*

The crowd chuckled.

"Synchronicity was an imposition." Dugen pointed to one member of the crowd.

"Was it your idea?" Dugen pointed to another member of the crowd.

"Did you authorize this?" Dugen began pointing wildly with both index fingers.

"Who approved this agglomerative aggregate of human effort into conformity?" Dugen held his fingers in the air, drew in a deep breath, and slowly lowered his hands.

"Because that's all this is, right? It was never done for you, or you, or you, or my good phone-a-friend Christina Starlight here. Synchronicity seemed like a worthy human endeavor, but it trampled over humanity in the process."

Dugen unlocked his wheelchair and again began to work the room from the outside perimeter.

"And it trampled over everything else in the process, seems to me. No single human could burn a hole through the ozone layer and kill off the coral reef. Synchronicity did that. No solitary man could poison the stream so the salmon run stops. Synchronicity did that. None of us acting in our own time, of our own volition, could destroy our home planet and call it progress. Synchronicity did that."

Dugen sighed. "Seems to me."

Dugen reached the front of the firehouse and began to wheel himself back down the center aisle. He always tried to time the big send-off speech with his grand procession through the congregation.

"So yeah, it's pretty good fucking news that we're entering into a new age, an age of asynchronicity. As each centralized system breaks down, and trust me... there's plenty of tears and ink spilled over them, there is also a release of all the time held hostage within that system."

Dugen pointed at each member while passing them along the aisle.

"Your time. Your time... Your time. Your time."

"FU-AP" they each replied.

"I'm calling to tell you that you get your time back. I'm calling long distance from the Age of Asynchronicity. It's the state of play. It's a state of mind..."

Dugen directed his wide eyes and clenched teeth at his audience.

"Will you join me, brother? Will you join me, sister?"

"FU-AP!" the crowd cheered with conviction.

Dugen reached his makeshift pulpit and turned back around.

"What will you do with all the time you didn't know you had? With all you've lost, and all those who have lost even more... don't forget what you've regained. As everything else falls apart, you finally get your time back."

Dugen sighed and felt a tear welling up in one eye. He couldn't always cry on command, but he was getting better at it each week.

"So I called Ms. Christina Starlight to tell her the good news. Synchronicity is breaking apart. We are entering the Age of Asynchronicity. Reclaim your time. Reclaim your life."

Dugen held up his hand phone and gestured as he 'hung up.'

"FU-AP, Pester Dugen!" the crowd cheered.

"And FU-AP to you, my unchurched brethren." Dugen clasped his hands together and nodded.

After a moment of silence, the seated congregation rose and began to mingle. Some exited right away, but others placed "offerings" on the kitchen counter top: a loaf of bread, canned soup, a bag of dried fruits, a glass bottle full of milk.

Christina waved bashfully at Dugen and smiled.

He blushed and tried to play off his flirtation with a stoic wink and a 'call me' gesture with his same hand phone. He hoped she would be back next week.

One by one, Dugen bid farewell to his parishioners and thanked them for their donations. Most weeks, Dugen found there was more than enough to sustain him and subsequently hand out leftovers to anyone who approached the firehouse in need.

The Moral Equilibrium in action.

Mac and Madison helped Dugen collect and put away the offerings. Without asking, Dugen found help was readily available after the service. He wished he had thought of this line of work much sooner and formed his own religion in concert with his many attempts at a college degree.

Not that he'd really ever paid taxes, but now he had no obligation to.

"Where do you come up with all this stuff? It's fascinating!" Mac asked as he arranged Dugen's fridge and cleaned out the expired condiments.

Dugen dipped a slice of bread into a fresh jar of marmalade.

"Oh, most of this has been knocking around in my noggin for

years. I would walk all over town and just muse about this thing or that. Maybe flashbacks from my nights riding hard on X-Delight at a place like End Party. I don't choose elevated states of conscious, but sometimes they choose me."

"It always gives us something to talk about for the week. And to talk about with our friends. Sometimes they say we're crazy. And I say 'thanks, we're trying.'" Madison said.

"Well, tell your friends to come next week! And tell them to bring cookies, because this is my third week of donuts and coffee and I could use some variety. Not that I'm picky!"

Dugen wiped his mouth with the crust of bread before eating it.

Mac and Madison gathered their jackets and headed to the exit as the last of the congregation shuffled out into the afternoon sunlight.

The cloud cover split in equal measure across the sky.

Dugen wheeled to the front of the firehouse to see them off. Since Homecoming, he never allowed anyone else to push his wheelchair, but a few nights he had passed out on especially potent moonshine and was given a courtesy escort back to his firehouse. It was understandable.

"So you really believe all that, what you said today?" Mac looked back at Dugen as they stepped onto the broken steps of the repurposed firehouse.

"Did it sound convincing? Did it make you think?" Dugen grinned with outstretched arms as his face caught the first rays of sunshine in many days. He closed his eyes and continued.

"It doesn't matter what I believe because this isn't about me. I'm unchurching others. If you disbelieve something because my words pestered your philosophical superstructure, that's what's important. That's what I believe."

"Ah. Yeah." Mac thought for a minute as Madison loaded up their two-seater bicycle towing a miniature trailer. Dugen looked upon it longingly. He reminded himself that his bike thievery career had probably ended with that shoot-out in the Timberlines.

"Truth is, I make it up as I go along." Dugen shrugged and held his arms out.

"I always have. And you know what?" Dugen leaned forward with a smirk. "So does everyone else... and anyone who says otherwise is deceiving you, themselves, and everyone they know."

Mac chuckled and pointed back at Dugen.

"Yeah man, I like that. That's truth, brother." Mac looked Dugen up and down. "So what happened to your legs, Pester Dugen?"

Dugen looked down to check. "Oh."

He looked up. "Nothing. Legs are perfectly fine."

Dugen laughed as Mac appeared confused. "No, no, I am not faking being a cripple to elicit sympathy... though I'm sure it helps with a certain segment of the charitable public."

"Truth is," Dugen continued, "I had too much fun in one weekend. Homecoming weekend. I jammed with the farmer's market hippies, kicked it with some country kooks, lost myself in the infinite expanse of waterfalls, and fucked the most gorgeous blonde ever to attend Salmon Springs College."

Dugen might have been exaggerating, but not by much. "Last

time I'd ever get properly laid." It was almost romantic when he thought of his late night tent indiscretions with Jill. Not that he was giving away any secrets here.

"And for all that fun," Dugen sighed for emphasis, "I paid the price." Dugen shifted in his chair and lifted up his cassock.

"I took a bullet for my best buddy. Two, actually." Dugen showed off his impressive bullet wound scars.

"So yeah, my legs are fine. But my spine is permanently busted. All things considered, it could be worse. I could still be walking around like a mindless zombie... paralyzed from the neck up!"

Dugen grinned and patted his legs. "I consider it an upgrade."

Mac looked back at Madison, who was patiently waiting. "Wow, this life is one hell of a ride."

"We all pay the price of admission in our own ways." Dugen leaned back in his chair.

"See you next week, Pester Dugen." Madison waved and rang her bike bell.

CLANG CLANG!

"Until then, may the liminal boundaries of the cosmos guide you in all things." Dugen pressed his hands together and bowed his head. It was a proper blessing and meant something significant to all who heard it. At least Dugen hoped so.

Mac and Madison biked down the road. Their next stop was the mushroom market and the monthly dart-throwing competition. Mac was a league favorite and Madison was gaining with every round.

Dugen stretched and poured the fresh milk into a plastic honey bear container with the bottom still full of golden liquid. Dugen closed the container and shook it, then sipped the frothy mix from the top of the plastic bear's creamy top.

Dugen picked up the audio recorder slung from his armrest and spoke into it.

"This is Pester Dugen, recording on April 7th, 2046 – whatever *that* means. Having traveled through the valley of darkness and decay, having walked and crawled through pits of fire and traversed great distances across mountains and under waterfalls... I have arrived at the land of milk and honey. And wow, is it sweet. Stay tuned next week for the first installment in a multi-part examination of illusory states of isolation and the underpinnings of the collective unconscious ego-self. Gonna be wild."

Dugen thought of Timo, the Greatest Go Fish Champion King Of All Time. Dugen howled like a wolf, "Ow-ow owwwwwwwwwwwwwww" and ended the recording.

[19 – Return to the Secret Grove]

The etching was near-perfect for a first attempt. Nate chiseled the final lettering on the granite slab as it rested flat against his workbench.

He propped it up and stood back, reading the epitaph under his breath.

CAITLYN LINARES MAGNUS
DEC 9, 2002 – MAY 18, 2036

KYLA
2033 – 2045

MAY THEY REST, MAY THEY JOURNEY
FROM THIS HALLOWED GROVE
TO EVERYWHERE BEYOND

With the basic chisel tools he gathered from around town, Nate had managed to embed a simple, graphical representation of binoculars for Caitlyn and a paw print for Kyla. It wasn't going to win any awards, but the art complimented an elegant headstone for his two great loves.

It was quite early and the April showers had just relented at some point during the night. Nate loved the sound of the pattering rain on his metal cabin roof. The cascade of soothing sound helped him sleep through many difficult nights.

He took Caitlyn's urn from the mantle, glancing once more at the framed photo of Nate, Caitlyn, and Kyla posing at the summit of the Timberline Peaks.

It was time. He packed the urn securely in the top pouch of his frame backpack.

Nate lifted the granite headstone and bent his knees, anticipating the arduous trek before him.

"You really gonna do this, Sisyphus?"

He lashed the headstone to his frame pack, which was otherwise nearly empty. Nate hoisted the pack onto the table top, nearly aligned with his waist. This allowed him to stage the fitting of the pack onto his body without bearing the weight on his body.

Nate sighed. He knew this was going to be hard. He had been training for it throughout the winter months. Now, the trails had cleared of ice and snow. He was ready to make the pilgrimage to the secret forest grove near the top of Timberline Bluff.

eeeeeeeEEEEEEEEEEEEEEEEEEEEEEEEEEEEEEEEeeeeeee

The tea kettle whistled.

Nate poured the piping hot water into his thermos and added some herbs, tea leaves, a scoop of brown sugar, and a dash of goat's milk from Fenix Farm.

He downed a hard-boiled egg (laid by a hen under Rooster Rodney's strict supervision) and was out the door by the first light of dawn.

It was slow-going.

Nate felt the weight of the granite slab bear down on his lower back. He adjusted the waist straps to better distribute the downward pull upon his body. He channeled the discomfort into a spiritual penance.

The winding mountain trail up the Timberlines was as familiar as ever. More blossoms, more budding tree branches, the rejuvenation of the spring season abounded – complete with its vibrant palette of bright green dashed upon the dull brown horizon of a dark winter.

Nate kept control of his breathing as best he could, keeping an even pace. He found it was better to find a casual hiking speed he could maintain for an hour, rather than a more aggressive pace that would leave him winded and pausing every ten minutes.

He wasn't in his 20s anymore.

But whenever he began to feel sorry for his sore thighs or aching back, his knees inflamed and his calves on fire... Nate remembered that Dugen would never feel any of that again.

The glorious pains of mobility.

It occurred to Nate that so much of his forward motion in life had been propelled by survivor's guilt. Of regret for not suffering the worse fate of those he cared for. Of seeing others set back while he marched forward. It was a cruel form of luck, yet one which never allowed for self-pity.

Who was he to feel sorry for himself? He was alive and well, sweating and heaving deep alpine breaths as the sun ascended through the pines.

He had made amends as best he could.

To Dugen, for putting him in the path of gunfire returned upon them. To Jill, for veering into a collision which fractured her legs. To Sasha, for turning a lovely Homecoming weekend into a nightmarish gauntlet through smoke and flames.

They had all forgiven him. Even Larry Blanton, in his pile of rubble. Even the gaunt man with his last dying breath. And in doing so, Nate felt a torrent of mercy in return.

Nate reached a midway point in the trail, where the incline leveled off and provided his grueling hike with requisite respite. His thoughts continued to swirl.

What made Nate worthy of so much forgiveness?

Did it speak well of humanity, or just poorly of him? Nate doubled back upon all the times he had forgiven anyone at all, even for when he accepted Kyla's puppy chewing habits upon his rubber boots and plastic tackle box.

Was forgiveness like a muscle? Could it be trained, could it be flexed, could it atrophy? Was it a skill? Was it a habit? Was it innate or learned?

"Nate the great and his late debate, a spate of fates bearing mighty weight."

He hummed to himself as he took on the last uphill climb through the winding treeline.

While the trailhead looked like spring was in the air, these upper altitudes of Timberline Ridge still bore the remnants of a cold, barren winter.

> *you will know when skies hang low*
> *that rains shall break*
> *the springtime skies cracked open*
> *only to reflect clear skies again*
>
> *I will return to mountainous mornings*
> *of grand horizons*
> *a gentle flower*
> *peaks and valleys*
> *of majestic power*
>
> *and between these mountainous mornings*
> *and those more distant to come*
>
> *I will retain the scent of rain*
> *I will know the shape of snow*
> *but when I find my way back*
> *to mountainous crags and whispering leaves*
> *I shall likely become awash much the same*
> *awestruck solace at clarity wilderness achieves*

"Transitions."

Nate muttered a single word as a placeholder for the many trains of thought leaving his station.

The seasons invited Nate to think upon each year, each decade of his life.

Moving around as a kid. Service work overseas, college

internships, life as park ranger. Caitlyn and Kyla. The losses, the despair, the rediscovery of his old friends.

The Homecomers.

Nate knew enough had happened beyond his ability to predict that he didn't know what would happen next. Life could be a cruel teacher, but it also never relented in the lessons it doled out. Nate should be so thankful.

He reached the overgrown path to the secret forest grove along Timberline Bluff.

Nate had nearly missed it. The morning light had shown the way to a subtle parting of the tree limbs, and that alone was the clue. Nate liked it that way. Perhaps this would be his last visit for a very long time, and that would be okay.

The secret grove was a mere quarter-mile from the main trail, if that. But as the overgrown path twisted and turned around the Timberlines, it truly became its own secluded destination apart from the rest of the rugged terrain.

With what felt like the last of his body's energy, Nate reached the circular clearing in the trees. An almost perfect circle. A symmetry which felt haunting, eerie for wild vegetation.

Nate fell to his knees and let the weight of the granite slab rest upon the grass as he unhooked his frame pack, letting it stand upright on its own as he shifted free of it. The burden on his shoulders and hips instantly lifted.

"Uhhmmmfff. Finally." Nate collapsed onto the wet spring grass, sprawled out like a snow angel after winter's retreat. He looked up at the sky in a blank, exhausted stare.
The clouds were moving quickly as the upper atmosphere churned from high pressure and temperature shifts. This was

the manifestation of something new, something decisive on the horizon. Nate took on meteorology as his own personal astrology sometimes.

"Ugh." As the fatigue lifted, the soreness lingered. He rolled over and managed to hoist himself onto all fours, taking deep recovery breaths.

Gradually, his vigor returned to him.

Nate crawled over to his pack, pulled his thermos from a side pocket, and sipped from his energy tea blend. It was still quite warm, but no longer piping hot.

"Ahhhhhh."

Nate sat on his knees and surveyed the task before him. He brought the same campsite shovel he had used to bury Kyla last fall. The mound of soil marking her grave was already starting to sprout greens again.

This was where he would dig a long, shallow groove to set the headstone.

First though, Nate pulled Caitlyn's urn from his bag. He stood and held the smooth bronze flask in his hands, against his chest, cradling it.

He knew Caitlyn was gone, he knew this was only symbolic. But it was symbolic not only of her body, but of her memories. He carried both with him this morning.

"Hey hun, I know you would've wanted me to do this a long time ago... but I wasn't ready to let go, not yet. And I didn't know when I would be ready. Maybe I was waiting for Kyla. Maybe I thought you both should be together again. Or maybe... I dunno, maybe I wasn't willing to release you from our home. I wanted you to live there with me for so much longer. We rebuilt it just for us. I wanted you to be there, and to share it with you."

Nate sighed. He wiped his eyes as the tears welled up. He looked around, as though anyone else would come here.

"Ugh, this is so stupid. You aren't really here. This urn isn't you. I'm not doing this for you. You're gone. Kyla's gone. I'm doing this for me. I'm doing this to... to somehow move on. To make all this hurt less, to accept how unfair it all seems... maybe to appreciate how good we really had it, even at a time when so many struggled with so much less."

Nate turned the lid and opened the urn.

He still remembered when Caitlyn's remains were cremated. He kept looking for her when he came home, expecting to see her sitting up in bed. Like it was just a bad dream. Instead, it was only the urn on the mantle next to a photo of who she was, what she represented to him.

"Maybe I've been holding onto this for too long. I'm no good with sentimentality. I know you aren't in this urn. I know I'm just talking to myself."

Nate looked around, taking in the deafening tranquility of this secret grove. No birds, not even a breeze to rustle the fresh spring leaves upon the tree branches.

"In a thousand years, this place will sound the same."

Nate shook off the tears and growled, a combination of catharsis and frustration.

"AGH. Okay. Let's do this."

He took several deep breaths, as though he was psyching

himself up to jump from a high cliff into the churning white rapids below. Emotionally speaking, it was exactly that.

"Goodbye, Caitlyn. You are finally where you've always wanted to be."

Nate emptied the light, powdered ash from the urn. Even with the still air, it seemed to billow and swirl in the morning light. Nate had seen enough sparkling soot and gaseous wisps of charcoal from wildfire burn sites to recognize the patterns in the ash.

Cremated tree branches or human remains, it fluttered in the breeze all the same.

"And in the end, she looks just like the forest around her." Nate whispered with a still, sullen gaze. "She becomes the forest. Just as before."

After a long, somber moment, Nate closed the lid of the empty urn and tucked it away in his pack. Perhaps he would wash it out and return it to town for someone else... to carry their remains, to ferry another soul from this mortal coil to the next.

He set about digging the trench for the headstone. The soil was soft enough, no longer frozen, and ready to accept his shovel. April was ideal for digging graves.

Placing the granite headstone in the trench, then shoring up the base with thick, wet soil, Nate stepped back and looked with satisfaction upon the sacred burial grounds for his little family.

He reached into his pack and pulled out his Ruger pistol. He looked it over, from the end of the smooth black barrel to the base of the etched metal handle, as though for the first time.

He remembered the last time he had fired it and the disastrous results which ensued.

This moment had played out in Nate's mind so many times. He had imagined all the ways he wanted to end his life, how this would be for the best. He would lie with his two greatest loves, he would be with his family forever. It was a beautiful ending.

But standing here, the pistol in his hand, it didn't feel like the ending he wanted, after all. Closure or no closure, spreading Caitlyn's ashes and setting the headstone for his partner and his pet was the final act of the life Nate was leaving behind.

Yet Nate remained.

His blood pumping, his heart racing, his lungs taking in the cool air of another season, another year.

Nate gripped his pistol and took off the safety switch.

He put his finger on the trigger.

He pointed the gun straight up.

The hammer struck the primer on the back end of the 9mm casing, igniting the powder inside the shell, propelling the bullet in a rifling spin out of the barrel at 1,200 feet per second.

BANG.

The shot reverberated across the Timberline Ridge and down into the valley below.

Then, it was quiet again.

The time was approximately 8:25am on April 7th, 2046.

Nate looked directly up as he lowered the pistol from the sky.

In theory, Nate could worry about whether the bullet would fall straight down and strike him at a terminal velocity because his 9mm handgun has a muzzle velocity of roughly 1,245 feet per second, which would apex at a height of about 4.5 miles before Earth's gravity pulled the bullet back to the planet's surface. But because the Earth rotates at approximately 1,037 miles per hour, it would be impossible for the bullet to fall back to the exact point at which Nate had fired it. These were the kinds of things Nate thought about, even at a time like this.

Nate looked at the pistol once more. By firing it into the air, he had marked the moment he had long considered to be his death.

The end of his old life. The one he had intended to physically end, yet now he was free.

To be someone new. To leave behind the person who walked into the forest grove and walk out as a different Nate Magnus.

Maybe no one else would even notice, but Nate would always know what happened to his former self on the morning of April 7th, 2046.

Nate put the pistol back in his pack.

He opened another zipper within his bag and pulled out his camera.

He took a few steps back, framing the forest grove evenly around the headstone and the green sprouts atop the mound.

He pushed down the button for the shutter. It opened and exposed the light from the camera lens onto the image sensor for one six-hundredth of a second.

CLICK.

Just one photo. That was all he wanted.

Nate bundled his camera and hoisted on his pack again, marveling at its near featherweight load upon his back now that the headstone was removed.

"It's all downhill from here." Nate laughed.

He found the overgrown path out of his secret forest grove. But before he set his pace for the return hike, Nate turned to look once more upon the resting place he had created for his deceased family, for his old life.

It was a dignified, sequestered home deep in the Timberline Bluffs. And it was perfect.

Nate found himself in a state of emotional shock on the return journey. If he was being honest with himself, he halfway did not expect to be walking back; he had made every preparation to end his life and for his remains to stay in the forest grove.

Perhaps it was the experiences of his Homecoming ordeal that put him back on the path of exploration, of possibility for something beyond the life left behind.

The day he happened upon Sasha, Jill, and Dugen in the run-down parking lot of the former Evergreen Shopping Plaza last October, he was loading up the granite slab to complete the final journey of his family.

They never knew what an intervention it turned out to be.

Nate whistled to himself as he made his way back down the trail, his legs feeling partially-filled with jelly and his knees aching.

He definitely overdid it today.

If he could draw a hot bath in his cabin, he certainly would after that grueling uphill journey.

The winter had been isolating, but purposeful.

After Dugen was in secure medical custody at Salmon Springs General Hospital, the four Homecomers parted ways again.

Their fifth, the little foundling named Cassie, went home with Sasha.

The Homecomers exchanged morose, exhausted hugs – and on terms more solemn than after the arbitration session 20 years earlier.

Nate hitched a ride back to his cabin and planned to work on the headstone outright, getting back on track for his original plan to end it all – before the winter months made setting the granite too difficult with frozen ground.

As it happened, the havoc and horror the gaunt man and his scrapper goons had wrought upon the Homecomers became the boon which set Nate on a path to longevity.

"How so?" he asked himself.

All of this began to connect in his mind as Nate hiked the familiar trail back to his cabin.

During those weeks after their Homecoming weekend, Nate kept thinking of his hollowed-out truck, still stranded at the trailhead to Timberline Bluff, like an orphaned child in need of rescue.

The anthropomorphization was a bit of a stretch, especially

compared to the gaunt man's own child being orphaned during the violent, fiery eviction of Salmon Stinks... but Nate had taken care of his old Frankentruck since after That Crash during their senior year of college.

It was sentiment bound up in pragmatism.

So Nate set about finding the parts needed to fire up the ignition to his sturdy Frankentruck and return it to its rightful place just outside his cabin.

It became a concrete, measurable goal. A challenge to a man who could immerse himself in projects. And in that immersion, Nate discovered something to keep living for.

Nate reached the foothills of the Timberline Bluff. It was only a short walk through the meadow and he would be at his cabin again.

But out of pure serendipity, Nate took a detour. He followed an ambling trail further down the hillside as the roaring springtime rapids of the Salmon Springs river grew louder with each step.

Upon reflection, it was never really about fixing up his truck again.

Sure, he needed a reliable ride into town each month, but there were enough other ways to make that happen, including a guaranteed seat in the Fenix Van whenever Nate needed one (Sasha had assured him of this).

Part by part, through trial and error, punctuated by swear words and hood-slamming, Nate restored the V6 engine and made a few improvements along the way.

When it finally ran, the six-cylinder purred like Tres Gatos fattened on goat's milk.

Restoring the Frankentruck was ultimately about the capacity for Nate to be driven again – not literally, but metaphorically. Nate had forgotten what it felt like to wake up in the morning with tasks on his mind and their completion being a source of satisfaction. He had surrendered that formation of purpose to the looming depression of grief, of loss.

The calamity of Homecoming 2045 changed all that. It was a series of unexpected adversities which revealed in Nate a resilience he didn't know he still had. And for all his faults, he still proved himself to be a survivor, a protector, and a true friend. If Nate could ever meet the gaunt man again, he would shake the scrapper's bony hands and thank him for saving his life.

Nate sighed and shook his head. "There's no way to know that the tragedies which befall us aren't actually good."

He headed down to the raging river, charged full by snowmelt and spring runoff.

Reaching the fast-flowing rapids of Salmon Springs river, the so-named feature of the town below, Nate sat in quiet contemplation.

He looked at this, and all things, anew – as an old baby born again after bearing witness to the rebirth of the world, after enduring the mortal blows to all he knew and cared for.

After a moment, Nate caught the first glimpse of a sight he never thought he would see again: bright flourishes of orange emerging from the white foam of the rapids!

First a single burst from the corner of his eye, then a few more, then a miasma of flashing orange streaks dashed upon the flowing river.

The Chinook "King" Salmon had returned.

Their spring salmon run was in full force!

It was almost too fantastic to believe, and yet it was though they had never left. The forever chemical nightmares of Titan Corp. were finally coming to an end.

Gathering his wits about him, Nate set aside his pack and took out his camera. He snapped several more photos.

SNAP.

SNAP-SNAP.

SNAP.

SNAP-SNAP-SNAP.

SNAP.

If he didn't capture it, nobody would believe him.

"Oncorhynchus tshawytscha. The king of salmon. Back after over 50 years without a sighting."

It was the first time in his life Nate had seen the salmon run in Salmon Springs.

He sat and watched the phenomenon for what seemed like hours.

The sun was rising high in the sky at this point, which only further illuminated the iridescent scales of each jumping fish as they swam upstream.

"Welcome home."

Nate felt the rumbling in his stomach grow louder. Perhaps he should return soon to catch some fish for dinner. He hoisted on his frame backpack once more.

As he turned to leave, Nate half expected to see a large grizzly bear emerging from hibernation to catch some fresh salmon breakfast from the river.

Surely this was the right reason to carry a pistol – just in case.

With each step towards his cabin, Nate increasingly thought about firing up his old photo printer and finally putting together an album: the rousing family photo at Fenix Farm, the selfie with his fellow Homecomers at Timberline Falls, the nearly-extinct spotted red deer in Buckson Park, his family memorial in the secluded forest grove, and now the spectacular comeback of the Chinook to Salmon Springs. Not prize-winning material, but a collection unlike any other.

"It's gonna make for an incredible story someday," he told himself as he patted the hood of his restored Frankentruck and reached the front porch of his cabin.

Nate turned. He looked out upon the dappled Timberlines as they tapered off into the budding forest sprawl of the valley below, sloping down into Salmon Springs.

"Wonder if anyone will believe it."

[20 – Anyone Still Listening?]

Finally, the sun was no longer setting at 3pm.

Jill always preferred to jog with the sun at her back, and that meant late afternoon runs. As mid-April goes, that necessitated pushing her run to just before dinner. She never ran after a big meal.

A mix of intact sidewalks, dirt paths, and broken-up pavement comprised the trail beneath her worn running shoes. It was roughly a two mile loop; she tried to keep under 15 minutes.

The winter months had seen a greater dispersal of tent encampments around the outskirts of Salmon Springs, including along the railroad tracks that cut through the old town structures and terminated at the edge of the city center.

With the Salmon Stinks encampment raided and burned to the ground by the National Defense Force, its former residents fled in all directions and setup camp along the river, under bridges and overpasses, in abandoned structures, and across blighted industrial properties.

As long as the encampment wasn't too concentrated or centrally organized, it was off the official radar for illegal occupation enforcement. And therein was the tragic irony: Salmon Stinks had provided an alternative community structure which, despite its flaws, had served many people well and met their basic needs.

The NDF enforcement actions had the unintended consequence of continuously driving homeless families underground, into more desperate, subsistence living conditions. Some believed it was intentional.

Jill's business analysis brain was always on overdrive during her runs.

Once she had overcome the shock, anger, and resentment of being surreptitiously fired by Suncoast Management, her free-associating thoughts organically shifted over time.

Staying the winter in Salmon Springs was her best decision in years. She found herself missing less and less of the loud, bustling, busy-for-busyness sake atmosphere of Wynhill Heights and all the pretentious platitudes that went with it.

Returning to her hometown wasn't without a strong dose of humility, however. After Homecoming weekend, Jill self-isolated for a long time.

Her mom had passed away when she was young, which probably explained a great deal about Jill's forced tenacity and grit. Her estranged dad was still living, mostly as a shut-in, with failing health. So that's where Jill went.

By the time winter's chill had affixed itself to the soil, Jill realized she was pregnant. She couldn't believe it. It was just one random, quickie bang-out of a hookup in a dark tent. Do people even get pregnant like that? Ugh.

Thankfully, it didn't take much asking around to find someone who could get her abortion pills. Since The Long Collapse, these kinds of emergency medications were stockpiled and stored cold, underground, away from government sweeps for immoral contraband. Shelf stable for 5 years, even 10 years with 90% efficacy. This is not medical advice.

It was an easy choice, and certainly not one that required a moral matrix of analysis. Jill had decided to remain childless long ago, when the world began to fall apart. Who was she to impose such foreseeable hardship on the next generation? And with some weirdo charity case, wheeling around spouting nonsense for a living as the father? With her own mother gone and father with one foot in the grave? And giving birth after 40 with the state of the medical system today? Could be fatal.

No. She took the pills, had a bad weekend, and moved on with her life.

Jill reached the top of the hill, a rolling trail's apex which overlooked the city to one side, railroad tracks winding along the horizon, and the forest's edge towards the Timberline Ridge to the other. This was also where Jill stopped to catch her breath, to reflect, and to have moments of pure isolation. She had never seen another soul up here in all her daily runs.

"Jill's Hill," she chuckled.

Sure, why not? Informally or officially proclaimed, this was her place now.

From mid-level corporate executive with an illustrious, upscale condo on one of the finest blocks of East Coast real estate... to a live-in home health aid in her dad's run-down, double-wide trailer home on the outskirts of a crumbling town in the Pacific Northwest?

That lifestyle swing took an especially grand act of swallowing her pride.

But Jill did it. And she was happy to do it. It wasn't worth writing the alumni association about, but Salmon Springs College was leveled by wildfires two years ago; surely the SSC Alumni Network had calibrated its own expectations accordingly.

It fit the situation she found herself in. And more each day, it also fit what she wanted from her life.

With the last traces of winter receding and the bright colors of spring popping up all over the valley floor, Jill felt the physical presence of new beginnings. It was an easy metaphor to adopt, given the contours of her life – given the unexpected fortunes and misfortunes within it.

Jill stretched and savored the cool evening air. The descending, golden sunlight would strike the man-made and natural structures across the Timberline Valley with just the right amount of glory each evening. If she timed her runs just right, this would be the view almost year-round.

"I could get used to this."

In her running shorts, the scars on her right leg were still visible, but only upon close inspection. Every time she looked at the twisted constellation of raised, bronzed skin, she thought about how That Crash had altered the trajectory of her life.

It was a convenient excuse for her setbacks and disappointments, but increasingly also a strange reminder of the serendipity of fate and unexpected fortune of calamity.

Jill began her brisk jog back down the hill, her hill. She'd put a pot of stew with red potatoes and chives to simmer on the oven range before her run. Surely it was ready to stir and serve by now.

She knocked on the front door as she entered. Jill had made a practice of announcing her arrivals and departures to keep Todd oriented. They were both still getting used to living together.

"Hey dad, I'm back. Ready for dinner?"

Jill looked to Todd as he half-smiled and moved his eyes, shifting his weight and holding out his arms so she could help him stand and move to the dinner table.

He hadn't spoken a full sentence in years, so Jill never expected a conversation after her greetings. But Todd always listened, always watched, and was alert whenever she spoke to him.

"Let's get you setup for mealtime. I'm hungry, I'm sure you're hungry."

Jill lovingly brushed Todd's wispy, white hair off his brow. His eyesight was very limited and his pupils were the blue-gray of storm clouds in the afternoon. But his sense of smell was quite keen and that was motivation enough for Jill to master cooking savory dishes for them both. Surely he could relish the taste of her best meals, as well.

Serving up two generous portions of stew with potatoes and some dinner rolls she had baked, Jill was becoming increasingly confident in her culinary abilities. It helped that her only taste tester was a muted invalid.

When Jill returned to Salmon Springs last fall, she was

conflicted about even going back to the Tavana family home. Did it confirm she was a failure? Was she relegating herself to repeat past mistakes and fall into slovenly habits?

She had left over 20 years ago with such determination never to return, to prove to herself that she could make it on her own. It didn't help that she had horrible shouting matches with her dad all through high school and right up until she moved out to attend SSC.

But now, all of that mattered profoundly little. It was a lifetime ago. It was before The Long Collapse, before the car accident, before her ascent and fall from the corporate ladder.

Todd wasn't even the same man now. His medical conditions softened his gruff edges and elicited from Jill a compassionate empathy which she didn't realize she had – let alone for him.

Sometimes, Todd would eat his own soup. Sometimes, Jill would feed him by the spoonful. He had his good days and his bad days.

"Don't we all?" Jill shook her head as she wiped his chin.

After a hearty meal and telling her dad about the local gossip and happenings of her day, Jill helped Todd back into his favorite reclining chair and rocked him gently. She turned on his favorite music station (which thankfully was still on air – being among the last active on the radio dial).

> *are you ready for the summertime?*
> *honey, let's get goin' tonight*
> *are you ready for the glamour time?*
> *honey, show me you're ready tonight*
>
> *shine up my shoes, kick off the blues*
> *fire up my Chevy, gonna get hot 'n heavy*

you know you ready for the summertime!
honey, we been cooped up 'till now
you know we gonna get into trouble time
honey, I'm whooped up for you now

Todd drifted off to sleep in his armchair with a western adventure novel in his lap, right by his favorite reading lamp.

On the same end table was an old framed photo: the Tavana family at the lake, circa 2012.

Jill looked long and hard at the eager little girl with missing front teeth and a blonde bob cut – courtesy of her late mom.

What would Jill tell that little girl if she met her? Could she prepare her for what would lie ahead? Or was it better to let the trials and tribulations run their course, unimpeded? Absent a time machine, it was purely a thought exercise – but an unavoidable one whenever Jill looked at her childhood likeness.

Hard to believe she was that same person. Maybe she wasn't.

In that very moment, Jill thought of Cassie, with an orange bow in her hair as she took heaping spoonfuls of gumbo in the chow tent, just before her world came crashing down in fury and flames.

In the next moment, Jill thought of Cassie, with a bandana wrapped around her head as Timo taught her how to milk the goats and collect the chicken eggs from around the coop at Fenix Farm.

What was childhood during The Long Collapse if not an accumulation of necessary resilience?

Jill looked at that blonde girl's beaming face in the photo one last time, then to her stern-faced father and gently smiling mother.

In truth, nothing could prepare that little girl for what would happen, no more than anything that could have prepared Cassie. Yet in the end, both little girls met their moment and found the people, skills, and strength they needed to carry on.

Maybe that's what she would tell her former self if they had met that July morning at the lake:

> *"Don't worry,*
> *you will find your strength*
> *in the moment of need."*

Todd was softly snoring. Jill turned off his reading light and cleaned up in the kitchen.

She had a few hours to herself before repeating her daily routine, so she had set a new habit which was intellectually engaging and somewhat therapeutic.

She started a podcast.

"Hello, my fellow travelers from across the land and beyond the sea, this is the Chill with Jill Podcast and I'm your host, Jill Tavana. Anyone still listening?"

Jill adjusted her headphones and leaned into her mic. She had turned the upstairs loft into an impressive, yet cozy, recording studio. And lest anyone was fooled into believing she was laying down vocals for a forthcoming album, she was strictly a talk radio personality.

Sipping from a hot cup of tea, Jill found it easier than ever to share her perspective, ranting and raving about her field of expertise – even as an outsider living in corporate exile.

"At least some of you are still listening because I have a few listener questions to answer... and we're also going over the massive sell-off we saw this week as yet another titan of finance declared insolvency and seeking to consolidate its debts before it reports quarterly earnings."

Jill tapped on her desk and cleared her throat.

"That's right, I'm talking about Hammershale Green and their shocking, but not surprising, admission that they've been losing revenue and shedding staff for the better part of a year now – more like the worse part of a year now!"

WOMP-WOMP!

Jill was getting more creative and added some soundboard effects as she recorded her show. Fog horns, game show fails, market bells, and much more.

As a freelance podcaster, she had no overlords to ingratiate nor advertisers to which she pandered.

"And wouldn't you know it? I told you right here on this scrappy podcast that Hammershale Green was going under. No special insight, no envelope under my door, no insider trading or whistleblower exposé. A shell game all along.

I just looked at the fundamentals.

I looked at the 6 month trends, the 18 month trends. And sure, you can say *'Jill is always bearish, she's always doom and gloom, eventually she's right about it... a broken clock is still right twice a day.'* Okay, but I was hearing from you back in December when I first started taking to the mic and I laid out my predictions for 2046. This was right up there. This was right up there."

Jill shuffled between papers she prepared for show notes, clicking through a window on her laptop.

Just then, the power went out.

Her lamp flickered.

A small battery backup beeped and flashed green.

"Oh yes, another rolling blackout. Well folks, wouldn't be a podcast series during The Long Collapse without a power outage in the place where an ad read would be. Am I right?"

Jill tapped on her soundboard app.

DING DING.

"And I would be happy to tell you all about my battery backup system here in the studio, but I don't have any sponsors yet. Wanna sponsor my show? I'm not for sale, but this twenty seconds of my podcast is, if you catch my drift."

CHA-CHING.

"Anyway. That's all I'm gonna say about that."

Jill got out her highlighter and a pen. The power kicked back on.

"Okay, so someone wrote in last week after the show wanting some advice. Like, first of all... my advice is to ask someone who gives better advice! Anyway, they wrote, '*my firm has had two waves of layoffs in two years. I know another one is coming. I think my position is going to be eliminated, but I thought that the last two times, as well. How should I prepare, or am I just getting worked up with dread?*'"

Jill paused and sipped her tea. "Well then, getting worked up with dread burns calories and keeps you looking young and healthy. More studies are showing this. That's all I got."

BAH-DUM-PSHHHHHH

"But seriously, folks. If you came here for the jokes, you'd be laughing at me already."

Jill traced the stack of papers with her pen and continued.

"Are the sound effects too much? I wanted to balance the bleak prognostications with some levity. Still trying to find that balance, I guess."

Jill reached down into the worn wooden desk and pulled out a bottle of whiskey.

She added a dash to her mug of tea.

"So look, I get this question all the time. As frequent listeners to the show are aware, I lived it. I was a senior-junior, being a mid-level executive. I oversaw several waves of layoffs – which we were trained in MBA speak to call 'right-sizing,' and it was always in the service of a doom loop of lost profitability and cutting labor costs, the snake eating its tail, you get the picture.

The saying goes, 'you're not paranoid if they're really out to get you.' And I don't know your situation, listener, but if you've survived two rounds of layoffs in two years, one of two things is happening. Well, three, really. The third is always that the company will turn itself around despite the longest economic recession-turned-depression in modern American history. Sure, there's always that. And Elvis could sing at your wedding. Does anyone get that reference? Practically a century ago by now.

But the two more realistic possibilities are: you are so fantastic at your job, your position is so essential, that you're 'layoff proof and you will have the unique privilege of watching everyone around you pack up their boxes and leave while you tend to the cup dispenser at the water cooler. That's possible. Seems unlikely when I put it that way though, right?

Because really, who is layoff proof? Even if you're an executive with a golden parachute and a diamond-studded landing zone, you still gotta jump sometimes. We all gotta jump sometimes. It's the way gravity works. And the myth of infinite growth cannot defy the reality of economic gravity forever. We're all learning that. That's why I'm recording this podcast and why you're listening to it. At least I hope so. It's not for the one-liners, that's for sure.

So yeah, you're probably gonna get laid off next time. Sooner or later, and probably sooner. Sorry it took me several bad jokes to lead up to this, but that's why you're asking. Asked and answered."

Jill took a drink and stretched. A sheep dog across the fence line barked as the rising moon bathed the Timberline Valley – all framed with picturesque calm in the Tavana's loft window. Jill could think of worse places to discuss the end of modern finance each night.

"Although the dread is totally optional, by the way. There's that old cliché about how 10% of life is what happens to you and 90% is how you react to it. Your percentages may vary. But you get the gist.

And look, I've been quite candid about how much I enjoyed my work, or at least I thought so at the time. After some reflection, some distance, a few drinks, being shot at by toothless wackos in the woods... well, I realized I felt good about my goal fulfillment. Goal fulfillment, right? I was completing the objectives I set out to complete. That felt good. In the abstract, as a core value proposition. Great.

But were my career goals getting me to where I wanted to be in life? I didn't know how to answer that question because I didn't know where I wanted to be in life. Maybe I thought I knew. I had one of the nicest condos in Wynhill Heights, a fantastic investment portfolio, fine dining, season tickets to art gallery openings, the orchestra, Broadway productions, um... I could get good dick whenever I wanted. You know, living my best life."

Jill sighed. She was debating how much she wanted to share to her undefined, anonymous global audience. What did she have to lose at this point? The question answered itself.

"But I knew I was on the run, psychologically speaking. Lost my mom at a young age, estranged from my dad since college, a car wreck cut short my running career, I was terrible at staying in touch with old friends, probably enough psychological issues to hire a full time therapist. My career papered all that over nicely. Won me praise, loaded up my bank account, the best credit card offers, exotic vacations to all the countries where indigenous folks fled their homes as climate refugees.

And weird as it sounds, all that became difficult to ignore. My personal accomplishments would stack up against the eroding conditions of my city, this country, our planet... and I was like, *what am I doing with my life? I help rich assholes get richer. I'm serving the top 5% of financial elites and I would never want to spend a minute with them outside a paid consultation in the company high rise.'*

So... dread? Dread of being laid off? Personally speaking, I wish I was laid off a lot sooner. It was the wake-up call I needed. I'm just glad that I packed up all my boxes and snapped out of it."

Jill cleared her throat and shuffled her papers, ticked off some items with her pen. Took another drink of her whiskey in warm tea. This was turning out to be a good episode.

"Okay, next question... probably the last one for tonight, honestly. I'm getting up early tomorrow to go help a friend out at her farm for planting season. Yeah, Jill the farmhand. Who knew, right? If you'd told me a year ago what I would be up to now, I would've filed a restraining order. Against *myself*!"

Jill laughed. The whiskey was kicking in.

"This listener asks, '*How do I know if I'm making the right choice in my career? I feel invested in what I'm doing, but honestly it seems more like a sunk cost lately. Is it too late to change course? I'm 38 and have been in my field since I was 20. Times are scary, change is hard. But will I regret it later if I switch things up and they don't work out?*'"

Jill shuffled her papers and then put them aside. She took a deep breath for dramatic effect. Surely her listeners could hear it.

"This might be a long way of answering a simple question. The question is basically about 'fear of future regret.' And I understand that completely."

Jill leaned back in her chair and brought her mic with her. Nate had helped her put together her home studio, including a mounted arm for her mic that could be set anywhere around her desk.

"Last fall, I had just about the craziest Homecoming weekend you could imagine, or at least I could imagine. Send me your craziest Homecoming stories – sad, weird, wonderful, felonious, whatever.

Anyway, mine started out awesome and ended up horrible. I'll spare you the details. Some of it made the national news bulletin. I cannot confirm or deny any particular facts, you get the idea.

Anyway-anyway, after that weekend, I was ready to get out of town again. I had seen enough, I didn't want to be around my hometown warts and uglies, and I thought coming back was a huge mistake.

So there I was, standing at the Salmon Springs rail station, end of the tracks, just waiting with my suitcase for a train to take me far away.

But I caught myself. I was running away. Again! I had been running my whole life, whether for scholarships or championships or whatever ship I could sail away from my problems.

I was afraid of regret. I was already filled with regret. I had put so much trust in Suncoast. I'm putting them on blast now, but whatever. Sue me... Um, so I put so much trust in my company, in the firm I had helped to build. I regretted it.

And yeah, just being honest, one time I put my trust in a random guy to give me a ride to class. I knew one of his friends from freshman year, and I didn't know this other weirdo guy at all. We got in a horrible wreck. Most horrible for me, took me years to get my legs back in decent shape for running. I regretted getting into that car.

I battled that regret all the way to the train station that day. But then the most mundane... yet, um, yet liberating thing happened: the train didn't come. No scheduled trains for a week, apparently. Too many wildfires in the region, not safe to travel.

So there I was, stuck at the station. I looked around, I felt sorry for myself, I felt upset with myself... for how entitled I had been the whole time. About all of it, even the tragic circumstances beyond my control."

Jill paused and sighed, processing so many emotions at once, so many memories at once.

"But regret was a choice. It was a choice I had leaned on when I found myself somewhere other than where I wanted to be... like in a hospital bed with my leg in a cast, packing up my office into boxes, or standing on that platform waiting for a train that would never arrive.

And fear of regret was a choice... one that had pushed me far away to begin with, chasing all these awards of recognition and promotions and corporate office suites. In the final analysis, it all brought me to that station at the end of the tracks."

Jill wiped her eyes and sniffled, regaining her focus and resolve.

"It wasn't some scheduled epiphany I was awaiting. It was... um, a function of necessity. I decided to stop running. Not with my feet, which I still love... but with my mind. I decided to face what I had been running from and stop, stop... trying to adopt some impossible fucking standard imposed upon me as my own.

Because the truth is, I never had to impress anyone else or prove anything to the regional performance manager at Suncoast. I had been holding myself to a set of expectations I could never, in fact, reach. And I could change that. That day at the train station, I did change that."

Jill sat up and adjusted the mic, finished her drink, and set down the mug.

"Or at least I'm trying."

She folded up the stack of papers and tucked them under her laptop.

"So just.. be honest with yourself, listener. Don't fear future regret. It may never come to pass, and if it does, you'll be a different person by then... if you want to be."

Jill clapped her hands and rubbed them together.

"And on that note," Jill laughed nervously to break the tension. It felt strange to talk to an invisible audience with such candor, only to remember she never physically left her small studio loft.

She composed herself and restored her best business podcast voice.

"... On that note, we're wrapping up this episode of the Chill with Jill Podcast. I promise to lay off the soundboard next time. Just a little bit. I was proving to myself that I know how to use it. Impressive, right? Don't answer that.

So stay safe out there, whatever step of your career journey you're on, whatever personal trials you are facing. We're all in this shit together. We don't have to face it alone. Be good to each other, be kind to yourself, and be ready for something new. Because whatever we've gone through, apart and together... if you're listening to this, you are one of the lucky ones.

Goodnight."

Jill ended the recording, saved the session file, and closed out her audio software.

She softly crept down the stairs, avoiding the familiar creaks she knew so well.

Jill took the rustic quilt her mom had stitched when Jill was a baby. Jill held it up. She walked over to Todd and wrapped it around him as he slept in his favorite recliner.

Jill stepped out onto the front steps of her family home as a white sliver of moonlight ascended through the bulbous rows of beaming cloud formations and into the vast expanse of starlight above.

April 7th, 2046 had been a busy Saturday for everyone, filled with new beginnings and putting the past to rest. But the world kept turning, whether its inhabitants were ready or not, and the rising sun illuminated a new horizon each day.

What would historians call the era after The Long Collapse? Who would be there to witness it?

In their search for answers to their own questions, the four Homecomers were helping to write the larger explanations for many greater mysteries. Perhaps they would get their own nature park, their own statue and monument, their own recognition?

Perhaps in due time.

By the first light of morning, Jill rode her bike along the winding country road until she reached the big green gate. A nearby post displayed a rainbow painted onto a wooden slat, with WELCOME TO FENIX FARM in big, bold letters.

Jill opened the gate and entered.

Rylar was just getting the kids out of bed and ready for breakfast. Tres Gatos bounded through the field together, playfully searching for mice or moths or anything that caught their feline eyes. The goats slowly ventured out of the barn and into the pasture, basking in the radiant morning sun. Rooster Rodney sat atop his perch. Same proclamation as the day before:

"Err-err-err-err-errrrrrrrrrrr!"

"Err-err-err-err-errrrrrrrrrrr!"

"Err-err-err-err-errrrrrrrrrrr!"

Sasha was out on the farm plots, plowing rows of dense, rich soil with her garden hoe. Jill waved and set her water bottle next to her bike. She was ready to help Sasha prepare the field for planting. This row was going to be bok choy and arugula. The next would be kale and spinach.

After putting in their morning work on the farm plots, there would be fresh blackberry muffins for everyone, baked with the berries Jill and Acacia had picked last fall. They already smelled so good!

THE END

www.ingramcontent.com/pod-product-compliance
Lightning Source LLC
Chambersburg PA
CBHW030638260626
47157CB00007B/2382